D0975897

A SKY
FOR US
ALONE

A
SKY
FOR
US
ALONE

KRISTIN RUSSELL

KATHERINE TEGEN BOOKS
An Imprint of HarperCollins Publishers

Lyrics on page vii used with permission from the songwriter, Cory Chisel.
2009, Black Seal/Sony
Katherine Tegen Books is an imprint of HarperCollins Publishers.

Library of Congress Control Number: 2018938294
ISBN 978-0-06-269702-8

Typography by David Curtis
18 19 20 21 22   PC/LSCH   10 9 8 7 6 5 4 3 2 1

First Edition

For Finn

This story started with a song.

Tennessee

By Cory Chisel and Adriel Denae

Just swing across the southern sky
And lift a match to my morning eye
Well we'll all die young if we're lucky babe
You'd hate the dark to prove the dawn
Need me no more and I'll be gone
I'm dying to love somebody like you love him
And you look just like my darling Tennessee
Do you think she'll know or see me now like the broken man I am
Doing a little bit more than the best I can
Still she's gonna need a little more
So cast your light into my room
Kiss me deep or I'm leaving soon
We're far too young to be dying now
Just draw me down with every word
Till we find what we deserve
I know I cannot pay my debtor's fee
But you look just like darling Tennessee
Do you think she'll know me or see me now like the broken man I am
Doing a little bit more than the best I can
Still she's gonna need a little more
I would stand in disgrace
I would spit in my savior's face
My coat tattered and torn
Just to know that my love will be reborn
And our days pass like autumn wind
And the world spins around me again
And you look just like darling Tennessee
Well we'll all die young if we're lucky babe

CHAPTER 1

HEAT MAKES PEOPLE DO crazy things—hate does too. The summer I turned eighteen was the hottest we'd ever known in Strickland County, least in the years I'd been alive. Those scorched months felt like God threw us all in a greased-up skillet and cranked the gas on high just to see what might happen. And everything that had been simmering low finally exploded into plain sight.

That year, Mama set my birthday party at Mohosh Pond because it was too hot to be anywhere inside. The window unit in our trailer had given out and we were still waiting for Daddy to replace it. From Mohosh that day, we saw the mountains that hover over our valley on all sides and the creeks dividing our hollers instead of streets. Mama invited the Draughns, and my best friends, Jacob and Red. Nathaniel and Daddy were there too, off from the mines since it was a Sunday.

"Here, I got a little something for ya." Nate handed me a

rectangular box he'd wrapped in a cut-up brown paper bag and masking tape.

I tore the paper open and felt everyone's eyes land on me. "Wow." I was confused when I saw the label on the box but didn't want to make Nate feel strange about the gift in front of everyone. They were blades for a jigsaw, but I didn't have the saw that I needed to use them.

Nathaniel laughed when he read the look on my face. "It's waiting for ya at home," he said. "I didn't want to lug that thing over here. It's heavy."

"What? That's way too big," I said. "The price, I mean, not the size."

"Nothing's too good for my little brother on his eighteenth," Nathaniel said.

"Are you sure?" I watched his eyes for a flinch.

"I'm sure." His gaze was direct and his smile steady. He set his hand on my shoulder and said, "Don't take all of the fun out of this for me. Jacob showed me the one you wanted. You boys been using that worn-out handsaw in the backyard for your projects for too long. Hurts my neck watching you haw away out there. Everyone else pitched in some too," Nathaniel said.

I knew that last part wasn't true, because no one there had any cash to spare, but I also knew he wanted me to take the attention away from him before everyone else could start in making a fuss. "Thank you," I said, and gave him a big hug.

"Just make me a chair soon and we'll call it even." He patted my back. At six foot five, Nate had a hard time finding things that fit him. Clothes, car seats, beds—everything was always too small. I was pretty sure that Strickland was starting to feel that way to him too, with the amount of time he'd been gone from the house.

"I'll do my best," I said. "Gotta finish the table first, and then I'll get to the chairs."

"Deal," he said. "Feel any different now that you're a man?"

"Not yet. Should I?"

"Probably not today," he laughed. "It'll creep up soon enough."

"If it's the mines you're talking about, it can stand to wait," I said.

"I wasn't," he said. "I told you I'm working out a plan, but this isn't the time or place. Later." He took his phone out of his pocket and checked his texts.

"All right, I'll hold you to that," I said.

"Harlowe, I think you know what's coming next," Mama Draughn said to me, and bent down to reach inside the picnic basket on the ground beside Mr. Draughn. Mama Draughn wasn't blood, but she was family all the same, and there was a time she'd taken care of me when my own mama couldn't.

"Happy birthday to you." Mama D started the song after she lit a candle on her famous caramel cake that she'd been keeping as cool as possible inside the basket. Everyone else followed her lead and sang too.

Mama helped Mama Draughn carry the heavy cake toward me. Staring at the flame of the candle, I remembered Jacob saying he was gonna talk to his rich uncle in Lexington about some money for us to start our furniture business. We still had a lot to learn, but were hoping to get a start during our senior year. Before I blew the flame, I hoped for that money to come through.

"Did you wish for a bigger shed to go with that saw?" Daddy asked.

"Not too far off," I answered.

"He can keep the saw in our room if there's not enough space out there," Nate said. "I need to clean some stuff out of the shed anyway."

"Y'all hush about all that now," Mama said. "Let Harlowe enjoy his day. Can't believe my baby's grown."

I felt a little sick when she said that. Most everyone I knew was ready to get the hell out of school, but all of a sudden less than a year seemed like it might be too short a time to come up with work other than the mines. No one talked about what would happen to all of us when they were finally shut down, but I guessed at least 90 percent of Strickland would be out of work.

"Hate to run, but I told Clarice I'd give her a break from

the baby," Jacob said. He patted my shoulder then whispered in my ear, "We'll celebrate proper, the three of us, later. I'm just trying to do the right thing by her these days."

Red overheard him and rolled his eyes, then opened his mouth to say something—probably along the lines of *should've done the right thing first and worn a condom*, which we'd all said plenty, Jacob more than anyone. Red seemed to think better of it and kept his mouth shut.

"Wait, take some cake with you," Mama Draughn said. She shot a look to Mr. Draughn that he clearly understood. He reached into the basket for the paper plates and napkins that she wanted.

Mama Draughn passed Jacob a big piece of cake so he could get over to little Suzy.

"See ya later, man," Nate said to Jacob.

"Yeah, good job on that saw. Can't wait to use it." Jacob smiled at me.

"Hey, you goin' to Ryan's party this week?" Red asked Jacob before he walked away.

"Course. Isn't everyone?"

"Didn't know if you had the baby or something."

"No way. Clarice knows I won't miss it," Jacob said.

The summer before, there'd been no baby, and we'd all tore it up pretty good at Ryan's. He had the party at the end of every July, and every year it was bigger, and louder. People from Griggin County and even farther drove in for it.

I finished saying goodbye to Jacob and then turned to take the piece of cake from Mama Draughn, more out of the desire to make her happy than any amount of appetite. Everyone else had lined up in front of her with hungry eyes, though. Everyone except Nathaniel, who I didn't see anywhere.

"Did Nate leave?" I asked Daddy.

Daddy looked at everyone in our group, and then scanned the surface of Mohosh Pond and the mountain on the other side, up to where their boss, Amos Prater, lived in a huge brick house.

"Suppose so. He must have slipped away without saying anything. Probably had some work to catch up on."

"Seems like he's always working these days," I said. I was a little mad that Nate had taken off in the middle of my party, but reminded myself I'd need to work just as hard if I ever wanted to give him a present like he'd given me.

CHAPTER 2

"HARLOWE, THROW ME THAT oven mitt, would you?"

I grabbed it from the edge of the sink and tossed it to where Mama stood. She leaned over the open oven and took out a casserole dish, her damp red curls sticking to the sweat on her face. "Shit," she said, wiping her forehead with the back of her wrist. "I knew I was forgetting something. Left the peas out this time."

I was going to say "don't worry about it" but jumped before the words could leave my mouth. A loud thud banged against the planks of our front porch. I looked at Mama, wondering what made the sound, then rushed to the door. It felt heavier than usual when I pushed it open, like someone was leaning against the other side, and part of me didn't want to know what I would see.

In front of me, Nate's body lay bloody, crumpled in a heap on his side. I fell to the planks beside him, and my eyes swept up to the truck in our driveway where Amos Prater's son,

Tommy, looked straight at me from the window. "Hey!" I yelled, and started down the porch stairs toward his truck, but he pulled out and drove away, dust clouding his wheels and our driveway.

Mama screamed from behind me and then dropped to her knees, wailing. She rolled Nate's body over to see his face and cried, "No, no, no, no, no, no, no," tears pouring onto him, her voice sounding like it had dropped and shattered in pieces we'd never find. "Call the sheriff," she stuttered through her crying.

Only when I tried to answer her did I notice that I couldn't speak because I'd forgotten to breathe. My hands shook like I was palsied, but I reached into my pocket for my phone. Before I could take it out, Daddy walked out onto the porch and yelled, "What? Who? No!" standing over Mama and Nate before he too fell beside them because none of us could stay upright under the weight of it all.

"Please," Mama said. "Please somebody call the sheriff." She cradled Nate's head in her lap and rocked back and forth. It seemed to calm her down a little with him closer to her, but it split me in two to watch her hands run over his hair like he was a young child with a fever. I wanted to both forget and remember the sight of them together like that. Nate's chest was soaked in blood from a gunshot, but his face told no story of the way he died. If I just stared at his face, I could imagine that he was still okay. His face looked the same as it had only a few hours ago at my birthday party.

When Daddy walked inside to make the phone call to the sheriff, I wondered how much time had passed between Mama asking and him getting up to go. I had already forgotten her words, or maybe I only ever imagined her asking him to call, I couldn't be sure. I wasn't certain of anything except that Nate was lying dead on our porch and I wanted to make it untrue.

Suddenly I felt like Mama and Daddy were strangers and Nate had left me alone with them. How could he leave me without telling me what I was supposed to do next? He said he had a plan for us, but I was sure this wasn't what he meant. I was mad at him for deserting me and then even more mad at myself for feeling that way, because I knew it wasn't his fault. All the feelings mashed together until they became one huge dark shadow that I knew would stay with me for a very long time to come.

Then Sheriff Powell's car was in our driveway and he walked toward us, mumbling questions that made so little sense, it sounded like he was speaking in tongues, like at the tent revivals Mama used to drag us to when we were kids. I stood up from the porch.

"It was Tommy Prater," I interrupted whatever he was spouting. "I'm sure of it."

"You're sure of what?" Powell asked.

"I'm sure Tommy did it. He's the one that killed Nate."

"Did you see him do it?"

"No. But I heard Nate's body land on the porch, and then saw Tommy pull out of our driveway."

"That doesn't mean much."

"How?" I asked, feeling again like neither of us understood the other. "Because he's a fucking Prater? That's what you mean, isn't it?"

"No. But isn't that why you assume that he did it? Because Tommy is a Prater? Maybe it was a hunting accident. Maybe he found Nate somewhere and did the right thing in bringing him back to his family," Powell said. "As anyone with a sense of right and wrong would do."

"They got nothing of that sense, and you know it," I said, the words coming from me without any thought.

"Shouldn't you be rushing off to arrest that boy?" Mama yelled from where she sat holding Nate.

"That's a decent question," Daddy said. "If Harlowe said he saw him, I'm sure he's telling the truth."

"Look," Powell said. "Y'all know there's a system we have to follow here, even if it's different than most. I understand your concern when it comes to the law and the Praters. I promise we'll look into everything. Do you want me to call the morgue for you?"

"No," Daddy said. "We'll bury him here with us." A while

back, home burials were banned in a bunch of neighboring counties, but it was still the way we did things in Strickland. Almost all of Mama's family was buried out front. As far as we knew, the land where our trailer sat had always belonged to them, and she intended to keep it that way, and all of us on it.

Powell nodded. "Did Nathaniel mention any trouble with Tommy or Amos at the mines?" he asked Daddy.

"Nothing that stands out." Daddy rubbed the back of his neck. "But I know he's been worried lately. Think anyone would be with the amount of paperwork and pressure he's been under, though." He was talking like it was still Nate's job, like this was going to blow over and the two of them would go back to the same routine they'd had every day before this one. Nate had worked his way up from being underground to operations on the strips and then into the office. It was a job most Strickland men only dreamed of, one that paid well and posed little risk of getting hurt. Until this.

"Hmm," Powell said. "I'll look into everything. Let me know if any of you remember or hear anything else. I'm real sorry for your loss." He said that last part like it was a Bible verse he'd learned but no longer believed.

Mama looked up at Powell with a mixture of anger and despair. The color drained from her face almost as fast as it did from Nate's. Dizzy, I felt my own doing the same. I steadied myself against the arm of an old chair covered in soft-edged boxes. I couldn't make sense of Nate lying there in Mama's lap. He'd always been the one to take care of everyone else. My throat was closing, and I coughed to push my breath through the tight space.

"Help me get him inside," Mama said to me and Daddy once Sheriff Powell had left.

Together, the three of us carried Nate into our bathroom.

"Unless you need me in here, I'll go call about his casket and stone," Daddy said. His face was white, and he backed out of the bathroom into the hallway, seeming anxious to get some air. I understood. The tiles were tight around us and Nate barely fit in the tub. I wanted to run out of there too, but Mama couldn't do this part by herself. So I helped her undress him, and together we washed the blood from Nate's body.

I kept adjusting the temperature during his bath, until I realized that he couldn't feel it anymore. The sobs took over and I had to sit back on my heels beside the tub until I could breathe steady again.

"It's all right," Mama said, her voice pulled thin with tears. "I remember Granny saying after Pop died that the strongest love ever shown a person is at their birth and then again at their death. It's God's way of reminding us still living to do better during the in-between part. I should have done better for him," she said quietly over Nate, rinsing the soapsuds from his hair.

"Shhh," I said, and rubbed her back for a few seconds. "You did the best you could. He knew that."

"There's a lot I wish was different," she said.

"You can't think about all that right now, Mama. You just can't." I knew she wished Nate had never had to help her as much as he did when she stopped with the pills. It was almost six years ago, a year after her back surgery when Nate was a senior and Daddy couldn't take off work. It was a bad time for all of us, but we got through it.

"Tell your daddy we need help carrying him out," she said.

Once we had Nate dry and on the couch, Mama taped the wound on his chest with duct tape so that he wouldn't bleed through his one nice blue shirt and dress pants that we'd bury him in. His secrets were taped shut in there too. I still needed for him to tell me so much.

CHAPTER 3

DADDY ANSWERED THE KNOCK at the door and then led the Murray brothers into the room with the casket. It was already getting light outside, and people would be arriving for the service very soon. When you bury at home without the stuff to preserve a body, things have to happen fast.

"Might be a little tight," Bobby Murray said, looking at Nate's body on the couch, "but it should do."

He was right, Nate barely fit inside the coffin. I knew he would have hated feeling so cramped, and wished that I could set him free. It wasn't a fancy casket, and it wouldn't have taken the Murrays that long to make a bigger one.

"I think it's best if we say our goodbyes to him before everyone else gets here," Daddy said. "If we leave it open, we're only asking for more chatter from the neighbors." He gave the Murrays their money, asked them to wait outside, and closed the door behind them.

Mama stood over Nate's casket and covered her mouth as

if to muffle the sounds that were trying to come out of her. Daddy tried to steady her, but her trembling was too strong for his hands. When the crying took him over too, he hunched over Nate's casket, covering his eyes. I stood a few yards from Nate's feet, feeling like maybe Mama and Daddy needed to say some things to him without feeling that I was listening. He was their firstborn, and there were memories only the three of them shared before I came along seven years later. After a few minutes, Mama looked up and motioned for me to come closer. The two of them scooted aside to make room for me by his head, and then stepped farther back to give me a little of my own privacy with him.

I thought that seeing Nate in his casket wouldn't be any harder than seeing him on the porch or in the tub, but I was wrong. It made it even more real that he was leaving me. That he was already gone. I sat down beside his coffin on the floor and cried, my thoughts still trying to catch up with the spin of time. There were so many things I wanted to say to him, but none of them seemed good enough. Finally, I just started talking because I knew we needed to bury him soon. "Remember when you took me to see *Avatar* in Griggin when I was, like, ten or something, and while you were getting popcorn that kid made fun of the coat I was wearing—one of your old ones? All you had to do was walk back over to me, and he apologized before you could even ask why I was upset." The tears slid down my wrists while I held my face in my hands and talked to him. "That was how I always felt with you. As long as you were beside me, everything was okay. And now I—" I looked at his face and mine drew so tight with crying that my head pulsed against it. "I should have been there to help you the way you always helped me."

The front door opened and Betsy Lawry, Mama's best friend, walked through carrying a Piggly Wiggly bag of white roses. She rushed to Mama and then looked down at Nate's casket and me on the floor. She wrapped her arms around Mama, and then wiped away her own tears from her face.

"Can you give us another minute?" Daddy asked her.

"Of course. I'll just tell anyone who comes to wait," Betsy said, and went back out onto the porch.

"We should get cleaned up now," Mama said to me, and I followed her down the hall. Daddy began to nail the lid shut. Each hit of the hammer echoed through my insides and made them ache. Mama stepped inside the bathroom and grabbed some cleaner to scrub the tub. When she leaned over, the container and white powder spilled across the floor, the sharp smell of it flying into my nostrils. Her hands shook so hard that she couldn't keep anything in them.

"Go lie down a spell," I said. "I'll do this part."

She didn't answer but squeezed my arm before going to her room. I fought getting sick while I cleaned and scrubbed as fast as I could. The powder mixed with Nate's bloodstains, and I looked away while the pink swirled down the drain. I did my best to get rid of any traces, but there were some spots that just wouldn't ever come clean.

I picked Nate's clothes up off the floor, and before carrying them to our room, felt the weight of his phone and wallet in the pockets. I took them out and left them on our desk, then showered and got dressed for his funeral.

Daddy had already taken Nate's casket outside with the Murrays' help, and Betsy was making coffee in the kitchen. People started filing in, and soon covered our table with casseroles, sweets, and bottles of liquor and shine. I was polite and thanked them for their kindness, but really I just wanted them all to go away. I wanted everything that was happening to stop and disappear. Daddy and Mama came back into the kitchen in fresh clothes and I moved over to the couch where I would be less obvious and wouldn't have to talk as much. The Draughns walked through the front door and Mama Draughn gave the room a fast once-over. She walked straight toward me as soon as her eyes landed on the couch.

"Don't get up," she said, leaning over and pulling me into a hug. "I hate it, Harlowe," she said. "I hate it."

I wiped my eyes, but they filled again before I could finish. "I can't see anything straight," I told her.

"You just hold on to us until you can."

Pastor John from Strickland Baptist called everyone's attention and said it was time for the service. The air in our trailer was already hotter than it would have been without all of the bodies crammed inside, and I felt dizzy and nauseous from the heat and no sleep and the constant pang inside my chest that my brother was never coming back.

As soon as I got to the bottom of the stairs, Jacob and Red found me. Jacob hugged me first. When he pulled away, his eyes were swollen from crying and he chewed the inside of his mouth. "God, Harlowe. I don't know what to—" he said, and stopped, looking like he wanted me to finish the sentence for him. Nate had always been like a big brother to Jacob, too.

"I know," I said, because it was all I could manage.

"We'll get through this." He wiped his nose. "Won't we, Red?" he said. "Nate would want us to look out for you, now. I know that much."

Red looked up at me and squeezed my shoulder. "It's true. Same as y'all did for me." It was less than a year since his daddy died in the dragline accident at the mine.

The pastor gathered everyone around Nate's grave next to Grandma Smithson's in our front yard. While I walked toward it, part of me felt like it wouldn't move with me, but was staying behind. Listening to the pastor's voice and looking at our friends and neighbors, time sped up and slowed down, all at once. The words came to me through a long tunnel, and only some of them made it all the way, the others lost where I'd never remember them. I spent most of Nate's funeral thinking that it couldn't really be happening. I had seen him, held him, and cleaned his blood, but all of those things felt like a movie I should have never seen. Pastor John led the group in singing "This World Is Not My Home" and then said a final prayer. I wanted to scream that it was too fast a goodbye, that it couldn't really be over, but I stared straight ahead, swayed on my feet, and wiped the mix of sweat and tears from my face.

"You all right?" Jacob cleared his throat. "You look like you might pass out. Should we get you out of here?"

"Yeah," I said, wishing I could just lie down. "Let me tell Mama." While I walked through the crowd, I nodded at the people brushing my shoulders and offering condolences, but kept my sight straight ahead on her.

In her hands she held one of the white roses Betsy brought and looked down at Nate's casket, already in the ground. She pulled me to her side before dropping the flower on the cedar box. I hugged her and wished that I could say something to make her feel better, but I knew those words didn't exist for either one of us. I was just about to tell Jacob that I'd changed my mind about leaving when she said, "You were strong, Harlowe. I know it was awful for you to see him that way."

"Not any worse than it was for you though," I said.

"You need to get away from the crowd now, don't you?"

I nodded.

"Just promise me you'll be careful. Stay to yourself, understand?"

"Of course," I said. She meant don't go looking for Tommy.

While I walked over to Jacob's wheeler, I realized that Amos Prater hadn't come. You would have thought that he'd at least show up for the funeral of one of his best employees, especially if he cared anything about clearing Tommy's name from it.

CHAPTER 4

JACOB DROVE US UP to Falk's Crag. I put my feet on
the dash and closed my eyes. The wind cooled my skin a
little but couldn't soothe my mind. Red tapped my shoulder
from the back seat and handed me a lit joint. I only took half
a hit before passing it over to Jacob. Getting high wouldn't
unscramble my thoughts, and adding paranoia to the mix was
sure to make everything worse. Jacob drove pretty fast up the
trail, and I jumped at the sound of low-hanging tree limbs
snapping above us. When he parked in our usual spot in the
middle of the clearing, I took a deep breath and cleaned the
red dust from my face with the edge of my shirt.

Without saying anything to either one of them, I got
out and started walking. We'd all been here together only a
week before, drinking and goofing off with some fireworks
left over from the Fourth. Now, it all seemed like a waste of
time. I stopped walking where the trees opened, and looked
down across our valley. To the right lay the mines and two

big swaths of brown rock where the mountain had been cut clean into for the coal beneath it. They were each almost a mile across, speckled with a few of the twenty-story draglines that carry the rubble away to the valley fills spilling out onto the surrounding land. I'd never seen a twenty-story building before, and when I'd first heard the phrase as a kid I thought it meant there were twenty different tales about how those things got so big.

Nate and Daddy had said there were plans for a couple more surface mines before next year. Soon, it seemed there'd be nothing left of our mountains to remove. Used to be, you couldn't see anything from here but trees that grew tall and thick. Now there were patches and holes of brown where once there was only green. The replanting efforts didn't last long, even though it was supposed to be upheld by law. Like most things in Strickland, no officials ever came back to monitor it. I guess in the grand scheme of things we seemed too small to matter much.

"You're standing a little close to the edge there," Jacob said.

"I was just thinking the same," Red added. We started calling him Red after he spray-painted daisies in place of red roses and left them in Missy Higgins's locker for Valentine's in sixth grade. When she opened the door, the flowers fell on her new white jeans and left red streaks all down her thighs that sent her screaming. Red didn't get the girl, but his nickname stuck better than the paint did.

I took a few steps backward. "Thanks," I said. "I didn't realize."

"We got ya covered," Jacob said, and took a flask from his pocket. He wiped his mouth after a sip.

When he passed it to Red, the open cap rattled in his trembling hand. I could tell he was trying to hold things together for me as best he could, but it was getting harder for him to do.

"Do you need to talk about last night or anything?" He looked down at his feet.

"No. I don't think so. Except. Powell was wrong. If Tommy found Nate somewhere and brought him home to us because it was right, then why wouldn't he have said something? Nate was shot in the chest, not in the head, and there's no way that he would ever—" My voice rose and then cracked, and I stopped to steady it. "He had too much going for him, he just wouldn't." I realized I was rambling, trying to piece my thoughts together as they came to me, however jagged the edges were.

"Was anyone else with Tommy?" Jacob asked.

"No, he was alone. Unless someone was hiding in the truck. He didn't seem worried about me recognizing him, though."

"Because he knows you can't do shit. Nothing ever sticks to Praters," Red said.

"Last time Amos was in prison was a joke," Jacob said. "They held him for, what, two days for killing his brother Charles on Christmas at the founders' parade? Self-defense my ass."

"They got everyone on their line one way or another. For mine jobs, pill poppers, and whatever else Amos is bringing in now," Red said.

"You can't say all the pills are coming from him," Jacob said. "That's like saying all the shine in Strickland comes from one mill, when everyone here can make it with their eyes closed. There's the pain clinics, and doctors, too."

I rubbed my forehead to try to make the ache go away. "Still, I'm sure they're making more from pills than the mines or logging or anything else now," I mumbled, wishing I hadn't brought any of it up.

"Seems like all it would take to put them away is one person knowing where they keep everything," Red said. "At least by the FBI, or someone like that."

"No. Amos is too smart to have some warehouse they could bust wide open," Jacob said.

I turned away from them and looked out into the holes of our valley again. I wanted them to stop talking, but what Red said got me thinking.

I jumped when he shrieked behind me. "Did you see that?" Red pointed to the brush ahead when I turned around.

"It's just a garden snake," Jacob said, and took another swig from the flask, then coughed. "No rattlers out here in the open."

Red was terrified of rattlers, with good reason, since his grandfather was a snake handler who finally died of the fate he'd always tempted. "Let's get out of here," he said. "Sorry, Harlowe. You can come to my place if you don't want to go home yet."

"It's all right," I said. "I'm ready to go. Drop me at the Sip N Sak if you don't mind, Jacob." The conversation and the sun against my back made me feel sick. "I need a cold Coke and a different view."

CHAPTER 5

THE PAINT ON THE side of the cinder-block building flaked away, and where there used to be letters spelling "Sip N Sak" there were now only gray spaces left behind. Mrs. Devin leaned over the counter and flipped through a magazine. She looked up at me over the rims of her glasses when she heard the door chime, and pity filled her eyes. I had hoped that maybe we wouldn't have to talk about Nate, but I also knew I'd be answering a lot of questions for a while to come.

"Get over here, Harlowe," she said, and stepped out from the register to hug me. "Won't ask you how you're doing. I can't stand it when people ask questions when the answer is plain enough."

Since her husband, Kenny, died in a blasting accident—got trapped after an explosive went off and then died from the fumes, the report told her—Mrs. Devin was always the first one to support mine widows, but also anyone who suffered tragedy in general.

She went in for the hug and I let her, even though it made me feel a little worse. I hoped I wouldn't stay stuck in the sadness the way she had all these years. I was sure Nate wouldn't like that at all.

The bell on the door chimed, and I broke the hug before she did. I didn't turn to see who was there, but instead scooted over to the back aisle of pickled vegetables and eggs in case it was someone I didn't care to see. I stared at the dusty jar of pigs' feet and wondered how long they'd been there and who the hell still ate them.

"Can I help you?" Mrs. Devin asked, which meant she didn't know who had walked in. That never happened. Nobody came through Strickland on the way to somewhere else. It was a dead-end street that ran straight into the mines.

"I hope you can help us," a girl's voice said. I couldn't see the door from where I was hiding behind the pickles. "My little brother might chew my hand off if we don't get something for him fast. Omie, give this lady our list, please."

I stepped around the edge of the aisle only long enough to steal a quick look at them. There were two heads of blond hair. Hers was long and straight, and the little boy at her side had a thick bunch of it sticking out in all directions.

"Let's see what you need here." Mrs. Devin straightened her glasses and held up the piece of paper. "Well, we don't have everything, but we got most," she said.

"As long as it's not moldy or expired, it will do for the night."

I glanced back at the dusty pigs' feet again.

"I'm sure we look a mess right now," the girl added. "We've been traveling all day."

"You got Cocoa Puffs?" The little boy stood on his toes and shouted up at Mrs. Devin.

"Hush," the girl said. "Remember what we talked about."

"Mind my manners," the little boy said, and swung one of his feet back and forth in front of the other.

Part of me wanted to sneak out the door without them noticing. I was red-eyed, worn down, and in no state to make a good impression, but the rest of me wanted to stay and find out more about them. It felt a lot better than it would back at home.

"Harlowe, will you come on out here and help them find what they need?" Mrs. Devin yelled, and settled my question for me.

I looked down at the wheeling dirt on my shirt and ran my hands over my mussed-up hair, then walked over to where they stood. The little boy smiled up at me right away. The girl looked aside from the piece of paper she was holding, with a funny expression on her face that made me realize my mouth was open, so I shut it fast. I must have looked as surprised as I felt. I couldn't help it, because the blue of her eyes was startling. That along with the fact that she was the prettiest girl I'd ever seen, and I don't mean just in Strickland—prettier than anyone on TV too. It was a lot to take in. On that day in particular.

"Here," she said, and handed me the list. "Or if it's too much trouble," she said when I kept looking at her wondering what I could possibly have to say, "I'm sure we can manage."

"Sorry," I said, finally taking the list from her hand, and telling myself to pull it together. "Cocoa Puffs, huh?" I said to the kid, and grabbed a basket.

"Yep!" He nodded his head up and down and followed me as soon as I started walking.

The girl caught up with us, leaned closer to me, and whispered, "Don't worry if there aren't any. The sugar makes him even more excited, if you can believe it." Her hair brushed across my arm. She smelled like suntan lotion and strawberry lip gloss.

"Think cereal's over there." I pointed to the aisle.

"Have you worked here long?" she asked.

"I don't work here," I said, and realized it must have been confusing why Mrs. Devin would ask me to help otherwise, even though I saw the answer pretty clearly. "Uh-oh. Nothing chocolate here." I pointed at the boxes of cereal.

"Honey-O's will do just fine," she said, and grabbed the box. Her little brother stared down at the floor when he heard the sad news, and she petted the top of his head.

"All right," I said, holding up the list again. "Milk, bread, fruit—you'll have to go into town for the fruit," I said.

"Sorry," Mrs. Devin yelled our way, obviously listening to every word we were saying. "Produce don't sell fast enough. Think there's some applesauce over there, though. And maybe some jars of peaches too, next to Fanny Reid's jams."

"Thanks, we'll make do," the girl said, and grabbed a loaf of bread, then walked over to look at the jams.

I couldn't help but stare at the tanned backs of her legs and the way her shorts rode up against them when she reached for the blueberry jelly.

"You got family here?" I asked.

She set the jar in the basket I was holding and looked up at me like she was trying to judge if I could be trusted.

"Sorry," I said when she was silent. "We don't see many new people around here. I'm not the best at small talk, either."

I turned to the cooler and grabbed a carton of milk.

"I'm starting to realize that," she said. "About the small town, not small talk, I mean. No, put that back!" I froze in motion and she laughed. "Sorry, I was talking to Omie." She hurried over to her brother, who'd found the candy section a few feet away. "He's like a little hound dog puppy. Always finds the sweets before anyone else does."

I opened the cooler again and held up a pack of bologna. "Maybe this would help?"

"Thanks," she said. "That might help fill him up, but I'll

tell ya, it would be more than a small miracle." She started walking toward the counter and I followed her.

She still hadn't answered my question about her family, but I was clear on the fact that she didn't want me nosing around too much.

"Want to start a tab or pay up now?" Mrs. Devin asked the girl when I set the basket on the counter.

"I'll take the tab since it's an option," the girl said.

"As long as you got someone who lives here vouching for you."

The girl looked at Mrs. Devin, then over at me. "Our dad is the new foreman at the mine. We just moved here—at least for a while, it seems. Will that work?" She didn't look too happy about sharing the information.

"Sure will. Have him come in this week and we'll get your account set up. We look forward to seeing more of you." Mrs. Devin glanced at me when she said it, then wrote the prices of all the items in a notebook and handed it to the girl to sign.

When the girl leaned over, she pushed her hair to the side and a gold locket fell from her neck and swung back and forth like a magnet over metal. Her brother pulled at the frayed edge of her jean shorts. "Let's go eat," he said. I watched her hand move across the paper while she wrote.

"Almost." She took the bag from Mrs. Devin and set it against her hip, then reached out for her brother's fingers. She turned to me and said, "Thanks for helping us."

"I'm around. If you have any questions about anything here."

"Like the county gossip?" She smiled. "I'm sure we'll run into each other soon. From what I've seen so far, it'd be hard for anyone to hide for too long."

"That's a lot more true than you know," I said, and then realized it sounded creepy, but couldn't say anything else because they were already standing at the door, ready to leave.

As soon as the door chimed closed behind them, I turned right away to the paper where she'd signed her name and read her neat signature: "Tennessee Moore."

"Well now." Mrs. Devin sounded proud, like she'd roped them into the store for me on purpose.

"Wonder why Amos brought an outsider in for the foreman job instead of hiring someone from here."

"Is that really what you're worried about right now?" She laughed. "Listen, I saw the smile that girl brought to your face. Nothing can erase sorrow, but don't spite the good things that come your way, Harlowe. Wish I'd known that sooner."

"Thanks, I'll try to remember that," I said. "Shit, it's getting dark." I finally grabbed the Coke I'd come for and reached into my pocket for some change.

"It's on me," Mrs. Devin said. "Don't leave just yet, I want to throw some things together for your mama."

While she scurried around the shop I stared outside the

door and wished I'd seen which direction Tennessee and her brother had gone. I hoped they didn't have too far to walk, and that Omie could eat a big bowl of cereal soon, if that's what they were having for dinner.

Mrs. Devin started putting things in a bag: some lotion (for Mama, I guessed), Little Debbie snacks, Kool-Aid mix, some ramen packs and peanut butter crackers.

"Give her my love and tell her I wanted to be there today," she said.

"Yes, ma'am."

"And Harlowe? Just one more thing. Looking for any kind of revenge won't bring Nathaniel back now."

"Even if it was wrongdoing that took him?"

"Personally, I still believe two wrongs don't make a right."

I took the bag from her. "Thank you," I said. "I'm sure this will all be put to good use."

CHAPTER 6

WHILE I WALKED HOME, the dark orange sky seeped into an even deeper pink. I didn't feel like the sun should be setting, even though it cooled the air just a little. The day was ending and so was the way everything had been before Nate died. I didn't imagine we'd ever find a new normal without him.

Betsy Lawry was still at Mama's side when I got home. The two of them sat at the kitchen table, a bottle of whiskey and a pack of smokes between them, and a bunch of leftover food spread all around. It was the same setup as when Mama used to have people over for Bible study when I was little, except for the whiskey maybe. At least not until most everyone had gone home.

"Where've you been? I was worried," Mama said. Her words bled into each other.

"I went with Jacob and Red. Didn't Mama Draughn tell you?"

"Oh yeah, that's right. Couldn't remember if that was today."

"It's been a very long one for you, sugar," Betsy said. "I'll start putting things away." Betsy scooted her chair out from the table and started wrapping whatever was still uncovered before putting it into the fridge.

I wasn't hungry, even though I hadn't eaten anything all day. I knew I should put something in my stomach, and grabbed a brownie off the plate before Betsy carried them away. I remembered the Sip N Sak bag and moved it beside Mama. "From Mrs. Devin," I said. "She sends her love."

Mama took a look inside and said, "You'd think she'd know to send cigarettes at a time like this."

"I thought it was nice of her to send anything at all. From the looks of it, she's hardly breaking even. Where's Daddy?"

"No idea. Left hours ago." She rested her forehead in her palm and swirled the glass in front of her. If there had ever been any ice in it, it had melted by now.

"Would you like me to go to town with you tomorrow?" Betsy asked her.

"For what?" I said, looking at the brownie in front of me, thinking if I stared at it long enough I might want to eat it.

"Nathaniel's insurance," Mama said.

"Through the mine," Betsy added. "Either parent can sign."

"I'll be fine, sweetie, but thank you," Mama said. "Harlowe will go with me, won't you?"

"Of course," I said.

"All right. I'll check in tomorrow afternoon. Call if either of you need anything at all. Don't get up." She put the last covered dish in the fridge and hugged Mama's shoulder from beside her chair.

I followed Betsy to the door and then watched her walk to her car. Nate's headstone shone in the floodlights. It'd be the first night that the two of us didn't share a room, and I felt bad for leaving him outside with the other dead people.

"Give me a hand?" Mama asked once I'd turned the lock, her fingers still wrapped around the glass. She leaned on me more than she should have as we walked to her room.

When I helped her to the edge of the bed, I spotted the orange bottle on her nightstand. "What's that?" I asked, even though I knew, and the sickness in my stomach I'd felt earlier returned.

"Could hardly walk today after everything. I won't take them for more than a few days, don't worry."

"That's a real bad idea," I said. "You had to go through so much last time, I know it wasn't easy. They say it can be even harder the next time you try to stop, or worse."

She didn't answer me but lay down on the bed in her funeral dress and closed her eyes. Prissy, the cat, ran in and jumped up beside her. Whether Mama was already asleep or just ignoring me, I couldn't tell. Either way, she wasn't going to talk with me about anything else that night.

I stood in the hallway outside her room for a minute, trying to decide if I should sleep on the couch or in my bed or if I should just get some air for a while. I really didn't feel like being in our trailer at all. But I knew I'd have to get used to my room again sooner or later, so I went and slid into Nate's bunk, feeling a little closer to him for it.

He'd taped pictures to the boards above the bed. I couldn't stop looking at the one of us taken the only time either of us had ever been out of state. Daddy took us to visit our aunt and uncle and our cousin Beau in the Florida gulf. In the photo, I'm ten and Nate's seventeen. We're standing on either side of a sixty-pound wahoo fish that we caught together, with some help from cousin Beau. The fish was as big as I was then. We'd talked about going back to visit and see the bait-and-tackle shop Beau ran now, maybe go out on one of his fishing tours. I hated that we never made it back there together.

I rolled onto my side and the edge of something poked through the sheet. It was a small notebook, the kind you were supposed to write in for class. I opened it and didn't see anything at first, but kept flipping the pages. Soon, I found Nate's handwriting and pages of dates and places.

- 2/21 Huntsville

- 3/14 Columbus

- 3/27 Smithville

- 4/09 Hazard

That's all there was, rows and rows of it, with no explanation of what it meant. For a second, I wondered if I should give the notebook to the sheriff, but knew that would do about as much good as shouting into a storm to try to make it stop. I sat up and bumped my head on the bunk, remembering that I'd left Nate's things on the desk. I looked inside his wallet first. There was a twenty-dollar bill, three ones, Nate's miner's card, and his driver's license. When I picked up his phone, it still had a little battery charge left, and also a passcode, I was frustrated to find. Four digits. I typed in Nate's birthday, 10/27—still locked. I tried my birthday, and then Mama's. After my third failed try, a message popped up that said "phone disabled." I found the charger cord underneath the desk and plugged in Nate's phone, setting it back on top of the desk beside my own.

I flipped through the notebook one more time, looking for anything that I might have missed. I kept thinking that somewhere between the lines, he might have scribbled something small to give me a clue what the places meant to him. He hadn't been to all of them, I was sure of that. I would have noticed him being gone overnight so much. We'd shared a room our whole lives except for the few times one of us stayed at a friend's house or Nate slept over at a girl's, but he always let me know. And those times weren't near as frequent as the dates in the book. He couldn't have been away from the mines that much anyway.

I realized that I was tired beyond exhaustion and might just be making something out of nothing to find some sense in the last twenty-four hours. I looked at the picture of us with the wahoo one more time before closing my eyes. To stop my brain from skipping across the lines of numbers and places, I remembered the way Tennessee looked at the Sip N Sak. For the ten minutes I was with her, the shadow of Nate's death didn't feel quite so big. Or at least I felt I could see out from under the edge of it. I wondered if maybe she'd been at least a little glad to meet me. Either way, I needed to find her again and make sure that my second impression was better than the first.

CHAPTER 7

"HERE YOU GO." I set Mama's coffee mug beside the cigarettes on her nightstand. "Post office will open soon. I thought you'd want to get going."

She rubbed her eyes and pulled herself up to a sitting position in the bed. "Thanks. Did you sleep?"

"Think I got a few hours in. You?"

"Slept hard. Needed it." Her sentences were one long word, the "S" barely making it out of her mouth. She looked away from me and down into her coffee, knowing that I recognized the medicated fog in her eyes.

"I'll leave you to dress," I said, wanting to say much more. "It's already getting hot in here," was all I could add, for the moment.

I stepped over the rug on the porch that covered Nate's bloodstain. To the side were piles of old broken toys and boxes of clothes us boys had outgrown years ago. Earlier that spring, Mama made plans to clear things out and repaint the porch. It might be something we could do together soon, once she was able.

When she came outside, I was glad to see that Mama had finally changed out of the dress she wore to the funeral. Her curls were wet and clean, and her T-shirt was tucked neat into her jeans. She took a pair of sunglasses from her purse and said, "You always fear you'll get that call from the mine. I never guessed it would be something else that took him." She tripped over the first stair on her way down and tumbled forward, but I managed to catch her at the bottom.

"Give me the keys," I said, once we'd made sure she hadn't broken or sprained anything.

"I'm fine to drive," she said. "There must have been something on the step."

"No, Mama. You're still loopy from the pills. I'm driving."

After I started the engine, I rolled down the window. The air conditioner was out in the car too. It seemed these things always broke when you needed them most.

"I tried to talk with your daddy about putting a fire under the sheriff with Tommy," Mama said. "But he won't talk with me about it. Maybe you could try."

"I'll do my best. Guess he's scared of losing his job, or worse." Red dust flew up around us and into the car while I drove.

"It's not okay," Mama said, "ignoring the right thing to

do. People used to care more about each other around here, I know that much."

"How so?" I asked.

"You always knew others were looking out for you, in a good way. Nowadays you don't know who you should trust. Everyone's out for themselves. Scared—you're right about that. Everyone's scared."

We drove past the trailers off Kinley Road and then Mohosh Pond, out from the shadows of the mountains above us. Kinley dropped toward town, and after we turned off of it, we saw solid brick houses with clean yards. They weren't big houses, like Amos Prater's sprawled out on top of the mountain, but they were solid, and everything had a rightful place in a garage or carport or basement, instead of spread over porches and yards like ours and most of our neighbors'.

While we were stopped at a light, I noticed the fuel tank was near empty. "I'll drop you at the post office and fill up," I said. "Unless you want me to go inside with you."

"Pretty sure I only need to sign my name. I think I can handle that," she said, but still I wondered when I saw she was fighting to keep her eyes open. "Get a carton of smokes while you're there?"

"I need cash," I said.

She looked into her purse, then handed me a crumpled twenty.

"That won't cover gas and a carton. I'll get you a pack instead."

"Wait." She dug deeper into the corners of her bag and found a five. "Get the carton."

I wanted to say that more cigarettes meant less gas for the car, but I knew better than to fuss with her about it anymore.

When I pulled up to the door of the post office, Mama patted her hair and tried to fix whatever had blown loose along the drive. I waited until she was inside and I couldn't see her anymore, then I drove to the only gas station on the strip. One of the two pumps was free, and I pulled up alongside of it. I had barely put the car in park when a thud shook the car so hard that my seat belt pulled tight against my chest and a horn blared loud behind me. I caught my breath then leaned out the window. A truck had run right up against my bumper, and a man with a pissed-off look leaned out the window, motioning for me to come toward him.

I turned the car off and got out. "Sorry," I said. "Didn't see you behind me. Thought I had the right of way. I won't take long."

"Come here, son," the man yelled, and leaned even farther out the window.

"Just one minute." I turned to the pump, my hand shaking. I wanted to speed things up and leave without talking to him at all. I'd never seen him or his truck before, and hoped

I never would again.

He slapped the side of his truck. "Get over here, now."

I thought about ignoring him and going about my business, but he didn't seem like the kind of person who'd accept that, or anything else I might do in the situation. So I did as he said, and walked over to his truck. He snapped the gum in his mouth and wouldn't look at me, but stared ahead, into the back of our car. Before I could see it coming, his hand flew straight out of the window for my throat. I inhaled fast when he grabbed me, but his grip was so tight that I lost my breath. I couldn't swallow, and all of my muscles froze solid. The heat rose from the cement, and my feet slipped on something wet beneath me. I reached for anything to hold on to, but found only air. He pulled me even closer and my body slammed against his truck. My rib ached with the impact and so did the lung beneath it. The man pushed his face right up next to mine, close enough for me to see the scar that ran from one edge of his eyebrow to the corner of his mouth, and pulled his lip into a smile that chilled the sweat dripping down my spine.

"I don't wait for the things I need." He squeezed my throat even harder.

His hand was so tight that air couldn't get through to my brain. My skull pulsed. His face faded from my vision. The next thing I knew, I was hanging over the trash can, where

I must have fallen when he let go. I touched my neck where he'd wrung me like a washrag, and looked up into the station windows, hoping someone had seen what happened and would offer me some help.

"Go on. Damn it, do I need to move your car for you?" he said.

I didn't look back at him but stumbled toward the car and managed to put the shaking keys into the ignition. I couldn't drive away from there fast enough, and sped back to the post office, where I found Mama waiting for me outside. I wrapped my hand around my neck and waited for her to get in the car.

"What happened to you? You're drenched all the way through," she said after she took the seat.

"We still need gas," I said. "And your smokes."

"You didn't run into Tommy somewhere, did you?" She gripped her seat and stared at me, shaking almost as much as I was.

"No. Just an asshole looking to pick a fight with someone, I think. You might as well cash the check now while we're here at the bank, if that's what you wanted to do with it." I wished that I didn't have to point out the sensible thing to her.

At the drive-through teller, she took the pen from the round plastic container in the vacuum and signed the back of the check. "Seven hundred and twelve dollars. That's what the mine says his life was worth, with Amos Prater's signature at the bottom to make it all official."

It was the most money we'd ever seen at once, but it still wasn't enough to give us what we really needed.

After the bank, I drove back to the gas station, and breathed a little easier when I saw the man was gone. I turned off the engine and Mama walked straight inside while I got out of the car to once again try to pump the gas. The numbers finally clicked on the pump after more trouble than anyone should ever have with something so simple. I looked over my shoulder to where the man's truck had been. Remembering the scar on his face dizzied me again and I leaned against the car to catch my balance.

Mama walked up beside me and tore the plastic off the carton.

"I'm all right to drive now," she said. "Thought we could get some Blizzards at the Dairy Queen before we go back?"

"No, Mama. I want to get the hell out of here. Did you see what that guy did to my neck?"

Her face fell and she took a pack of cigarettes from the carton. "I'm sorry he hurt you. It just feels good to be out of the house for a minute. Being there only reminds me that Nathaniel isn't."

"It'll get better with time. That's what everyone says, anyway." I still didn't feel like she'd seen the mark on my skin or cared all that much about it.

She lit a cigarette. "They only tell you that because they don't know what else to say."

We were both quiet on the way back. Mama looked out the window through her sunglasses and let the wind blow against her face.

CHAPTER 8

I DROPPED MAMA OFF at home, then drove the car straight over to the Draughns. Their place became my second home when Mama was pill-sick years ago, and now with Nate gone, I knew I'd need them just as much again. Walking up the stairs to their porch, I found Mr. Draughn sitting in his rocking chair. He hummed a tune with his eyes closed and his mandolin laid across his lap. He didn't play it much anymore, after Chuck Gibbons, his fiddling buddy, passed a couple years back, but he still liked to keep it nearby. I used to love to listen to them play their old-timer tunes. I stood square in front of him and he opened one eye and smiled an almost toothless grin, but before he could say anything to me, Mama Draughn threw the screen door open. "I was hoping I'd see you today," she said. She held the battered door while I walked inside. It hung halfway off its hinge, loose from years of her hearty welcomes.

As soon as we stepped foot inside, I recognized the familiar

scent of her greens, black-eyed peas, and cornbread, all cooking in bacon fatback, which she insisted was the only way
anyone should ever cook anything. She wiped her hands on
the apron tied around her waist, hugged me, and said, "Set,"
then pointed to their kitchen table in the middle of the room.
Her oak walls were painted white, and the yellow curtains
over her windows were open to the sunlight. While I sat, she
walked to her old icebox, brought out a pitcher of sweet tea,
and poured two glasses for us. I looked at the photographs
and clippings of her daughter, June, on the back wall. June
the beauty pageant queen, now gone off to California and
living the life of a movie star, Mama D said. Only I'd heard
that someone spotted her in a titty bar two counties over
not long ago, and that she already looked near fifty. I didn't
blame Mama D for lying about June, if she really knew the
truth. I think she was only saying out loud what she wanted
most to believe.

Mama D handed me the glasses of tea when I stood to
help. "I got the rest," she said. I watched her fill the plates
with food, including thick slices of tomato she slid off her
cutting board.

"Where do you get those?" I asked, pointing to the
tomatoes left on the counter. "Not from the Sip N Sak,
that's for sure."

"Farmer's market over in Griggin, almost every week. I'll

take you with me sometime. Didn't used to have to travel at all. We'd have more vegetables here than we could eat in the summers, and spent many nights canning and pickling all the extra. Soil's changed now, and things have been coming up too spindly and weak." She set the plates on the table and took the seat across from me.

"Is Mr. Draughn not eating with us?"

"You know he runs on his own watch these days. After all the hours he's clocked underground, the last thing he needs from me is a schedule. Plus, he knows I want some talking time with ya."

"This is the first I've felt my stomach growl in days with the heat and then—" I said, looking at all the food on my plate.

"Well, go on, then. But it would be smart to save a little room for pie." She picked up her fork and waited for me to do the same.

"I didn't see one on the counter, but you know I was hoping for it." I went for the collards first, then picked up the buttered cornbread.

When I tipped my glass in the air to drink some tea, she pointed at my neck and said, "That ain't a love mark on your neck. You get in a scuffle?"

I didn't want to think about the gas station, especially when her food was already making me feel better. "It's just a scrape. You heard anything about this new foreman at the mine? His kids came in the Sip N Sak yesterday. She seemed nice. I mean, they seemed nice. Both of them."

Mama Draughn laughed and wiped her mouth with a napkin. "You mean nice as in pretty, don't you? I knew you stopped in for some reason other than my cooking. I heard about them, all right. He left a mess behind in Chatham."

"I figured you'd have the story for me."

"I'll save it for the pie."

She knew that would focus me on eating dinner, and laughed a little when I bent over the plate and set to work with my fork and knife.

"The pie's not going anywhere, ya know," she said. "And neither am I."

"I know, but now you've got me thinking about it." Well, the pie and also hearing everything she knew about Tennessee. "Can I take the rest of this home? I don't want it to go to waste. Got just the right amount of room left in my stomach for dessert."

"Of course. Was planning on fixing you a to-go bag, anyway. Stay put," she said, when I tried to get up.

I saw that she'd hardly touched her plate, and felt bad when she took both of them over to the counter. "Sorry, I didn't mean to rush you," I said.

"I wasn't all that hungry," she answered. "Hazard of being in the kitchen all day. Watching you enjoy the food brings me a lot more pleasure than eating does, anyway. All right then." She turned toward me with a pie in one hand and two forks in the other. "Tell me what you think of the filling. I tried something new to you."

She set the pie between us and handed me a fork. "Well, go on," she said, waiting for me to take the first bite.

"You don't want to cut slices of it first?"

"Nope. Sometimes you have to break some rules along with the crust. Tastes better that way, I think."

I didn't waste time and broke a small piece off the edge. Some of it crumbled on the way to my mouth, but the part that made it melted on my tongue. "Damn," I said. "Every single time." Then I stuck my fork right in the middle of the pie, watching her as I did it to see if she'd squirm at my rule breaking, but she giggled and nodded, waiting for me to take my first real bite. The color was a bright red, but it wasn't cherry, and the texture wasn't your typical strawberry either.

"Go ahead. Eat it, don't just stare at it."

I did as she said, and closed my eyes before I swallowed. "It's perfect," I said, and reached for another bite.

"Bet you never thought you'd love vegetables for dessert. Rhubarb-strawberry."

"I'd eat this all day every day," I said. "But you're right. Wouldn't have guessed it was a vegetable pie. I'll say it again, you should sell these, you know. You'd make a killing." The last word didn't sit right with either one of us, but I was glad she didn't say anything about it and moved along.

"I've no interest in that. Haven't made a rhubarb one since my mama died. That's her recipe, right there, and she got it from my granny. Reminds me—those children you were speaking of, the Moores. Their mama died, but I don't know all the details about it. I heard that soon after she passed, their daddy got his leg cut off in the Chatham mine for the disability check."

"That don't make him any different from a lot of people round here."

She took a bite of pie and then a sip of her tea. "No, but it's only the desperate that go and do a thing like that on purpose. I think they've moved around quite a bit, and wherever they went, he always lived up to the reputation that preceded him. Word is, he got fired after leaving a mantrip running and collapsing half the mine on account of it."

"I wonder why Amos took him on, then."

"Maybe he sensed the desperation would make him more loyal. You can be sure he had some reason for it, whatever it was."

I rested my fork and lifted the cool glass of tea. It dripped onto the table and ran down my arm. "Amos doesn't need a reason to do anything. Just wanting something is enough. That goes for all of the Praters."

"I agree that it's not right how they wield fear. Amos

didn't used to be so bad when he was young, but somewhere along the way his bad choices outweighed any of the good ones he ever made."

"I don't care about any of that," I said. "It won't bring Nate back."

"No, it won't," she said. "But I wish I could."

"I know you do." I wiped my mouth on a napkin. "Might as well tell you—Mama couldn't walk straight enough to drive this morning." I rubbed my neck again and looked at her, waiting to see the understanding come across her face. It was one of the things I loved most about her, that I never had to spell things out.

"Oh, Harlowe. And you think it's pills again?"

"I know it is. She didn't even try to hide them from me. I'm hoping she won't take any more, but there's nothing I can do to stop her."

"No, we've already learned that. I'm always here, whatever you need."

"Knowing that keeps me sane," I said, and took one more bite of pie. "Any chance you know where the Moores are living?"

She crossed her arms and leaned back in her chair. "If I say, you didn't hear it from me."

"Course not."

"And if I tell you, you have to be good. We don't need more babies sprouting up around here before their time."

"Come on, Mama D. If I wasn't already scared enough, watching Jacob go through it all would do it for me." I didn't tell her about the phone call a couple years ago from Victoria after I'd lost my virginity to her. It was just a scare, but I'd sworn that if she got her period I'd never go without a condom again.

Mama Draughn rolled her fingers against the table like each one was a decision. "You'll find out one way or another, so it might as well come from me. They're in Baxter Creek Holler. Back by Widow Hemlock's place."

"The Arrowwoods' old trailer?"

"That's the one. Guess the Arrowwoods are living with her mother now, in Harlan."

"Thanks," I said.

"Don't go and disappear completely for a silly crush, now. I'm old. Can't compete with a young pretty thing."

"I'd never do that to you."

"Never say never." She looked back at the pictures of June. "But I believe you. You wouldn't go without saying goodbye, at least."

"Doesn't June ever call?"

Mama D shook her head. "Just too busy, I reckon."

"I'm sorry about that. I promise I won't ever take off without telling you first."

"Well, I can guess where you're headed as soon as you

leave here," she said. "Come back by for your leftovers on your way home."

"You spoil me. The only thing I can figure is that June didn't know how good she had it with you. Thank you. I really needed this today." I took one last bite of pie and stretched my arms above my head to make walking space in my too-full stomach.

"Wait." She went to the oven, brought out another pie, and wrapped it in foil. "Take this to the Moores as a welcome. It's already cooled. And tell your mama I'll come visit next week. That's when people start dropping away and things get too quiet. I'll leave a bag for you on the counter."

"Can I help clean up before I go?"

"No. But you sure did the right thing by asking." She stood on her toes and kissed my cheek.

When I stopped beside Mr. Draughn on the porch, he took off the hat shielding his eyes from the sun and looked up at me. "She get some of that talking energy out?"

"Yes, sir," I said. "You might have a quiet afternoon now. Don't hold me to that, though."

"I know better than to expect that. Truth is, I wouldn't know what to do without her chatter."

"You and me both."

"Careful out there. Saw a flock of crows earlier, and there's a new moon tonight."

"Murder of crows."

"What?" He leaned closer to hear me better.

"Isn't that what a flock is called? Murder of crows?"

"Nah, that's superstitious hogwash."

"Oh. Well, thanks, I'll be careful, as you said."

"That's right," he said, and placed his hat over his eyes again.

CHAPTER 9

BAXTER CREEK WAS LESS than a quarter mile from the Draughns', and it would have been a waste of gas for me to drive, even though the sun blazed against my back. I held the pie carefully while I walked.

In place of a sign for the holler, there was a deer-crossing symbol on a pole. The sun shone through the dozen bullet holes polka-dotting the metal animal. I guess our lack of road signs was one more way we told others that if they didn't know where they were going here, they shouldn't go any farther. I passed Widow Hemlock's place, her yard cut neat and her birdbath collection full of water and fat, lazy birds. There were no cars in front of the Arrowwoods' old place, and the brush was still overgrown. I hoped Tennessee was there, despite the empty look of things, and wiped the dripping sweat from my face onto my jeans before walking up the drive.

With the pie balanced in one hand, I knocked with the other. I waited and listened to the rhythm of my nervous breath, then cleared my throat. No sounds came from inside. The pie wobbled, and I caught it, but felt one edge crumble under my grip. I was just about to knock again when the door opened.

Tennessee looked confused when she saw me, then surprised, then a little happy—I was pretty sure that's what her smile meant. She looked even more beautiful than when I saw her the first time, with the same jean shorts, but now wearing a blue tank top that brightened her blue eyes.

"Who is it?" a man's voice yelled from behind her, inside the trailer.

"It's fine, Daddy. I got it," she shouted, turning behind her. "Hi," she said when she looked at me again.

"Mama Draughn wanted me to bring this over to y'all. It's really good. I already had some. I mean, not out of this, a different one, but it was the same flavor, I think." I told myself to stop sounding like a freak.

"Your mother made this?" She took the pie from my outstretched, sweating hands.

"No, we all just call her that. You'll see why when you meet her. If you want to meet her."

"She sounds really nice, and she's the first person to give us a welcome present, so I'm sure I'd like to meet her."

"Oh, good," I said. My mind went blank while I looked at her standing in front of me. I hadn't thought of what I would say next.

"Well, be sure to thank her for us," Tennessee said.

"Everyone says she makes the best. Pies, I mean. If you like sweets." I couldn't remember the last time I'd felt so jittery.

"Who doesn't like pie?" she said. "Actually, I have an uncle who doesn't like anything sweet, but he's a miserable old man. Obviously Omie did not get that gene from him." She rolled her eyes and put me a little at ease. "I'll have to hide this somewhere safe or he'll gobble it up before the rest of us even have a chance to taste it."

"Wanna go for a walk?" I blurted out fast, and hoped for the best.

"Where would we go?"

I scavenged my brain. "The pond isn't far."

She tilted her head to the side and looked at me the way she had in the store, squinting, deciphering. "I'll walk with you for a little while. We'll see how it goes."

"Sounds good." I felt my face turn as red as my hair, and couldn't hide my smile, either.

"Let me put this inside, and I'll meet you up at the road in just a minute."

"Take your time," I said, even though I didn't want to let her out of my sight. Before I stepped off their porch, I noticed a car and the tails of two trucks sticking out from the brush around the side. Her daddy fit right in with everyone else in Strickland, more rides than he could use or were probably running.

I walked out of the holler toward the road and tried to think of things I could talk about with her. She was smarter than I was, I could already tell that, and seemed different from any of the other girls I'd ever known. I'd only had the short thing with Victoria and a couple of other hookups, but I'd never spent any time worrying about what I'd say to those girls.

I waited for Tennessee up by the deer-crossing sign, and kicked some rocks down the side of the road. Mr. Crowder drove past in his logging rig and waved hello. I was glad he couldn't stop and have a conversation with me, because I wouldn't have been able to get away once he started talking. I was beginning to feel like I'd been standing there for a long while, and wondered if Tennessee might have changed her mind about meeting me. I looked down the holler road, but saw no sign of her. Then I heard a "Hey!" come from the elderberry bush where the road dropped below, and I ran down into the field to meet her.

"We can go the back way, if you like," I said.

"Yes, I would. I get the feeling people around here watch and do a lot of talking. No offense, or anything."

"None taken. Your instincts are right." I hoped my smile looked as smooth as I meant for it to. The fact that she intimidated me didn't make her easy to flirt with. "Sorry again for prying yesterday about your family. I understand not wanting to answer people's questions."

"I guess it comes from moving around to a lot of small towns," she said. "I shouldn't be away from them for too long, just so you know. I told Omie I'd teach him how to draw a bunny later, and I still have *The Heart Is a Lonely Hunter* to finish. Have you read it yet?" She moved the thin purse strap from her shoulder to across her body.

"It's next," I said, remembering my summer book list still crumpled at the bottom of my backpack. I made a mental note to call the library and see if they had a copy. I cared more about having something else to talk with her about than I did about getting a grade. "You just let me know when we need to turn around, okay?"

"Thanks. I'm glad you came by, sorry if it seemed otherwise at first. It sucks always leaving friends behind, hoping you'll make new ones in the next place." The sun caught her collarbone and the gold necklace just below it.

"How'd you get your name?" I asked, trying not to be disappointed that she'd used the word "friend." "I've never heard it before. I mean, there's the state, of course, but—"

"Yeah, that's what most people say. I've only met one other Tennessee, an older woman. She said she grew up as a trapeze artist with her family in the circus. My story isn't nearly as exciting. Pretty silly, actually," she said.

"I'm listening," and would for as long as she could talk. Her voice was soft but throaty—the kind of voice that carried in a whisper, but could yell something powerful.

"All right, here goes. Mama and Daddy had this long-standing disagreement between them over their choice of liquor. Daddy loved Tennessee whiskey—Jack Daniel's. Mama always favored Kentucky bourbon, the really smooth kind, and saved it for special occasions like birthdays, holidays, a quiet night with a book, which was always a very rare thing for her. Daddy made such a big deal of it and said that everyone, except Mama, knew that Tennessee whiskey was the best. Not that he'll ever pass on a jar of good shine, or any kind of beer, for that matter. It became this weird thing he wouldn't give up, even though there was no logic in it, but just an opinion he could carry on and on about forever."

She sounded and looked like she should be in a movie and have had a famous actor walking beside her instead of me.

"Anyway," she said after taking a deep breath, and slowing down a little, "when Mama was pregnant with me, Daddy said they'd name the baby Tennessee if it was a girl, and Kentucky if it was a boy, and somehow that would settle the argument between them once and for all."

"Did it?"

"I guess in Daddy's mind it did. But Mama stopped arguing with him long before that, because she knew there was no point in it."

"Why didn't they name Omie Kentucky so they could both win?"

"Mom said one child with an odd name was enough." She

moved the locket back and forth across the chain and peered at me over it.

I couldn't stop staring at her lips, and I also couldn't tell if she was joking or not. "Uh, can't say I've heard of that many Omies, either," I said.

She laughed hard and touched my arm for a split second. "I know, right? It's an even weirder name, but it's from Mom's family, so I guess it seemed normal to her."

"That's pretty," I said, pointing to the locket, but still thinking about her mouth, and feeling an extra pulse of energy from her touch.

"This was in her family too," she said, and pressed it against her chest, but didn't say anything else about it.

I worried I'd hit another sore spot, and picked up the pace to distract from the chance that I was right. The pond trail lay just ahead of us. I really wanted her to see Mohosh before she had to go. She hadn't mentioned leaving yet, so I kept the pace. She was taller than most girls I knew, and even though she was thin, her long limbs held muscle, like she'd always climbed trees and swam in the summers.

"Down here," I said, and pointed to the path, holding a branch back for her.

She stopped and looked at me, then back behind us—I figured it was to see how far we'd come and if she should turn around or keep going. "They'll be okay for a little while longer," she said, more to herself than me, and ducked under my arm and onto the trail.

"Look out for the roots," I said once the brush closed behind us. "They'll pop up and trip you flat if you're not careful." The path had grown narrower than I'd ever seen it—the kudzu vine had grown over everything else, which meant that not many people were using the trail this summer. I scooted in front of her again, clearing space for us to walk. When our way widened, and we could see the pond sparkling ahead in the clearing, I heard Tennessee sigh next to me.

She stood still and looked out over the water, then raised her eyes to the mountain beyond it. "It feels so different here than anywhere else I've been in Strickland so far," she said. "I bet you come here a lot."

"I used to. I'm sure I will again. I don't really have a normal right now, if that makes sense."

"I think I know what you mean. Right now I feel very in-between. Waiting to settle into the new, but missing the old."

"Yep, that's it. I can't guess what it will feel like on the other side of things yet. Hey, if you want to sit and rest a minute, there's a flat spot over there." I pointed.

"Okay." She followed me but then stopped and leaned down to pick something up off the ground. "I think this is a geode," she said, and passed the rock to me.

"It feels light. Wanna break it open and see?"

"Not now," she said. "I want to imagine what might be inside for a while longer. Could be anything."

I held it out for her to take again, and when she reached, our fingers brushed for an instant.

"Isn't it crazy that we can change things just by touching them? All the tiny holes in this thing where water seeps in and mixes with minerals and oxygen to make crystals—what if just now we planted a crystal seed or changed the color of one?"

"I had no idea that's how it works. What do you hope is inside?"

She rolled it around in her hands and thought. "I have a pretty nice citrine one, and azurite. I only have a fragmented amethyst, so I'd be happy if this was another one of those, more intact. Or smoky quartz—those dark gray crystals are really amazing." She sat down beside me and crossed her legs. "Really any kind of crystal is pretty great with me." There was a sliver of air between our knees. If either one of us moved the slightest bit we could touch again. The possibility hung in the air like a question.

"What is that?" She pointed to the biggest house in Strickland, up on the side of the mountain.

"Somewhere you never need to go."

"Why? It looks incredible. Who lives there? The mayor?"

"Might as well be." I thought of warning her about the Praters, but told myself to hold back. I didn't want to scare her too much, and she'd find things out soon enough. "You said your daddy's the new foreman at the mine?"

"Yes. He told me that he got an offer he couldn't refuse."

"You can understand why, looking up there. It's where his new boss, Amos Prater, lives."

"He must have a lot of children. Not to mention money," she laughed.

"Yes to both, but not many of his kin live there anymore, believe it or not." I swatted away the mosquitoes and other things I wanted to say about Amos.

"You obviously don't like him. The look on your face makes that very clear."

I laughed. "You and Mama Draughn are going to get along just fine."

"I like everything I know about her so far. But back to that guy." She tossed her head at the mansion. "What's his story?"

I opened my mouth to speak, but then bit the inside of it. All of a sudden, I saw Nate lying in his blood like it was happening all over again right there in front of me, Tennessee, and Amos Prater's mountain. Even in the shade, the heat seemed to rise an extra twenty degrees, but my skin went damp-cold. I swallowed against my tight throat, remembering the gas station earlier that day, and then Nate lying dead on the porch. Too much had happened in too short a time, or any amount of time, for that matter.

"You look pale," Tennessee said, and lightly touched my arm. "Stick your head between your knees and breathe." She moved her hand to my back. "Tap your fingertips against one another like this. I know it sounds weird, but it helps. We're sitting right here on this rock. That's all that is happening. Just breathe."

She was right. I started to come back—first through new air in my lungs, then her touch, and then my own fingers tapping together. "Sorry," I said. I wished I hadn't given her so many reasons to think I was a disaster.

"Does it have something to do with that house up there?"

I was in too deep already. "My brother's dead," I said. "Tommy Prater did it."

She looked at the house again and was quiet for a few minutes. Then she turned and looked into my eyes. "Why?"

I stared at the expensive brick and windows and hardened my jaw against them, but there was nothing I could do to stop the tears. They sprang on me, not caring where I was, or who I was with.

"Never mind," she said. "You don't need to talk about that right now."

I was glad she knew the right thing to say, and also what to leave unsaid.

"Our mom died last year." She turned the geode in her lap. I inched a little closer toward her, and our knees finally touched. I thought about reaching for her hand, but they were both wrapped around the geode. I wondered if she was changing it again right then. "Has it gotten any easier?"

"No," she said immediately, then laughed a little. "Not really. Honestly, I'm so busy taking care of Omie that I haven't even thought about what's easier or more difficult, because I don't have a choice but to keep going. But when I have a minute to stop, or Omie asks me about Mom, and I realize he is starting to forget her—it hurts almost worse than before. Sometimes there are days that I think of her and smile instead of crying, so I guess that's the good news."

"Yeah. That helps a little."

"She used to tell us these stories that came down from her great-grandfather. He was Scottish. There was one about a mermaid and a fisherman. Apparently Scottish mermaids are also half-seals, in case you didn't know." She laughed a little. "This one mermaid left her seal skin on the beach, because she wanted to take a walk with human feet. The fisherman saw her and stole the skin so that she would be bound to him forever, but she always wanted to go back to the sea. Years later, one of her kids found the hidden skin and returned it to her, and then she ran back to the ocean, finally free."

"That's kind of sad. What about her kids?"

"I know. That part's tough. But Omie and I like to pretend that now Mom is someplace where she always wanted to go back to. Maybe she was only meant to be ours for a little while."

"I guess I can see how that helps." I don't know if it was that she'd trusted me with so much right then, or if I was just excited to find someone who seemed to understand, but I leaned toward her lips without realizing it. We were less than an inch apart, our heat and shadows mixed.

She quickly jerked away and blinked like she'd forgotten where she was, and how she ever got there.

"I'm sorry," she said, and jumped to her feet. "I have to go. They'll be getting worried by now." She straightened her clothes and tucked her hair behind her ears.

"I wasn't trying to—" I said.

"No, it's okay. I just really need to hurry now." Her guard flew up again in a flash, and I felt awful for trying to kiss her. Whatever door she'd opened for me now seemed closed. I hoped she hadn't locked it for good.

I led Tennessee quickly to the path and then out into the field. She was silent, and I figured I'd irritate her if I tried for any conversation, so I kept my mouth shut too. As soon as we got close to Kinley Road, she said, "I can take it from here."

"Let me walk you home."

"No, it's best if I go alone," she said, and took a few steps past me.

"Wait," I said. "When can I see you again?"

"I don't know. I hardly have a minute to myself, and I really shouldn't have been gone this long."

"There's a party tomorrow night. Biggest one of the summer."

"It's been a long time since I've been to one of those," she said. "That sounds great, but I doubt I can get away. I feel like I'm more of a mom than a teenager most of the time."

"I understand." I looked down at the purse by her side. "Do you have a phone?"

She nodded. "You?"

We exchanged numbers.

"Thanks for taking me to the pond. And talking," she said.

"I probably said too much."

"Nope, just enough. I mean that. Okay, I really gotta run now." She turned and started walking, and then jogging, the geode still clasped in her hands.

CHAPTER 10

A GROCERY BAG HEAVY with leftovers sat on her counter, right where Mama Draughn said it would be. The loud sound of a spinning metal fan came from their bedroom; neither one of them were anywhere to be seen or heard. I figured they were sleeping and didn't want to wake them, so was careful to not let the door bang on my way out.

I was too stirred up after the time with Tennessee to go home and sit still in our trailer, so I texted Jacob, Around?

Pick me up, he said.

He was waiting outside when I got to his place. "Mind taking me to Ryan's?" He leaned through the passenger window. "The wheeler's on empty, and my mom is gone for the day visiting Gran at the old folks' home."

"Sure, I guess. I could use a couple of bucks for gas, though."

"No problem." He handed me a five. "Come hang with us. I'm helping Ryan get ready for the party tomorrow night. We gotta pick up the keg and a bunch of ice."

"I need to take this food back to Mama. Anyway, I get the feeling Ryan likes hanging out with you solo. You know he's always been weird to me since the thing with Victoria."

Jacob got in the car and handed me a beer. "Oh yeah, forgot about that. Bet he's over it by now, though."

"No thanks, it's a little early for me," I said to the beer in his hands. He looked like he'd already had a few, the way he slumped into the seat and leaned against the door.

He popped the top on the beer, and I started driving. "I guess Ryan's always been jealous of you, come to think of it," he said after he took a sip.

"I don't know what he'd be jealous of. He's the one with all the stuff."

"Yeah, but he don't have many friends. I mean real ones. Everyone comes for the booze, but they don't show up unless there's a party or something."

"If he hadn't stolen everyone's lunches in first grade, he would've made more friends."

Jacob laughed. "Oh my God, I forgot about that."

"Hey." I wondered if I should speak my question or keep it to myself. "You heard about the new girl yet?"

"Hell yeah, everyone's talking about her. Boyd said he saw her chasing her little brother around. Said she has an ass like a peach and the rest of her is even hotter. What'd you hear?"

"Did he talk to her? What about him and Ellie? I thought

they had gotten all serious by now." Even though I knew everyone would be after Tennessee, it already drove me crazy to think about Boyd or anyone else talking about her that way. I sat up straighter in my seat and leaned closer to the wheel, my shoulders tight across my back.

"I don't think Boyd's serious about anything but his dick. Why does it matter, anyway?"

We were getting closer to Ryan's. "She's different," I said. "She's not like Victoria or Clarice or any of the rest of them."

"Watch it," Jacob said, and finished the last of his beer. "You're talking about the mother of my child." It was weird how he'd get defensive over Clarice when most of the time he was complaining about her. "Of course you'd fall for the new girl," he said.

"I won't be the only one, and that's what worries me. Just keep those idiots away from her, okay?"

"Hey. I always got your back, you know that," Jacob said. "It's just been crazy lately with the baby and all. I got my hands full, but I know you need me more now that Nate's— Listen, we should go see my uncle in Lexington soon, so you can meet him. And we can get back to working on that cherry table with your new saw."

"That sounds good," I said. "It'd be nice to get out of here for a while. Get back to thinking about what's up ahead." I pulled up to Ryan's brick house.

"Sure you don't want to come in? He said the pinball's up and running again."

"I'll see it tomorrow night."

"All right." Jacob hopped out and leaned down where I could see him. "Lexington," he said, and pointed at me. "Next week, maybe. Just need to clear the baby schedule."

"You got it," I said, even though I didn't have the money for a road trip and I figured he didn't either, but maybe his uncle would float us, or I could borrow some cash from Mama now that she had the money from Nathaniel's check. Maybe even Tennessee could somehow come along.

When I got near home, Daddy's truck was parked in our driveway. I carried the bag of food from Mama Draughn inside, and found the two of them sitting at the kitchen table, talking serious over something.

Daddy looked up when I came through the door. "Where you been?"

"You know, kids aren't supposed to spend summers indoors," Mama said.

"He's not a kid anymore."

"Mama Draughn sent a few things," I said. "And she'll come see you sometime next week, she wanted me to tell you."

"She's such a saint," Mama said. I saw her roll her eyes a little. "Wish I had a quarter teaspoon of the stuff she has that makes her that way."

"I think she just loves taking care of people," I said.

"Whatever it is, I'm sure neither of you would mind if I could cook like she does."

"We're fine the way things are," Daddy said. "I'm already fat enough, don't need any more on me."

"Mr. Draughn's pretty skinny. Guess it's all those vegetables they eat," I said.

"Expensive to eat that way. I don't know how they afford it. Social security don't buy health food, and the mine retirement sure as hell don't."

"I suppose they figure it's worth the cost."

"Food is food," Daddy said. "It all comes out the same way in the end. I've got to get back. New foreman's tightened things up, trying to make a good impression."

"What's he like?" I asked, anxious to get his take on Tennessee's daddy.

"It don't matter what I think of him. Time will tell if he'll last. Takes a long time to learn Amos's ways. How to choose the right battles. We'll see if Moore can manage that."

"Are you trying to say that Nate should have just stayed out of his way and kept his mouth shut?"

"I wasn't aiming to, but I sure wish he had."

"Have you talked to the sheriff again?" Mama asked.

"I told you I'll get to it," Daddy said.

"I don't think you will," I said before thinking. "You just

said people shouldn't upset Amos. I know you don't want to risk your job for it."

Daddy brought his hand against the table and the slap echoed through the kitchen. "Don't put words in my mouth and don't talk about things that you don't understand, boy. When you're paying the bills for everyone, then you can speak. Not until then. You'll find out soon enough that all you can do in life is choose the best way to take care of yourself and your own. Simple as that."

"Speaking of," Mama said, rubbing her forehead and then around her eyes, "you got the grocery money?"

Daddy looked at her and laughed, once, before saying, "You've got plenty. Did you really think I wouldn't know that you cashed Nathaniel's check? Both of you are so goddamn thick-headed right now."

"This is my trailer, and my land," Mama said. "You better keep doing what's right by us. If you won't—"

"Then, what? Harlowe will? You know as good as me that the only way he'll ever do that now is if he gets in right with Amos, and he needs me for that. Especially after everything with Nathaniel. I'd be careful with that money, Sarah. And careful of what you say to me."

"Both of you stop," I said. "It's only been two days. You think he'd want this?" I stood and left them to fight each other if they had any energy left for it. They'd drained all of mine.

In my room, I took the big box Nate left in the corner for me on my birthday and finally opened it. I'd never seen a saw shine like that one did. No dust on it yet, the engine sparkling. Every piece, big and small, had a purpose. I'd dreamed of holding it in my hands and there it was, bittersweet. Nate was right, it was heavy, but not the way he'd meant it. He'd added an expectation I only hoped I could meet. I set it down and took my phone out of my jeans pocket, snapping a pic to send to Jacob. We needed to see his uncle Lexington, and even more than that, get our asses back to work.

I put my phone back in my pocket and then walked over to the other side of the desk where Nate's was still charging. His notebook was on the desk, and I flipped it open, scanning the dates and places he'd written, looking for any numbers that jumped out. Since they were only months and days, most of them were three digits instead of four. But there was one that stood out to me: 12/25, Strickland. Nate had never missed a Christmas with us, and it was the only date that was at home. I punched the numbers into the phone. The screen shook and said "failed attempt." I popped my knuckles and looked down at a piece of mail Mama had left for me a couple of weeks ago. I hadn't opened it because it was from Arizona State University, one of those stock letters they sent out to everyone. I wasn't going to apply anywhere—I didn't have the grades or the money to go to college. "Harlowe Compton, 1613 Kinley Road," the label read. It was worth a shot. With my thumb, I typed the numbers of our address into Nate's phone. My stomach flipped when it opened. With a deep breath, I wondered how Nate would feel about me digging into his business. But if things had happened the other way around, I was sure he wouldn't stop searching until he'd set things right.

CHAPTER 11

I SCANNED THE LIST of names on Nate's screen. Mine was there, so were Mama's and Daddy's, and a handful of other people I recognized, along with a few I didn't. At the very top was Tommy's. I clicked on his name right away. He had sent the last text to Nate, and it said **2:30, at the office.** I read the date, 7/21—my birthday, right around when I noticed Nate had left the party. My heart beat faster, and my mouth went dry. I scrolled all the way back, looking for anything else that pointed to that day or any other trouble between them, but there were only a few earlier texts about standard job stuff like when the reports were due. At least I had proof now that Tommy wanted to meet Nate the day he died. If I couldn't get the sheriff to pay attention to that, I'd have to find someone else who would.

Since I had already gone that far, I figured I might as well read all of Nate's texts, especially if I was going to offer his phone up as evidence. I guess I could have done without seeing the naked photos Missy Higgins sent him, even though she looked really good in them, but I was more glad he'd skipped returning the favor to her. Anyway, I went ahead and erased the thread from her. It seemed like the right thing to do. I made my way through the rest of his messages without finding anything shocking. The last name was Jacob's, and there was only one text. It was from Nate to him and it said **Remember, Woodvale Friday.** The message itself was weird, but so was the fact that there was only one. I knew they had sent other texts about the saw, or times we'd all met up together. My pulse quickened again. I put Nate's phone down on the desk and picked up his notebook. Flipping to the last page of his writing, I read "7/19, Woodvale." The pages shook in my hand. Nate must have erased their other texts, as easily as I had Missy's nudes. I needed Jacob to tell me what it all meant.

Looking at my own phone, I saw that he still hadn't texted me back after I sent him the picture of the saw. I snapped photos of Nate's notebook pages, and also the text to Jacob on his screen, figuring an extra record of both wouldn't hurt. Then I bit the inside of my mouth and sent a text to Jacob that said **Need to talk,** from Nate's phone.

CHAPTER 12

I TURNED THE WATER in the shower as cold as it would go, thinking if I froze myself under it, the heat wouldn't feel so bad when I got out. But as soon as I toweled off, I started sweating again. It was ten thirty in the morning. Jacob still hadn't texted me back from the night before—on either phone.

I looked in the mirror and combed my hair, thinking I should have buzzed it a few weeks ago because it was starting to curl, but I didn't want to do it right before Ryan's party that night. Jacob would be there, and I'd make sure he couldn't avoid me then.

I thought I'd find Mama in the kitchen, but when she wasn't there, I knocked on her closed bedroom door to tell her about the text from Tommy. A rustling sound came through the door, and I knocked again.

"What is it?" she said, sounding half-asleep.

I didn't want to shout through a closed door, so I turned the knob and opened it. She was still in bed and pulled herself up, then blinked at me. When she reached for her cigarettes, she knocked the full ashtray all over the floor.

"God damn it," she said, and rushed out from under the sheet to clean it up. She crouched on the floor in only a too-small tank top and underwear. I turned away, embarrassed to see her like that.

"Did you take another one last night?" I asked, and wished Nate could tell me how he'd dealt with the pills the last time. I remember her sleepy and stumbling after the surgery. Nate found her out cold one morning, and after the medic came to revive her with Narcan, she finally agreed to stop. That was when he sent me over to Mama Draughn's for a few weeks so I wouldn't have to see the worst of it.

"That's none of your business," she said. "I don't have to answer to you, or anyone else, for that matter."

"Does Daddy know about it?" I asked.

"There's nothing for him to know." I heard her dump the ashtray into the trash can by her bed, and then get back under the sheet again. "I appreciate your concern, sweetie, but," she yawned, "I'm a grown woman. I can take care of myself."

I turned around to face her again. "Have you talked to the doctor? Did he give them to you?" I asked, even though I knew it didn't matter where they came from. Legal or not, pills did the same thing once inside a person.

"Go put on some coffee for me and I'll make us breakfast"

was her only answer. I changed my mind on telling her about the texts. She wasn't in a state to hear about Tommy or Nate. It would probably only make her worse.

By the time she made it out to the kitchen, the coffeepot was full, and I'd already scrambled some eggs because I was hungry and tired of waiting on her. She squinted and closed the curtains I'd opened to let in the light.

We spent most of the day in front of the TV. I wished the hours would go faster so I could get out the door to the party. Mama loved watching *Wheel of Fortune* and dozed on and off between cigarettes and during commercial breaks. A woman jumped up and down, squealing at her good luck. I wondered what she would do with the twenty-five hundred dollars if she didn't lose it before she had to go back home. Maybe she'd sat with her mama at night watching the show like I was then, just hoping to find some way out.

"Mind grabbing some beers?" Mama asked. She'd never allowed me to drink in the house before, but I wasn't going to remind her of that.

While I was at the fridge, one of the phones in my pockets vibrated. Tennessee's name on my screen shot through my veins like the strongest shine.

CHAPTER 13

Does the invitation stand? her text said.

Yes. Want me to pick you up?

Let's meet at your place.

Great. 1613 Kinley Road. Anytime.

I stared at my phone for a couple of minutes, the fridge still open, waiting to see if she'd say anything else. The heat of our trailer stuck against my back but there was a nice chill on my arms from the fridge and her text. I grabbed the beer and went back to the couch.

"It's been a while since I've seen that smile," Mama said, looking up at me when I handed her the can. "What'd I miss?"

"That foreman Daddy was talking about? His daughter's coming by here and going over to Ryan's with me tonight."

"Right now? I should get dressed, then. The place is a bad mess," she said, and set the recliner down.

"It's fine, she won't stay long. And she knows what's happened. She understands."

Mama didn't hear the last of what I said because she was already in her room. I heard the water running in the bathroom. I was glad she finally had a reason to get up and get moving. Maybe she wouldn't need the pills if she had something every day to look forward to. I nursed the beer and my surprise that Tennessee was on her way. It wasn't long before I heard a knock at the door.

Tennessee's light blue dress grabbed my attention and her smile put me at ease. "I wasn't lying," she said. "It really was a fluke that I got away."

"Come in," I said. "You look great. Is it okay for me to say that? You look great." I could feel myself blushing. "I said that already. Damn."

"Thanks." She laughed and followed me inside.

"Do you want a beer?"

"No thanks, I'll wait. Our neighbor, Mrs. Hemlock, has been asking if she could watch Omie sometime. Daddy's out of town for a meeting, and I remembered the party, so—"

"Yeah, I'm really glad you did. It should be a lot of fun, especially now that you're coming." I'd just have to find some time to talk with Jacob alone, but that shouldn't be too hard.

"Thanks," she said. "Trust me, I'm excited to get out for a night."

Mama came into the kitchen with damp curls pinned on top of her head, wearing clean clothes and a little too much makeup. "Oh gosh, you're already here. I was hoping I could straighten up. It's not always this messy." She offered her hand to Tennessee. "Just call me Sarah. The 'ma'am' and 'Mrs.' stuff gets to me sometimes. Doesn't seem I should be that old. I don't know how it happens so fast." She smiled. "Aren't you lovely?"

"Oh, thank you. I love that lipstick you're wearing," Tennessee said, noticing her effort.

Mama touched the back of her neck and looked pleased. "Harlowe, why don't you get that Tupperware Betsy put the sweets in and meet us at the table where we can talk a little?"

They chatted while I grabbed the brownies and cookies and poured two glasses of Kool-Aid for Tennessee and me.

"Wow, it's so very blue," Tennessee said when I set one in front of her.

"You don't like it?"

"I do sometimes, I guess; I was just thinking about going to the party with a mouth full of blue teeth," she laughed.

"Right. We don't want Smurf teeth. I'll get some water for us." I took the blue glasses to the sink.

Mama made use of every second I was gone to ask Tennessee about her family, and where she was from. I tensed when I heard Tennessee talking about her mom dying, and hoped she didn't feel like she had to explain anything she didn't want to.

"I'm so sorry," Mama said. "You've got a lot on your shoulders looking after a little brother so young."

"Not any more than you're carrying. I heard someone say once that losing a child is the worst grief a person can know, and I'm sure that's the truth," Tennessee said.

Mama nodded and looked down at the table until she touched her cheek and looked at the tears on her fingertips like she was surprised to find them there. "I'm sorry. They come without warning." She reached for a napkin. "Anyway, it's real nice to meet you. Looking at the two of you sitting here reminds me of when I was young. I forgot how exciting summer nights used to feel. Like something magic could happen any minute."

"And did it?" asked Tennessee.

"Sometimes," Mama said. "Enough to always keep me hoping for more."

Her face seemed a little lighter than it was before Tennessee came, even with her tears. I imagined what she must have been like at our age, or even younger, before she met Daddy. I'd seen pictures of her then, but this was the first time I saw traces of the girl she used to be.

"I could sit here and talk with you all night, but the two of you should get outside in the air and enjoy yourselves."

I stood, happy to have some alone time with Tennessee before we saw everyone at Ryan's.

"No driving, Harlowe," Mama said before we left. "And Tennessee, you come back here anytime."

"Thank you, I will. You made me feel right at home," Tennessee said.

CHAPTER 14

"I HOPE THAT WAS okay back there," I said once we were walking down Kinley Road together.

Tennessee's purse tapped against her leg and her hands tucked into the pockets of her dress. "It was great," she said. "Your mom's very kind."

"She is. I worry about her."

"Of course you do. I'm sure she leans on you even more now."

"Yeah, I think she does. I don't know how much I can help her, though."

"Well, from here it looks like you're doing a great job." Her smile caught the light of the moon above us.

I didn't want her to think that I was a downer all of the time, and tried to come up with something else to talk about. "How's the reading going?"

"Almost done with the Carson McCullers. Think I'll dive into *Hamlet* next. Oh, and Omie and I are reading

Winnie-the-Pooh before he goes to sleep at night."

"Can I borrow that first one when you're done? Haven't been able to get a copy of it yet. You're going to Berry Grove, right?"

She shook her head. "They said the kindergarten there is full. Omie and I will take the bus over to Wilson."

"Oh." My stomach dropped and our pace slowed.

"Why'd you say it like that?" she asked.

"It's nothing. I just assumed we'd be in the same class and thought it'd be pretty great." There was more to it than that. Amos owned Wilson Academy. Plenty of kids from other counties went there too, but he opened the school so that his own family, and anyone else he wanted to, could get diplomas no matter what their real grades were like.

"We'll still see each other," she said. "I came tonight, didn't I? It was a little hard to leave Omie at home. I've gotten so used to being the one that takes care of him. Mrs. Hemlock's a good person, right?"

"She is. Keeps to herself, but I've never heard a bad word about her. If there was any reason to worry, I'm sure I'd have heard about it."

Tennessee nodded. "Well, I bet you've heard some things about us. Dad caused some trouble in a few places. I think Mom planned to leave him once she could find work of her own, but then she got sick." She looked down. "Go ahead, tell me. I might as well know what they're saying."

"I heard about his leg, and the explosion. You shouldn't worry about it, though. I'd never make it out of the house if I thought too hard about what people say." Which made me think of Mama hardly ever leaving.

"You're right, it's a waste of time," she said.

Red's place was up ahead, right past Macnab's old cabin.

"Wait." Tennessee stopped walking. "What's that? It sounds like a duck is dying."

I couldn't help but laugh. "It's Peter Macnab, playing his bagpipes. He's a little strange, doesn't talk much to anyone."

"It's such a sad song. He lives by himself?"

"His wife died years ago. His kids are grown and moved away. They all wanted him to sell his land to Amos, but he never gave in. Recognize that?"

I pointed up the mountain, behind Red's trailer after we'd passed Macnab's.

"It's the Prater house we saw from the pond," she said.

"Yep. Macnab owns all this land that backs up to the mountain. Some say Amos wants to build on it, others think he wants to blast because there's more coal underneath."

"No offense, but why does Macnab want to stay here? Seems like he could make a bunch of money and go somewhere else."

"That's what I'd do, for certain. That land will go to ruin sooner or later anyway, sitting as it does by the mines. Guess he's used to the way he's always done and can't imagine doing it different."

Soon, we were close enough to Ryan's place to see the flicker of lights and hear the bass thumping hard. We took a right turn down the dirt road packed with parked cars on both sides. The music grew louder the closer we got, until we couldn't hear each other over it anymore. There seemed to be even more people than there were the year before, and I scanned all the strange faces for some familiar ones. Ryan was circled by a group of girls standing next to a new black Dodge Ram.

"Hey!" He motioned once he saw me. "Come check this thing out!"

"It's yours?" I stepped through the herd of girls leaning against the truck and made sure Tennessee was still close at my side. I could already sense other guys looking at her and closing in around us.

"Sure is." He handed beers to Tennessee and me. "I'm Ryan." He offered her his other hand.

Tennessee gave him a firm shake and said hello. When she turned her head to look out over the crowd, Ryan nudged me in the ribs with his elbow and wore a look on his face like whatever he wanted to say about her was going to be messed up. I shook my head before he could say anything out loud and walked even closer to her.

"All right then," he said. "I see. Y'all have a good time. Let me know if you need anything." He turned his back to us and faced the group of girls again.

"Hey," I yelled behind him. "Where's Jacob?"

He looked at me over his shoulder. "Round here somewhere."

Tennessee opened the door before I could reach it. The house was full of people and cigarettes and dope. She elbowed her way through the room and I followed her, thinking she must have been to parties much bigger than this one before. A hand touched my shoulder and someone yelled my name. I jumped and turned around quick, only to find it was Red, half-drunk, trying to throw me with a weird voice he'd made sound deeper than his own. I tagged his shoulder and he laughed, but stopped whatever he was about to say when he saw Tennessee. "Oh," he said, straightening. Tennessee shook his hand with the same strong grip as she had Ryan's.

"Everyone's heading downstairs, let's go check it out." Red started walking, and we followed him through the crowd into the kitchen, then down the stairs to the basement. Electric guitar blared through the speakers. People sang and danced, holding their beers high and spilling them all over the floor.

"Shit. Where did all of this stuff come from?" I asked Red. The basement was as loaded as the arcade at the Griggin movie theater.

"Don't know. This is the first time I've seen any of it. That pool table is epic, though." He stood on his toes to see over the crowd and handed me the joint in his fingers. I passed because I wasn't sure how Tennessee would feel about it. She reached over my shoulder, took the joint from Red, hit it once, then handed it back to him.

"Bet I could beat you," she yelled over the music, and pointed to the pool table.

"Only if I let you, and I can't do that," I said, though I'd never played pool before in my life, only seen it on TV. But I'd fake it and hope for the best rather than telling her that. The three of us walked down the stairs and pushed our way toward the table. The smoke was so thick it covered all of our faces like a mask. I waved my hand through the air and it cleared just enough for me to see Jacob through the crowd, holding a pool cue.

CHAPTER 15

"LOOK," RED SAID, AND pointed through the haze.
"Original Pac-Man over there." He bolted toward the corner,
but only made it a few yards before a girl two inches taller
than him caught his eye. He tried talking with her, but mostly
stared at the cleavage spilling over her bra.

"This way." I held my hand out to Tennessee. She looked at
it like it wasn't something she needed, but took it anyway and
wrapped her fingers around mine. I walked as fast as I could,
and squeezed us around and through the crowded bodies. I
didn't want to let go of her hand just yet, but felt her fingers
slipping from mine.

We stood right in front of him, but Jacob acted like he
didn't see us and leaned over the table to shoot. A cigarette
hung from the corner of his lip.

"Did you get my texts?" I asked him.

He missed his shot and stood the cue on end. Finally he
turned to me. His eyes were bloodshot and he looked like he

hadn't slept or stopped drinking since I dropped him off at Ryan's the day before. "No," he said. "You know the service is shitty here." He smiled at Tennessee, ashed his cigarette on the ground, and looked back at me again. "Aren't you going to introduce me?"

Tennessee jumped in and said hello, sensing something was off between us.

"How'd he talk you into coming with him?" Jacob asked.

"He didn't have to," she said.

"I need to talk with you for a minute," I told Jacob. I thought I heard him chuckle a little, like he'd recognized the words I sent from Nate's phone. I was getting more and more frustrated with him, but didn't want to make a scene in front of Tennessee.

When he leaned over the table again, Tennessee stepped back and made room for his cue. The sound of his shot cracked the air and he hit two balls—one went in a left pocket, and one into the right.

"That's better," Jacob said. "Grab us another round, Lowe, and you can tell me all about whatever's bugging ya."

I wanted to tell him to get his own beer but turned and asked Tennessee, "You all right here?"

"Yep, but I'll come if you need a hand."

"I got it. Keep an eye on him, though."

Jacob laughed a little too loudly and patted my shoulder when I walked past him on my way up the stairs. Melting ice and floating beer filled the kitchen sink. I grabbed three cans.

Yelling sounded from the basement and I froze. It wasn't party yelling, but the fighting kind that quiets everything else. By the time I stood at the top of the stairs, the crowd had pushed against the walls. Jacob stood beside the pool table in a circle of empty space. My stomach dropped.

"Get out!" he screamed. "You ain't welcome here, and you know it!"

Tommy Prater stood at the other end of the pool table. I pushed the beer onto someone beside me and ran down the stairs. Once I was on the floor, I rushed toward Jacob. Tennessee stood behind him and backed away into the crowd, her arms crossed over her purse.

"What's going on?" I whispered to Jacob.

"Stay away from this, I got it," he said.

Tommy wore a tight T-shirt and a look that matched. "Thought I might find the two of you here together," he said. The sound of his voice and the easy smile on his face brought my stomach into my throat. I saw Nate's blood in the tub again, swirling down the drain.

"Why's that?" I asked.

"Harlowe, don't," Jacob said.

"You can play dumb if you want, but it won't change anything."

"What is he talking about?" I turned to Jacob.

"Later," he said to me, under his breath.

"Wait," I said when he started forward, but he'd already left, the cue ball gripped tight in his hand, and flew at Tommy. They were on the floor by the time I got to them. Tommy screamed at him, and swung.

Jacob's knuckles were so tight that they matched the white ball. He kicked his way on top of Tommy and brought the ball hard against the side of his skull. Blood ran down Tommy's face and into his eye socket but he managed to flip Jacob onto his back.

"Stop!" I yelled at them, but Tommy's foot kicked me backward and I crouched over my stomach till I caught my breath. Everyone else in the room froze. The ball rolled out of Jacob's reach. Tommy pulled his arm back and punched Jacob so hard I could hear it over the music from where I stood. Blood dripped from Tommy's fist onto Jacob, and Jacob's own blood started to pool beneath him.

"Is this what you wanted, you sick motherfucker? You want me to beat the shit out of you?"

My insides burned and my vision went red. I rushed toward the two of them again but couldn't find a way to tear them apart. "Leave him alone!" I screamed at Tommy, my voice cracking. Tommy wouldn't look at me. I was invisible to both of them. "I gave you a choice," Tommy said. "This is all your fault."

Jacob tried to block the punches but couldn't. His head

slammed against the concrete floor over and over. Every time I heard it hit, it felt like Tommy's fist went straight to my stomach.

"Stop!" I screamed again, and looked around for something to knock over Tommy's head. I caught sight of Tennessee moving along the wall toward us, but then someone pushed me out of the way and I fell against the cinder blocks. When I was able to stand again, I saw Ryan holding a shotgun, standing over Tommy and Jacob. He jammed the barrel into Tommy's head. "Get the fuck out of my house," he said.

Tommy sat up, his full weight against Jacob's chest. He ran his hands through the blood in his hair and spat pink onto the ground, then looked up at Ryan. "Real nice stuff you got here," he said to Ryan. "This ain't all come from the mine. I know what your daddy makes." He stood up, Ryan's gun still pressed against the back of his head. Once Jacob was free of Tommy, he rolled onto his side and coughed out more blood.

I jumped when a hand touched my shoulder, but then saw it was Tennessee's. "Are you okay?" she whispered. I nodded and tried to find words again.

Ryan walked Tommy to the door. "If I see you on my property once more, I'll shoot," he said.

"One week," Tommy shouted on his way out.

Jacob lay on the floor, unable to get up. As soon as Tommy left, everyone rushed to help him when they wouldn't before.

I got down on the floor beside him.

"I need to get back to Omie," Tennessee said behind me. "We'll talk later."

"Just a minute," I said.

"No, do whatever you need to do. I'll be fine," she said.

"I can't let you walk home by yourself, especially not with Tommy wandering around out there."

"I'll stay off the main roads," she said.

Red walked up beside us. "Shit."

"Mrs. Hemlock will take care of him. She wouldn't want you walking home alone, and neither do I. I'll only be one minute."

She took a deep breath and nodded, but looked at the door like she was thinking about leaving anyway. I couldn't blame her.

When I got to Jacob's side, he held his hand to the back of his skull and brought it out full of blood.

"I'll fucking kill him, Harlowe."

"Let me take a look; you might need stitches," I said. "Then you have to tell me what the hell is going on."

"I'm fine." Jacob's face had swelled. The side Tommy punched had turned purple and black.

I leaned behind him to find the back of his head slick with blood. The gash was bad, but the blood was clotting, and his skull wasn't cracked. "Come on. Let's get you home," I said.

"No way. I can't let Mama see me like this."

"You're not taking him anywhere." Ryan walked up beside us and stood the shotgun on end. "I'll clean him up, then we gotta leave."

"Where?" I asked.

Ryan didn't answer. I felt Tennessee beside me, and her need to get back to Omie and away from all of the crazy I'd brought her into.

"One of you tell me what's going on! All of you know something, but my brother was the one that got killed for it."

"Drop it, Harlowe." Jacob leaned on Ryan and looked at me. "I mean it. Stop asking questions. You'll only get hurt. Or worse."

"Go home," Ryan said to me. "Stay out of Tommy's way. We'll deal with it."

"No," I said. "I need to know. What was the Woodvale text about, Jacob?"

"Please." Jacob's voice cracked and his eyes filled with tears. "Drop it, okay?"

Before I could say anything else, Ryan started walking Jacob up the stairs.

We both needed air. I took Tennessee's hand, walked past the blood on the floor and through the door. I knew she felt the tremor in my fingers.

"I'm sorry," I said once we were outside. "I wouldn't have taken you if I had any idea."

"Are you okay?"

"I found some things last night," I said, and then stopped, remembering Jacob's face before Ryan took him away. I didn't want to get her involved.

"Tommy is the one you told me about?"

I nodded. "I've probably already said too much. I don't want you to worry about this. Just trust me: I don't know what's going on here."

"Why didn't someone call the cops?"

I sighed and tried to calm the mix of anger and adrenaline that had built up inside of me.

She dropped my hand and slid her purse strap higher on her shoulder. "Because his dad owns everything," she said, answering the question herself.

"I bet you're thinking all kinds of things right now," I said. "But I can tell you this—I'm not trouble. I wanted to hit Tommy as much as Jacob did, even more. But I'm not that stupid."

"Is that what Nate did? Went after Tommy?"

"I don't know. I think he might have known some things about Tommy that he wasn't supposed to."

"And Jacob did too?"

"Yeah, it looks that way."

She looked down at her feet while she walked. "What if Tommy comes after you?"

"I think he would have already done that if he wanted,"

I said, but didn't tell her I was scared that he still might if he didn't get whatever it was from Jacob.

She was quiet and didn't ask any more questions. We were in Baxter Creek Holler by then, and soon could see Mrs. Hemlock through the curtains, asleep on the couch.

"Omie must have worn her out," Tennessee said.

"I'm really sorry about tonight," I said again. "Can I call you?" I asked.

She nodded, but looked off to the side like she wasn't so sure. Before I could reach out to hug her, she was already up the stairs and standing at the door. "Please be careful, Harlowe," she said. "You're my only friend here right now."

CHAPTER 16

THE DARK WALK HOME by myself felt too quiet, and I quickened my pace, trying not to think about where Tommy might be. When I finally reached the light of our porch, I saw that some of Jacob's blood was still on my hands, and I wiped them on an old bag of sprouted seed.

"How was the party?" Mama asked when I walked inside. The TV was too loud for my nerves.

"Hang on." I walked to the sink and washed my hands, then I checked my clothes to make sure there wasn't anything she would notice.

"Tennessee sure is pretty," she said when I sat on the couch.

I reached for the remote to turn down the volume. "She is," I said. "And she's really smart."

"Well, you say that like it's a bad thing."

"No, it's a great thing. Just not sure I'm up to snuff, as you like to say."

"Don't talk like that. Of course you are. You met her daddy yet?"

"Not yet. I guess that will happen sometime soon. It might be time for me to go by the mines, anyway."

"That's a good attitude," she said. "I know you've never wanted to be a miner, but it doesn't have to be forever. Just till something else comes along."

I couldn't tell her that it wasn't a job I was looking for.

Mama rested her head against the back of the chair and closed her eyes. I looked at the orange bottle beside her.

"Jacob left town for a while," I said.

"What about baby Suzy?" She yawned.

"She'll be fine with Clarice, I guess. She'll have to be." I stood up and turned off the kitchen light and then spread myself out on the couch beside her. I lay there wondering where Jacob and Ryan had gone and if they weren't going to answer my questions about Nate, who could.

I jumped when the front door swung open and banged against the wood paneling. The morning light flooded in around Daddy. Mama fumbled with the handle of her chair.

"What time is it?" Mama asked.

"Past the time respectable people are awake." He closed the door and stood over the two of us, hooked his thumbs in his belt loops, and watched me clear the sleep out of my eyes.

"I'll make coffee," Mama said, and got the recliner down.

"Looks like you both need it," Daddy said. He didn't help her up.

Mama walked to the counter and peeled the lid off the coffee can.

"Heard about last night," Daddy said to me.

"You mean the party? How?"

"What are you two talking about?" Mama said from the kitchen. I didn't want her to know about Tommy and Jacob or anything else that could make her want to take even more pills.

"Let's go outside for a minute," I told Daddy.

"We can talk right here. No need to keep secrets. I don't know what you're messing with, boy. But I'd like to think you know better."

"I didn't do anything!" I yelled at him. "All I know is that Jacob and Ryan took off. Just like I told you last night, Mama." I lowered my voice again.

Confusion spread over Mama's face at the coffee maker. Daddy came toward me and grabbed me off the couch by the neck of my shirt.

"That's not what I heard," he said.

"What is going on here? Don't act like I can't hear both of you." Mama spilled coffee grounds all over the floor.

"Everything is fine," I said. "There's no need to worry."

She looked at Daddy, then back at me. "One of you answer me right now." The empty scoop shook in her hand.

I stared Daddy in the eye. He didn't have to deal with her every day the way I did. He'd given up trying long before Nate died.

"It's out of my hands," he said. "You're gonna do whatever

the hell you want to, I can see that. But I'll tell you this: if you hear from Jacob, you best tell him to stay wherever he is. He should have minded his own and kept his head down. Same goes for you, now." He reached into his wallet and took out two twenties, laid them on the table, and walked out the door.

Mama took a few steps toward me, balancing with her hand along the counter. "What was he talking about?" she asked.

I took the can and the scoop from her hands and filled the coffee filter. "Jacob had a little trouble with Tommy at the party. Nothing too serious, but that's why Ryan thought it'd be best for them to lay low for a spell."

"Was he hurt?"

"Not bad, no."

"Did Tommy try to hurt you?"

"No. Just wants to scare everyone, that's all."

"You can't tell me that after everything. I'm not an idiot. Why is everyone trying to keep me in the dark?" She leaned against the counter like she might slip into the ground otherwise.

"I'm not, Mama. Just doing the best I can. Like you."

"Not one bit of this makes sense to me. I don't know when the world went upside down and why no one else seems to notice."

"I noticed. I'm trying to set it the right way up best I know how."

She looked out over the sink window. "You know I wouldn't

make it if anything happened to you. I'm not sure I can bear it as it is."

And that's why I couldn't tell her the truth. "Nothing is going to happen to me," I said. I gave her the answer she wanted. "I need to get some work done. Maybe Betsy could come over for a while."

She shook her head. "Think I need to rest after all that," she said. "Can't seem to catch up on it."

Our fake-wood-paneled walls closed tight around me, and her stale cigarette air made it too hard to breathe. I hurried to my room and grabbed the saw and box of blades.

CHAPTER 17

THE BLUE PLASTIC TARP still covered the sawhorse where Jacob and I last left it. The only good thing about the summer drought was that I didn't have to worry about wood getting wet. Otherwise I crammed as much as possible into the shed. It would be nice to have a garage someday so I could keep several projects going at once. Better yet, a workshop. I took the padlock off the shed and found the electric cord. After I plugged it in at the porch outlet, I put on my goggles and gloves.

The new blade sailed through the plank of cherry. It would have made Nate happy to see me using his present. A clean-edged plank fell to the ground when I sliced through to the other side. The fight at the party tugged at the back of my mind, but the sound of the saw humming through wood pushed it far enough that I could mostly ignore it. Making something real and solid felt good. I'd do it every day, but people in Strickland didn't care about paying for the time it took to make nice things anymore. I figured if you're going to sit at the same table for most of your life, it should look as good as it is strong. I'd been reading about some techniques some guys were using to season wood with blowtorches and then varnish. It made the surface dark and shiny, but left the grain visible everywhere else. It was on my list of things to try when I had more space and equipment to experiment.

When I finished the next cut, I saw Red standing only a few feet away. "You can't sneak up like that," I said, then turned off the saw and slid my goggles off.

"Didn't know the best time to tell you I was here, was scared I'd mess you up," he said. "How is it?"

"A beast. Want to try?"

"You know I'm no good at stuff like that," he said.

"That can change. Heard anything from Jacob?"

"No. Was about to ask you the same."

"God, it's hot," I said. Sweat soaked my shirt. "Come over here to the shade." I climbed up the side of the porch and cleared some boxes off a couple of chairs. Red sat in the one with the hole in the bottom before I could offer the other. "He ever say anything to you about Nate?"

Red looked out over Kinley Road. "What kinds of things?"

"Hang on," I said, and went inside. I grabbed Nate's notebook, his phone, and two glasses of ice water for us.

Red sat and listened to me and held the glass against his neck when he wasn't drinking from it.

"Does this make any sense to you? Know anything about Woodvale?"

"It's right outside of Lexington, isn't it?"

"Yeah, but that's not what I mean. Ever heard either one of them mention it?"

"No, I don't think so." He stared into his glass and fished out a mosquito.

"Why do I get the feeling there's something you're not telling me?"

He took a deep breath and scratched the back of his head. "Did I tell you I'm skipping next year?"

"Of school? Senior year?"

"Yeah," he said. "Mama blew through everything Daddy left, then bought a bunch of shit off QVC she never uses. Credit cards are maxed. I need to start working."

"The mine?"

He nodded.

"It can't wait one more year?"

"No. Not sure I'd graduate anyway."

"Does Jacob know?"

"Haven't had a chance to tell him. He's been gone so much taking care of the baby."

I could see pushing Red for answers wasn't going to get me anywhere. Telling me about the mine was his way of saying that he couldn't risk poking at any questions, same as Daddy.

Still, Red helped me without knowing it.

"I should clean up," I said. "I've got an errand to run."

"Oh, all right. Maybe we could take some beer up to the Crag later or something?"

"Sure. I'll text ya when I have time."

CHAPTER 18

I LOCKED THE SAW and the rest of my things in the shed and ran inside to grab Mama's keys.

"Where you going?" she said from the recliner when she heard them jangle in my hand.

"See a friend," I said, and reached for the door.

"You're making me real anxious." She put out her cigarette. "Especially after last night."

"Your nerves are no fault of mine," I said.

She turned her head toward me, away from the TV. "I have half a mind to take those from you right now," she said, pointing to the keys, then slowly turned back to her game show, resting her chin in her hand. "But if you're going near town, at least grab me some smokes."

I wasn't, and left without saying anything else to her. I rolled down the windows before starting the car and then held my hand in the breeze while I drove. Clarice's parents lived a few miles past Baxter Creek, in Fulton Holler. They were tucked back in a grove of old hackberries that threatened to fall on their trailer with the next spring's storms. I wiped my face with a bandanna I'd left on the passenger seat before walking to their front door.

Clarice looked worn and frazzled when she opened the door, balancing baby Suzy on her hip. She was a lot thinner than she'd ever been, and I guess maybe that was what made her look so much older; her shorts hung loose around her hips. "I was just about to feed her," she said loudly over Suzy's crying. "Come on in."

"Thanks, I won't be long," I said.

She pointed for me to sit in one of the chairs at their plywood kitchen table, and opened a jar of green baby food. Once she'd strapped Suzy into the high chair, she fed her the mushy stuff. It smelled like old peas mixed with Beanie Weenies.

"I can guess why you're here," she said. "Krystal Travis told me about Tommy showing up last night."

"Yeah, it was bad. Do you know where Jacob and Ryan went?"

She rolled her eyes at me and wiped Suzy's mouth with the back of her hand. "Fat chance of that. Asshole hasn't talked to me in over two months."

"What? How's he seen the baby then?" I asked.

The spoon dangled in her hand when she looked at me, wide-eyed, like I was daft. "He doesn't see her," she said.

"Got it. Sorry. I'm just confused because it's not what he told the rest of us."

"Well, he's a liar," she said. "I learned it the hard way. I won't let her go through the same with him." She nodded at Suzy reaching for the spoon, and then gave her another bite of mush. "The only thing Jacob's good for is a handful of cash he leaves for us every once in a while under the mat, and I can't even count on him for that."

"Think I'm starting to get the picture," I said, so many other questions bubbling up in the back of my brain. "Thanks, and I'm sorry to bring it all up."

"That's okay. I'm kind of relieved you didn't know. Means you're not as much of a jerk as he is."

I wondered how much Nate had known about Jacob. "I'll see myself out," I said. "Mind letting me know if you hear from him?"

"Sure," she said. "But I wouldn't count on that happening."

"Okay," I said. "Seems to be the running standard lately."

CHAPTER 19

THE SUN WAS ALMOST down when I left Clarice's. I thought of all the times in the past couple of months that Jacob said he had to leave when we were hanging out, or couldn't make it at all, because of the baby, and I wondered where he'd really gone off to instead. It couldn't have been all of those places written in Nate's pages. I never went more than three or four days without seeing him.

After I started the engine, I told myself I was too close to Tennessee's to go home without trying to see her, though I didn't really need an excuse for wanting that. I parked just at the head of Baxter Creek, and once I reached their trailer, walked around to the back.

The light of a TV flickered from a window, and where the polka-dotted curtains parted, I saw a bookcase, its shelves full of books and a few stuffed animals. It had to be Tennessee's room. There was a pile of half-rotted wooden crates and old firewood against the side of the trailer, so I stacked them together and climbed high enough to peer closer through the window. Omie's yellow hair stuck out in all directions over the edge of a sheet on the bed. Tennessee blurred past the window, and I pawed at the screen. I felt the glass on the other side, and realized she couldn't hear me. I didn't want to yell, so I tapped my knuckles softly against the pane. She came to the window but looked straight over my head and didn't see me. I knocked again, a little louder. She jumped back and covered her mouth when she saw me. Then she tilted her head to the side, and a little smile appeared on her face.

She lifted the glass separating us, leaned closer, and whispered, "What are you doing?"

"Just wanted to see you."

"Is everything okay?"

"Yeah. I mean, as much as it can be, anyway."

She moved her head, and the lamp behind her glowed bright in my eyes, making it hard for me to read the look on her face. Then she turned to the bed to make sure Omie was still asleep. "Only for a minute," she said, lifting the screen.

I helped her through the window frame and onto the stack of crates. Once she was on the other side, she turned and pulled the screen down, leaving it open an inch at the bottom. "It sticks sometimes," she said.

After I hopped from the pile of wood to the ground, I reached my arms out to her. She took my hands and jumped.

"It's nice to see you," she said after she landed. "I've been a little worried since last night."

"You don't need to worry about me, you've got enough on your mind already. I was scared you'd be mad that I showed up before getting word to you."

"Well, you shouldn't make a habit of it, but now that you're here . . ." A thought flashed in her eyes. "There's something I want to show you. We have to hurry, though; I don't want to get too far away in case Omie wakes up." She took off toward the bushes and I followed at her heels. There was a small opening that she pushed wider, and then a narrow path on the other side. The moon was just bright enough for us to see the outline of things, and then only a few feet ahead of us. The path dipped down alongside the creek and then brought us up again to higher ground. Pine trees towering over us blocked the light, and Tennessee reached for my hand in the darkness. The bank steepened, and the creek below trickled softly. It was hard to hear the water at all, as it was near dried up. Tennessee started walking so quickly that we were almost running.

"Okay back there?" she asked.

"Yeah, great." I panted a little to keep up with her.

"Only a little bit farther. Oh good, there it is." A large shadow loomed in front of us. There was just enough light for me to catch a glint in Tennessee's eye when she smiled, but I still couldn't tell what it was that she wanted me to see until we got closer.

"It's definitely not perfect, so don't judge it too harshly," she said.

"Did you make this?" I asked, looking at the tent, or more like fort—fabric held together and lifted by a large wooden stake in the middle, pieces of broken crates, and the maple trunk behind as an anchor. It reminded me of the teepee Nathaniel and I made when we were little, where we spent as many nights as we could get away with.

"I sewed all the fabric together, and then we collected as much strong wood as we could find. It's definitely hodgepodge, but we like coming here. It's ours."

"I'm impressed," I said. "And a little jealous." I loved seeing how proud she was of what she'd made.

"Go on and take a quick look inside," she said, and parted a slit in the tarp.

I sat next to her on a quilt covering the plastic bottom and she threw me a pillow, then reached toward the back corner and clicked on a flashlight. There was a big jug of water, some books, and an unopened bag of chips together in a neat pile. Tennessee poured some water into a cup, took a sip, and then passed it to me. I wondered about the time and her hurry earlier, but then seeing her face in the glow of the flashlight, my pulse quickened, and all I could think about was how I could get even closer to her.

My hand traveled to the top of hers and I felt her fingers flicker under mine, not like she was trying to get away, but maybe that she was a little excited too. I scooted nearer and reached for her shoulder, scared each move might send her running, but she stayed where she was this time, even seemed to lean toward me a little. I followed the line of her neck with my fingers, moving my hand up into her hair. Whatever happened, I wouldn't let the moment get away from me this time. Before I could do anything else, she pulled my face toward hers.

I'd never been so thirsty for anything before in my life. I wanted to drink all of her in and hold each drop on my tongue as long as I could. She was stronger than any liquor I'd ever tasted. The more I drank of her, the bolder I became, until my body did all the reaching and my brain had nothing to do with it.

My fingers hooked her belt loops so tight that they went numb. Our tongues reached for every nerve ending on the other. She bit my lip a little, and it made me so crazy for her that I smiled while kissing her deeper. We fell to our sides, her hair wrapped around both of us and then falling against my face. I rolled her over onto her back and bumped my head on the stake in the middle of the tent. She laughed when I groaned, but neither of us pulled away from each other. The sounds that came from her were the best I'd ever heard—better than when Nate first played Led Zeppelin for me, or when folks used to gather around Mr. Draughn and Charles to hear their tunes.

My hand slid under her tank, then lightly over the top of her bra. Her eyelashes flicked open against my cheek and she moaned a little, so I moved my hand to her stomach. "No," she said. "That was good." She kissed me harder, her fingers running over my face and chest, and her legs tight as a kudzu vine around my waist. I pulled her even closer, hating the clothes that kept the rest of her hidden from me. There was no mistaking that she felt how much I wanted her or how ready I was.

Then everything stopped and she pushed me away, hard. I looked at her with my mouth open, about to ask what I had done wrong.

"Shhhhhhh!" she growled before I could speak.

"What is it?" I whispered. Then I heard it too—Omie's voice screaming, "Tennessee!"

She pushed through the tent and almost took the whole thing with her, sprinting toward his cries. We tore the brush down running, legs scraped and burned. Once we reached the trailer, Omie jumped through the window and straight into her arms.

"Daddy's real sick," he said once he caught enough air to speak.

"Okay. It's okay. Everything is going to be fine." She picked him up and then gave me a look over his shoulder that said *Help me*. I climbed through the window first, closed her bedroom door from the rest of the trailer, and then guided both of them inside.

Omie pointed to the door. "He's in the bathroom," he said.

Tennessee cradled Omie's head against her shoulder and nodded to tell me that I should go check on things.

The bathroom was right across the hall and the door was wide open. Omie must have woken up, needed to go, and then found him. Their daddy lay in a puddle of vomit on the floor, his body still and curled beside the toilet. All of his limbs were crooked and unnatural looking—neck bent and hands splayed; the angle of his leg was all wrong. I remembered what Mama Draughn said about his leg in the mantrip accident and realized the fake one must have come loose when he fell. I stepped over him and fought the spasms in my stomach and the sick coming up my throat. I reached around his neck and felt for a pulse, just as I'd done with Nate, except Mr. Moore still had one, even though it was slow. Something on the side of his face caught my eye, and I covered my mouth and nose so I could lean in to see it better.

Once I did, the room slanted and I fell against the shower curtain and into the tub. I wondered if Tennessee and Omie heard the commotion. If they had, I knew they'd be even more worried with the sound of things. I stood and looked at Moore's face again, just to make sure. There was no mistake. The scar ran from his eyebrow to the corner of his mouth where his lip pulled back in a cold smile, even passed out in his own vomit. I felt my throat where he'd squeezed it so hard that day at the gas station.

Remembering how Nate helped Mama when he found her on the floor out cold, and what I was there to do for Tennessee, I stepped over Moore, and went to find the phone in the kitchen because I didn't want to take the chance of my cell not working. The phone in my hand, I thought about the hatred I'd seen in his eyes that day, and for one instant, wondered if I should even dial. But knowing how scared Tennessee and Omie were chased all that stuff out of my head, and I called 911. "Yes, ma'am. Baxter Creek off Kinley Road. There's a deer-crossing sign at the turnoff."

After I hung up, I went to their room. Omie lifted his head from Tennessee's shoulder and peered into my face for an answer. "He's going to be just fine," I said. "The doctors are coming." Tears filled Tennessee's eyes. I saw more anger than shock on her face, which meant this had happened before.

The three of us sat on the edge of the bed, and when the sirens came, I said, "Sit tight," and closed the door behind me again. Two men walked through the front door wearing large square backpacks and carrying a stretcher between them. Red and white lights flashed outside, through the windows. When I pointed to the bathroom, the men went in, and I cleared space for them in the hall. I couldn't see anything from where I stood other than Mr. Moore's legs, both the false and real one stretched into the hallway.

"Give me the Narcan," one of the men said.

There were the terrible sounds of pumping and then more vomit. They yelled for me to steer clear of the hallway, so I moved even farther back into the kitchen. The stretcher came toward me with its wheels rolling, and straps holding Moore's body in place. His eyes were still closed, but he moved his head back and forth and mumbled. I was glad he didn't see me, and wanted them to leave as fast as they possibly could.

"It's a good thing you called. He was almost gone."

"What was it?" I asked, to make sure.

"Pills and alcohol, both. Which hospital?"

"I don't know," I stammered. *Just get him out of here.*

"Griggin's closest. You can call there and check in the morning. Sign here." I picked up the pen and scribbled where the man pointed. I probably should have gotten Tennessee to do it instead, but figured if Moore had been found somewhere else that another stranger would have done the same.

They left and I picked up the phone to call Mama. "Are you awake?" I asked when she mumbled into the phone. "I have two friends who need to stay with us."

Tennessee had me stay with Omie while she cleaned up the mess in the bathroom. When she came back, she grabbed some clothes from two different drawers and threw them in a black trash bag. We went out to the porch without saying anything, and Widow Hemlock walked over while Tennessee locked the front door.

"I heard the sirens," she said. "You children let me know if you ever need anything at all, hear?" She looked too feeble with her cane to walk very far, let alone help anyone, but she stamped the end into the porch a couple of times to let us know she meant it.

"Thank you," Tennessee said. "I'm sorry about the noise." Her voice was embarrassed and tired.

"I don't care about the commotion, just the two of you," Mrs. Hemlock said.

While I drove us home, I wished I could erase the memory of Moore's face from my mind. It would only make Tennessee feel worse if I told her about the gas station and what he'd done, like it'd make Mama feel worse if I talked to her about Nate.

CHAPTER 20

"WHAT'S HAPPENED?" MAMA ASKED after I let Tennessee and Omie through the front door.

"We'll talk later. Right now everyone's tired, and they should rest," I said.

"Of course," Mama said, and looked around the room like she didn't remember what to do with houseguests. "Are you hungry?" She picked up two empty beer cans from the table next to the recliner and carried them to the trash under the sink.

"No, ma'am," Tennessee answered for both of them. Omie was so sleepy on her shoulder, I don't think he heard anything that was said. "Thank you for letting us stay here tonight."

"Make yourself at home," Mama said.

Tennessee settled Omie into the recliner and he curled into a little ball. She helped me pull the sofa out, and stale cereal and chips fell to the floor while we unfolded the mattress. Mama ran over to the broom closet, embarrassed again for them to see how much she'd let the housekeeping go, but I knew they wouldn't be thinking about that after everything they'd just seen with their daddy.

After we got a sheet in place, Tennessee picked up Omie and brought him over to the mattress. He couldn't seem to get close enough to her. He tightened his grip on her neck, and tucked his head tight over her shoulder. Tears ran down her face and she wiped them fast before he could see them, even though I had. I could hear her quietly saying to him, "I'll never leave you alone with him again."

Mama walked up beside me, tapped my shoulder, and nodded down the hall, meaning that she wanted to talk.

"I'll be back," I told Tennessee.

The door shut behind us and Mama crossed her arms.

"I stopped by to see her and we found her daddy passed out on the bathroom floor. Sick from what he'd taken." I said it matter-of-fact and looked her straight in the eye. She looked down right away.

"There's not anyone else to help them?" She crossed her arms.

"No. They needed me, and I called the medic. You think they did this to themselves? You of all people should know it's not their fault."

"Watch it," she said. "It's how much you like her and the thought of them sleeping over that concerns me. We got enough on our plates. What if he's in the hospital for a long time?"

"Tennessee will figure it out. It was the right thing to do

for tonight, that's all. They were scared. You know how that feels. Makes it even harder to be alone."

"There's more to consider here," Mama said. "Don't act like I'm heartless. Her daddy and yours work together, and Amos—I don't know. I'm so tired of it all, I can't keep any of it straight. I just know we don't need to go asking for trouble."

"I'm not asking for it, and they didn't ask for this either. Have you already forgotten how Mama Draughn took me in when we needed her?"

She waved her hand in front of her and tightened her robe like she refused to hear anything more. "It's too late tonight. Go on and get some sleep," she said. "I'll make sure they're all right out there."

I lay on the bunk and listened closely for their voices. I knew the last thing Tennessee would want to do was talk about her dad, and I hoped Mama wouldn't push her into it. They didn't speak for long, and when I heard Mama's bedroom door close again, I went out to see them. Omie was already asleep, and Tennessee's neck was free of his little fingers. She spooned herself around him on the mattress, and I lay down behind her. When she settled her weight against me, I couldn't help but imagine how good it might feel to have her beside me every night. I reached for her hand and she let me take it.

"It's my fault," she whispered after a couple of minutes.

"No, it's not. It's your daddy's fault." I started to feel guilty that I wasn't telling her all I knew of him. The two impressions he'd given me at the station and then that night in the bathroom left little space for benefit of doubt.

"I knew better than to leave Omie with him."

"Does it happen often?"

"Once is enough to know better, and it's been more than that."

"Did he seem weird earlier tonight?"

"I heard him talking on the phone with someone, and he was angry, but that wasn't unusual. I didn't see him drink any more than his normal. Definitely not enough to make him pass out."

Omie rustled in front of Tennessee, and we both waited until we knew he was asleep again to say anything more.

"So liquor's his problem?" I whispered, trying to see how much she knew of his habits.

"Not only." She gave me a look that said we both knew more than either of us wanted.

I nodded. "Started after the mine accident?"

"Before that, even, but it got a lot worse after."

"He ever laid a hand on you or Omie?" I might have been crossing the line by asking that one, but I had to, especially after the way he'd been with me at the gas station.

"No. But I don't think my mom was as lucky."

I lightly rubbed her arm. "I'm sorry," I said. "It's horrible always wondering when someone might lose control."

"Yeah," she said. "I'm constantly on guard."

I smoothed her hair until she fell asleep. Next, I woke to Mama tugging on my hand and the sun bleeding light through the checkered curtains.

"What do you think you're doing?" Mama's whisper might as well have been a shout.

"Shhh." I swung my feet to the ground. "Don't wake them." When I got up, Tennessee stretched and without even opening her eyes, reached for Omie beside her.

Mama followed me into the kitchen and stood behind me while I made the coffee. "You know it ain't proper, being in bed with them like that," she said.

"When have things ever been proper around here?" I set the coffee filter in the basket.

"I won't stand for you sleeping with a girl in my house."

"Because why, the neighbors might talk about us? Jesus, Mama."

She grabbed my wrist and squeezed it hard enough to make me squint. Her eyes grew big and her jaw quivered like it was wound so tight that it might spring wide open and every thought would come pouring out. "Don't you talk that way to me. Ever. Understand? You sounded just like your daddy then, you know that? Some things stay sacred whether you believe them or not, Harlowe. This is my house, more than yours or anyone else's. I've served my time for it, and I won't stand any disrespect from you."

I slowly took my hand from her grip. "If you'd seen their daddy last night, you might have a little more sympathy for them." I took a deep breath and then added, "You might think a little harder about some other things, too."

"Don't draw comparisons. Her daddy's only part of the reason I'm worried about how close you're getting to her. Talk with her about staying somewhere else. I'm sure Mrs. Hemlock's watching everything pretty close, anyway, and she'd be happy to look after them."

"But I understand what they're going through more than anyone." I could tell from the look on her face that I'd been hitting too near the bone and she wouldn't take much more of it.

"Careful," she said. "One more night. That's it. And if you get yourself tangled up with a baby the way Jacob did, I won't be helping you out none. Needed to make sure that was said."

"I'm smarter than that," I said. "Anyway, you always acted like you love little Suzy."

She looked at me like I was a horseshit salesman on TV. "I won't spite any child. That would be hateful. But I'm not gonna pick up after you when you know better than to make a mess of things in the first place. I'm done raising children. When you get married and do it proper, I'll be as good a grandmama as any. Not now."

CHAPTER 21

OMIE WANDERED INTO THE kitchen with Tennessee close behind and I wondered how much they had heard. From the look on Tennessee's face, it was a lot more than I hoped.

Tennessee rested her hand on Omie's shoulder and he looked up into her eyes. "We don't want to cause you any more trouble, Mrs. Compton," she said. "Maybe it's best for us to go home and wait until he's back."

"No, sweetie, there's no need to do that," Mama said, changing her tune now that she had to say it to Tennessee's face. "I know things are hard right now and you could use a little help. You two sit down and I'll find us something to eat." She took a box of cereal from the cupboard, and I got the milk out of the fridge. I wished we had some eggs I could scramble, but I'd already used the last of them. Daddy was leaving less money than usual since Mama cashed the check, and Mama seemed to be keeping a tight lid on the cash.

Tennessee poured the cereal into a bowl for Omie, and

his eyes brightened when he saw the dark brown flakes fall from the box. It wasn't Cocoa Puffs or any other expensive brand he'd seen on commercials, but it was chocolate with a thick coat of sugar, and that was all he needed to make him happy.

"More!" He jumped up and down in his chair.

"That's enough for now." Tennessee poured the milk for him and then some cereal for herself and passed the box and carton my way. Before she could even finish her second bite, Omie lifted his near-empty bowl to his lips and slurped the leftover milk. Half of it spilled down the front of his shirt, and he set the bowl on the table, looked around at the three of us with a big grin, and said, "Now more?"

Tennessee turned to Mama before answering him.

"You can have as much as you like," Mama said to Omie. "I've been meaning to make a trip to the store, anyhow." She lit a cigarette and drank her black coffee.

I caught Tennessee's eye and smiled, hoping she felt a little better than she had last night. Her lips turned up at the corners, but her eyes told me she was plain exhausted, and from a lot more than one night of rough sleep.

Omie slurped and chewed, his grin almost big enough to make up for the worry on the rest of our faces. It would be nice if something as simple as cereal could always keep us as happy as it did Omie. There was a knock on the door and everyone, except Omie, sat up straight in their chairs and got silent.

Mama stood from the table, her robe open at the waist and her white slip dipping low against her chest.

"No." I stopped her from going any farther. "I'll get it." Walking to the door, I hoped Mrs. Hemlock hadn't done anything crazy like call Child Protection Services. When CPS came in a home, they often split up siblings, like they'd done with the Addison twins, Louisa and Charlie. And since Tennessee was eighteen, but Omie still so young, they could take him from her. I pulled the smoke-stained curtain back an inch from the window and felt relieved when I saw Mama Draughn's face on the other side.

"Perfect timing," I said when I opened the door and helped her with the two brown paper bags she carried.

"Told you I would, and that was even before—"

"Thank you," I whispered. I set the bags on the counter and started unpacking them. There were two dozen eggs, as if she'd heard my thoughts earlier, along with a homemade loaf of bread, some fat tomatoes, sliced ham, and a few other things. I looked up from the bag to introduce her to Tennessee and Omie, but she was already sitting next to them, talking.

"Oh, you're the one who sent us the amazing pie," Tennessee said.

Omie looked up at the word "pie" and said, "Yum."

Mama Draughn giggled with him. "I'm glad you enjoyed

it. Plenty more, and I can't wait to have you both in my kitchen soon."

"If you're willing to share your recipe, I'd love to learn," Tennessee said. "It tastes like one that's been in your family a long time."

"You got good taste buds, woman. Harlowe's been bugging me to sell my pies, but I don't have the energy. But if you two wanted to give it a go—"

"Really?" I interrupted her, excited to think about starting any kind of project with Tennessee.

"What are y'all talking about now?" Mama looked down at her cleavage and wrapped her robe tighter around her.

"We were just trying to come up with some ways to make a little cash," I offered.

"It'd be good outlet for Harlowe," Mama Draughn said. "For all of us, really."

"I used to bake with our mom but haven't done any since she passed. Your crust is like nothing I've ever had before," Tennessee said, sounding a lot more cheerful than she'd been before Mama D showed up.

"Glad to hear it. We'll start today, then. If that's all right with you, of course," Mama D said to Mama.

"That sounds just fine. It will give them all something to do," Mama said.

"My thoughts exactly." Mama D leaned over and whispered

to her, as if we couldn't hear, "And there's plenty of food in those bags that should keep you set for at least a few days, so you can just rest." Mama D was always warm with her, no matter the proud cold shoulder Mama gave her.

"That's very kind of you, as always," Mama said, and ran her hands over her curls. "I can't believe I'm not dressed yet. It was a long night, as you might guess."

"You have more reason than anyone to take your time these days. I haven't forgotten about our girls' night, so you know. We'll make that happen real soon. For now, enjoy a little quiet. I'll get these hoodlums out of your hair so you can take a nice long bath. Those always give me a new lease."

Mama smiled and squinted when she inhaled her cigarette. "That sounds nice," she said, but seemed a little put off by the advice.

I carried the cereal bowls to the sink, unpacked the food Mama Draughn brought to us, and put away anything that might spoil.

Mama pointed to the tomatoes on the counter. "I never see ones like that anymore," she said. "Don't know why they can't stock good ones in town."

"Costs too much, I guess," Mama D said. "Or people don't buy them. Next time I go to market, I'll make sure to bring you some, along with some peaches before the season's over. My friend Aida gets them off her sister's land in Georgia. You won't believe. Better than strawberry wine."

"Only if it's no trouble," Mama said. "You've always done so much for Harlowe. I worry you think he's not all right here, but he is. We're doing fine. Just takes time."

"I don't worry about that," Mama Draughn said. "I've always loved each of you, and nothing could ever change that for me. Just reflex by now, that's all."

"I'm sorry," Mama said. "My nerves are raw lately. Think they're all showing through my skin today."

"Don't cover them on my account," Mama Draughn said. "The three of you ready to go?"

"Just let us brush our teeth," Tennessee said.

I remembered Nate telling me to do the same, just before he took me and a bag of clothes to Mama Draughn's over six years ago. Now Mama was getting worse from missing him, and that made me miss him more, along with the advice he could have given me.

CHAPTER 22

ROWS OF WRINKLES DREW up around Mr. Draughn's eyes as he smiled at all of us standing on the front porch. "Well, Darla, didn't know you were going on a treasure hunt today," he said.

"Thought you might enjoy some company," Mama Draughn said. "These two are as golden as their hair."

Omie ran straight to Mr. Draughn's side, grabbed the arm of the rocker, and grinned up into his face. "Can I have a turn?" He hopped on one foot.

"Climb on up," Mr. Draughn laughed, his gums shining where his teeth had gone missing.

Mama Draughn whispered to me and Tennessee, "The three of us can have a little time to talk, now." Once we were standing inside the kitchen she said, "I don't know how much Harlowe's told you about me, Tennessee, but I wanted to ask if there's any way I can help, knowing only a little bit of what y'all are facing."

"Do you mind if I ask how you know?" Tennessee asked.

"You're sharp, that's good. Don't mind at all, but I can't answer your question except to say, somewhere along the way, I became that person people tell things to. This is a safe place, here. I've worked hard to keep it that way, and I suppose folk feel the freedom to tell me things because of it."

"I see," Tennessee said. "I understand why people feel at ease with you, I felt it right away. I really hope I didn't sound rude, I'm still learning the way things work around here."

"I only thought you sounded smart, certainly not rude. You've got a good head on some strong young shoulders. How are you holding up? Has this kind of thing happened before?"

"Yes. But Omie doesn't know that, and I'd like to keep it that way."

"Understood, but don't be surprised if it comes out at some point that he knew all along. I think he's got your spirit, and I'm guessing that part of y'all came from your mama. The intuition, I mean. Our Harlowe's got a hefty dose of it too."

"It's not always easy to feel things so much," Tennessee said, and looked a little sad.

"That's why our kind have to stick together. Got anywhere you and Omie could go if things got worse? Any family close by?" Mama D took a bag of cherries from the counter and began sorting through them, checking for any bad ones.

"No. Mom's family is still mad at us because Dad owes

them money, and we've never met any of his blood relations."

"Well, they can't stay angry with you over his faults forever," Mama Draughn said. "Let me add that they shouldn't."

"Mom's sister wouldn't even come to the funeral. That's how much they hate him."

"People act surprising when they lose someone." Mama Draughn filled a big pot with water and set it on the stove.

Before we could see him, we heard the patter of Omie's little feet running toward us on the wooden planks. "Mr. Draughn says bring him tea," he said.

"Oh look, Herbert finally got himself a little helper!" Mama Draughn laughed. "Hold tight just one minute." She reached into the fridge and filled a glass. "There you go. Ask him about the time he walked smack into a sourwood honey tree. Best honey there is, you know."

I'd heard the story at least five different times, and it still sent shivers up my back wondering how he escaped all the bees alive.

"Okay!" Omie shouted, spilling only a little tea on his way out the door.

"We might as well get to work in here," Mama Draughn said. "No matter how I tried, I could never get my June to bake with me. So I'm real happy to have someone who wants to learn." She scurried around the cupboard and grabbed tools and ingredients, then handed them over for us to set on the table.

"Tennessee, grab two sticks of butter from the fridge and cut them into little squares straightaway. Don't touch it too much though; we have to keep it cold. That's hard to do in these summer months, but it's the most important thing. I keep my flour in the icebox and that helps some. Looks like you got the touch," she said, peering over Tennessee's shoulder. "Harlowe, pour the flour into that bowl. We want to smear the butter in there with it, so you get flat leaves of butter covered in the flour—no powdery stuff left at the bottom, and no balls, neither. Do it fast, that's right—get on in there. Smear those big chunks there or the crust will tear."

"How does this look?" Tennessee lifted her floury hands so Mama Draughn could see inside the bowl.

Mama D sifted through the mixture a little with her fingers. "It's ready for the ice water now. Scoop your hand around to mix, just to the point when you can pull it all together without it falling apart, and then shape it into a ball. Next we'll set it in the icebox to rest and let it get good and cold again before it hits the oven. That's when the butter and flour make the real magic happen." She fanned herself with the recipe book and didn't notice when something fell to the floor.

I reached down to pick up the old photograph while Tennessee scooped the dough and began shaping it. When I held the picture close, I saw that it was of a young Mama Draughn, slim with curled hair, holding a baby on her hip, who I guessed was tiny June. On the other side of them stood an even younger-looking woman, with dark hair, wearing pants and an oversized men's work shirt. She had one hand on June's little arm, and the other around Mama Draughn's shoulder.

"Who is this beside you?" I asked Mama D, then showed the picture to Tennessee so she'd know what I was talking about.

"Wow, look at you." Tennessee pointed at the photograph, but moved her hand away quick so she wouldn't get flour on it. "You were so beautiful. I mean, you still are."

Mama Draughn laughed a little at Tennessee trying to cover her tracks. "It's okay. My looks certainly aren't what they used to be. No need to sugarcoat that truth. That there's my sister Nuna," she said, leaning into my shoulder when she looked closer. "Lord, we were so young. If I'd only known then, and all that hooey us old folk say. It's true though. It will hit you one day, and you'll remember me saying so."

"You have a sister?" I'd never heard her mention one before.

"We've only known each other for eighteen years, Harlowe. I don't believe you can ever know all there is about a person. I got more than one sister. The other two gone on ahead, though, and it's just me and Nuna still living. She won't come down off the mountain, though." She looked at the ingredients on the table and muttered, like she was eyeing what she needed at the next grocery trip.

"Why won't she?" I asked.

"Oh, she's still mad at me," she said, still making some kind of mental list and not looking up. I could see we weren't going to hear any more about Nuna that day.

"You could just tell me to mind my own business, you know," I said.

"What's the fun in that? I like to watch you try to figure things," Mama Draughn said. "Come on over to the stove and I'll show you how to cook the filling. Not for too long, or it will turn to syrup. Good for pancakes, but not the kind of thing we want for pies. The fruit should still have a crunch to it before it goes in the oven, but the bit of extra cooking thickens the sauce." She measured sugar and spices and stirred it all together with a spoon almost as big as my hand.

I looked at the piles of fruit sitting on top of the counter and thought she must have already spent a month's worth of groceries on all of the supplies for us.

"We'll jar whatever filling we don't bake in the pies. Herbert eats it with a spoon for breakfast. Puts it on everything. If you two decide to sell the pies at market, you could sell the filling too. Always nice to have more than one thing to offer people." She handed me the spoon and I took over the stirring while Tennessee measured ingredients for another crust.

The first pie we baked didn't seem anything like the ones I'd tasted of Mama Draughn's, and I wondered if we'd ever get close to touching hers. The next two came out a little better, and the fourth was finally sellable, Mama D said—a golden peach pie with decorations of leaves that Tennessee cut out of extra dough and put on top.

For the rest of the day, we worked more than we talked, our hands finding a kind of rhythm that made it hard to think about anything else. Omie ran in to check on us, following his nose once the baking was under way, and Mama Draughn sent him straight back outside with one of the ugly pies and two forks for him and Mr. Draughn.

Finally the three of us sat at the table and rested, wiping the sweat from our faces with old kitchen towels Mama D passed around, and sipping ice water. Mama Draughn looked at the photograph of her and Nuna again. Her expression held the same sadness on her face as when she looked over at the wall of June's photos.

"How are you feeling now?" she asked Tennessee after she set the photograph on the table and looked up at us again.

"A lot better than I did this morning. Learning how to do something new always seems to get me out of a funk."

"You should see how many books she has," I said to Mama D. "Got me beat in the brains department, that's for sure."

"Men often feel a need to state the obvious, don't they?" Mama Draughn said, smiling at me.

Tennessee laughed but then softened when she saw I didn't

join in the laughter. "At least with Harlowe it's obviously kind," she said.

"You given any thought to what you want to do in life?" Mama Draughn thumbed the edge of the photograph, but this time kept her eyes on the two of us, sitting across from her.

"Teaching, most likely. I'd love to write stories too, but with Omie, it's really hard to find the time."

"You'd be a great teacher, and with the stories—you'll find time if it's something you really care about. You're a diligent sort, I can see that even in your crust making." I knew these were the kinds of questions Mama Draughn wished she could still ask June about, and I was glad Tennessee didn't seem to mind answering them.

"I have so much to learn. And then there's the hope of getting to college . . ."

"You'll find a way. Plant your dreams carefully. Might take a while to find the right kind of sunshine and water, but remember even wiry thistles can sprout up through rocks."

"My mom would have really liked you," Tennessee said, and pulled pieces of dough from her fingers with a faraway look. Then she cleared her throat to bring her thoughts back from wherever she'd gone and said, "Did it take you long to get your recipe the way you wanted it?"

Mama Draughn filled both of our glasses with some more ice water from the pitcher on the table. "A lot of time and even more mistakes. Only thing I ask in return is that you remember my kitchen is a place of peace. I don't allow any trouble here."

Tennessee took a deep breath. "You're saying that because you've heard about our dad, aren't you? I don't plan on telling him about us taking pies to market, if that's what you're worried about."

"I'm not saying what you should or shouldn't tell your daddy about. I wish there was a simple way to know what secrets we should keep and which we should tell. Figuring that out can take a lifetime," Mama D said with a sigh.

"You seem to have it down," I said. "I bet you know more secrets than anyone in Strickland, but you've never had any trouble with the Praters, far as I know. That takes some skill, for sure. Any of them ever bug you?"

"No," she said, and knocked her apron free of some fallen flour. "I'll say this for myself, I can count on one hand the choices I made that didn't come out of love. If I can keep it that way for the rest of my days, I'll leave this world in peace." She carried her glass to the sink and filled it again, drinking almost all of it in one go like all of a sudden thirst had overtaken her.

Omie stumbled into the kitchen again, yawning this time, and we all smiled at him, Mama D included.

"Look at your sticky face." Tennessee pulled him to her side. "I'd say you made a new friend today." She tried to smooth his cowlicked hair. "Let's get you cleaned up."

While they washed at the sink beside Mama Draughn, Mr. Draughn set the almost-empty pie tin on the table. "Welp, you can count on us to eat up all your rejects, ain't that right, O? Think that little fella could win some pie-eating contests right good."

"You have no idea how true that is," Tennessee chimed in from the sink.

"Anytime you need a hand with him, bring him on over here. Been a long time since I had as good of company."

"You always wanted grandkids, didn't you," Mama Draughn said.

"True, but, I'm still plenty happy with the way things turned out," Mr. Draughn said, resting his hand on her shoulder. "I'm the luckiest fool I ever known, to still be here with you."

She smiled up at him. "We both know that you've had to put up with plenty with me," Mama Draughn said. "The two of us are equal lucky, and that's the truth."

After Tennessee dried Omie's hands, she carried the mixing bowl from the table to the sink, and I followed her with the dirty measuring cups, spoons, and rolling pin.

"Oh, leave all that," Mama Draughn said. "It will give me something to do later. Take the best pie home to your mama. I'll put a few jars of filling in a bag for y'all, too."

Omie leaned against Tennessee's legs and rubbed his eyes.

"We should probably start walking," Tennessee said. "I don't know how much longer he'll last. Thanks again for today," she said to both Mama and Mr. Draughn.

"No need for any more thanks," Mama Draughn said. "I enjoyed it as much as anyone."

"Well, I'm glad to hear that, because I have a feeling this one will be asking to come back very soon." Tennessee looked down at Omie.

"That's more than fine by me," Mama Draughn said. "Harlowe, come over here just one second." She pulled my elbow just before I followed Tennessee and Omie through the door. "I can see you've fallen for her, and all the reasons why, because I have too. But this business with her daddy has me worried about the kind of man he is."

"Is there something you're not telling me?"

"Nothing that would help you for the knowing of it right now. You already seen enough to recognize some things."

"Yes, ma'am. But if there was—"

"Hush," she said. "Just keep your wits about you, that's all I'm saying." She walked out onto the porch to see everyone off and left me to wonder what she'd already heard.

CHAPTER 23

MAMA PUT OUT HER cigarette when we walked into the trailer. From the looks of her tight curls and fresh clothes, she'd taken the long bath Mama Draughn suggested.

"Thought you'd be back long ago," she said.

"Takes each pie at least an hour to bake," I answered. "We brought you one. Did you have dinner yet?"

"I picked a little at some things. Happy to pull some food together for y'all, though."

"That's okay, I'll do it." I didn't want her to go to any trouble on account of Tennessee and Omie that she could later complain about. "Tell me what you think of the pie, first, though."

"If neither of you mind, I should probably give Omie a bath now, and then take a shower myself?" Tennessee said.

"Of course," Mama said. "Use anything you need in the bathroom."

"At this point I think just a little soap and water will do

wonders," Tennessee said.

"There's plenty of shampoo too. Help yourself." Mama glanced at the plate I set in front of her, and then the pie beside it. "Have to admit, that's fine-looking," she said. "You've always been good at making anything you set your mind to."

"Tennessee should get the credit for this one," I said. "Turns out there's a lot more to baking than I would have thought."

She picked up the fork and I watched her take a bite, waiting for her response. First she looked like she was concentrating real hard on a thought, but then her eyebrows lifted and she couldn't hide the smile. "Oh," she said, and took another bite.

"Good, isn't it?" I grabbed a fork myself and dipped into the center of the pan. "I think people would buy it."

"Can't think of anything I'd change about it."

"The crust isn't quite as flaky as Mama Draughn's, but it's almost. Nervous first-timer hands, I guess. We might have worked it just a little too much."

"Tastes just as good to me as anything she's ever made."

When Mama leaned over her plate to take another bite, her collarbones jumped at me from the edge of her T-shirt. I knew she'd lost a little weight, but I was shocked to notice how fast it was coming off of her. "Don't stop at one piece," I said. "We've had plenty to eat, and will be making plenty more."

"Going all the way to market sounds like a lot of trouble."

"It was my idea, and I think it's a good one. It'd be nice if you could hope for the best."

She took another cigarette from the pack. "You call your daddy about the mines yet? You'll be out of school before you know it."

"Not yet. He ask you to talk to me?"

She shook her head and blew smoke. "No. But as we've all said, what else are you gonna do?"

There were so many different things I wanted to say to her just then. But more than anything, I felt like she was giving up on me and saying that I might as well do the same.

Omie ran into the kitchen and slid across the linoleum squares in his pajama feet.

"All clean!" he shouted. "Tensee said she out in a minute."

I smiled at the way he said her name. "I'm guessing I already know the answer, but I'll ask ya anyway. Got any room left for dinner after all that pie you ate today?"

He looked up at the ceiling and put a finger under his chin like he was thinking hard, then nodded his head up and down, giggling. "Uh-huh!" Then he rubbed his belly, sticking out in his almost-too-small Bugs Bunny pajamas.

"I'll hook you up, then." I took the ham out of the fridge, and then sliced a tomato and two pieces of the homemade bread. I hadn't seen Omie turn down anything yet, and hoped it was a dinner Tennessee would approve of. As soon as I set it in front of him, he chomped down on the sandwich and smiled. Half the ham was hanging out of his mouth when Tennessee walked into the kitchen with her long wet hair combed, her tan skin a little shiny and pink from the shower. "Sandwich?" I asked her.

"Just some ham and tomato would be great, thank you. I'm still pretty full from all the tasting we did."

"Me too," I said, feeling the sugar crash coming on.

"I just tasted some myself," Mama said to Tennessee. "Better than anything I've ever made."

"Well. Not much can go wrong when you have Mama Draughn standing beside you every step of the way. It might be another thing when we try to do it on our own."

"We just need a little more practice," I said, and noticed that Mama looked bored with us talking about it all. "And a business plan. I'll work on that part."

"I see Mr. D again?" Omie asked, and then added, "Don't poke bees," and I laughed hard because I knew exactly what he was talking about.

"I said the same thing after he told me that story," I said. "And I've never gotten stung because of it." I knocked our old cheap cedar table with my knuckles and thought how much better the cherry one I was working on would be.

Mama yawned, and when she felt my eyes on her, covered her mouth. "I'm sorry," she said. "I know it's early, but I guess I'm still pretty tired from last night."

"We had you up too late," Tennessee said. "You've been so generous to have us here."

"Both of you are real sweet. You heard anything from the hospital at all?"

Tennessee shook her head. "Guess I'll call tomorrow if I don't hear something by then."

"That's a good idea," Mama said. "I'm sure he's doing fine and that he can't wait to see the two of you."

Tennessee forced a smile, but then chewed the inside of her cheek nervously.

"Bet y'all are pretty worn out, after all that cooking," Mama said. "Probably best if we all turn in early tonight."

Omie yawned as if it only took mention of sleep to flip his switch.

"Walk back with me, Harlowe, got something I want to show you," Mama said.

"Go on. I'll be there in just a minute," I said.

She looked at me for a couple of seconds like she was waiting for me to change my mind until she gave up and walked down the hall by herself.

"I'll clean up in here," Tennessee said.

"Come see me in my room after he falls asleep," I whispered to her.

Omie's eyelids started to drop.

"Okay, I'll try," she said.

Mama's door was open when I got to it. "Come in." She rubbed the back of her neck and grimaced, then laid both of her hands up on my shoulders.

"What is it?" I asked when she didn't say anything.

"Guessing you've noticed your daddy hasn't been round much."

I nodded, waiting for her to say more.

"Thing is, we're running a little low. I don't want you to worry too much or anything, but just thought that you should know. Just in case you end up making some money at the market, or—"

"What about the check?"

She took her hands off my shoulders and dropped her eyes to the ground. "I never said I was perfect."

"I'm not paying for your pills. You better talk to Daddy about that."

"I can't. You know he won't understand." She wiped the tears spilling onto her dark circles and displayed a look that was desperate and worn.

"How much is left?" I asked.

"Just under a hundred."

"And how much are you paying?"

She scratched the back of her head and looked away from me again.

"You can't pick and choose what you want to tell me, Mama."

"Thirty apiece."

I stared at her for a second, then closed my eyes and breathed in through my nose. It took effort for me not to blow up at the stupidity of what she'd said. "And who do you get them from?" I asked as calmly as I could.

"I don't know exactly, and that's the truth. Betsy's been taking care of that part so I don't have to get out. I just give her the money."

"Damn it, Mama. What about everything you went through last time?"

"It won't be that bad this time. I just need to get through the next month or so, start my exercises again. Muscles just seize up and there's nothing I can do to make them stop."

"I don't know what else to say. You know how I feel about it, but that's not stopping you any."

"I'm just asking for a little understanding and a little more time," she said. "Give me a hug?" Her eyes filled again and her hands dropped loose to her sides.

I walked closer to her and put my arms around her shoulders, partly sorry, but mostly beyond angry at how she was acting like she didn't have any choice in the matter. I know she felt me tense when I thought about all the things I could do to try to forget what happened to Nate. But there wouldn't be anyone left with any sense at all if I did. I let go of her and took a few steps back. "If you want my help while you're quitting, I'll do what I can, like Nate did. But I can't help you hurt yourself."

She wiped her face again and took a jagged breath through the crying, her shoulders inching toward her ears like she wished they would hide her face. "Just a little more time," she said again.

"I don't want to find you the way I found Moore last night," I said.

She looked at me like a kid that's been scolded. I hated sounding like the parent that done it. The order of things was all messed up. I told her goodnight and as soon as I closed her door, texted Daddy to ask when I could meet him at work. He was the one that should be having those talks with her, not me.

In my room, I lay down and closed my eyes to try to calm down. Things couldn't be the same everywhere else as they were in Strickland. I'd seen reality shows of rich kids in Hollywood and New York, with their perfect white teeth and brand-name everything. I knew there wasn't much reality in any of those shows, but there had to be someplace in between, where everything wasn't either a sad country song or a commercial for the perfect life. I felt like the worst person for thinking it, but I was jealous that Nate found a way out. I didn't want to die, but there were times it seemed that might be the only ticket away from everything. I'd never heard of anyone really leaving Strickland behind. Most everyone ended up like June one way or the other—making up stories for the folks back home but living the same sorry truth over and over. I heard my bedroom door open and then saw Tennessee walk through it.

"Hey." I patted the mattress next to me and scooted over for her to slide in the bottom bunk. "He's asleep?"

"Yeah. Right away. Makes me feel a little better knowing the other night didn't stick with him as much as it did me."

"He's gonna be okay," I said. "Both of you are."

"It can't keep happening," she said.

"I know."

She turned on her side to face me, and I propped myself on my elbow to see her better. Her hair was still damp from the shower and the skin on her cheeks and nose was a little freckled. I brushed away the hair that fell across her forehead and kissed her. I felt the same as I had in the tent with her before we heard Omie scream. As soon as our lips touched, I wanted more of her. I slid my hands to her hips and pulled her on top of me. She held the back of my head and brought my face even closer to hers, though that was barely possible. I wanted to get up and lock the door, but as soon as I was about to, she stopped and said, "I should go."

"I'm sure Mama's fast asleep by now," I said.

"I can't risk having her mad at me," she said. "You can't either."

I sat up and touched the back of my head where her fingers had been before. "You're right. But this is about to drive me crazy. I need some time alone with you."

"I know, I want it too," she said. "We'll find it soon."

She stood and walked to the door but I wouldn't let go of her hand until she turned around to give me one more kiss. After she left, I couldn't stop thinking about the way her tongue felt in my mouth and how incredible it would be when I finally could feel all of her. I lay for a while and waited for thoughts of her to take me into sleep. Instead, they kept me wide awake so I dove into them as deep as I could, and relieved my mind and body of the tension. At least for the night.

CHAPTER 24

I HEARD THEIR VOICES and the clink of forks on plates in the kitchen. Before I went to the shower, I pulled the dirty sheet off the bed and threw it in the back of the closet.

Plates of Mama Draughn's food and two smiling faces waited for me at the table. Though Mama looked as worried as she had the night before. Tennessee passed me the fried ham and finished eating a corner of toast. "There's still pie left too," she said.

"That's a miracle. I better get a slice before you know who—" I turned to Omie and he laughed at my wide eyes.

Mama sipped her black coffee, but ate nothing. "You were just like that when you were his age," she said.

"It's comforting to me that your appetite seems to have evened out," Tennessee said. "Sometimes I worry his will keep growing and growing even after he's older. He's never been chubby, but I keep thinking it'll either catch up with him or we won't be able to afford to feed him."

"He might get chubby for a little," Mama said. "Harlowe went through one of those phases."

"Mama," I said, and shot her an embarrassed look, which at least made her smile.

Tennessee covered a burst of laughter and then Omie joined her too.

"Hey, I need you to stick up for me, Omie!" I said. "You can't let them all gang up on me, now."

"I place with Tensee!" He held a cup of Kool-Aid in both hands and lifted it to his mouth. A blue smile remained after he set the cup down.

I'd already been around him enough to notice how he lifted everyone's spirits automatically, same as a cute puppy or a song that's easy to sing along to. I envied Tennessee having someone who looked up to her so much. I was sure Omie felt about her the same way I always had Nate.

But as soon as the front door swung open, the mood at the table changed. Daddy barged into the room with all of his usual noise, plus some extra.

"Brought grocery money for two of you, not four," he said. "What are Moore's kids doing here?" He didn't say hello or even look at them, but stared at Mama, then at me.

"Eating breakfast," Mama said. "Would you like to stay and have some too, like civilized folk do?"

"They're not a part of this family, and neither of you have

a right to step into their business."

"So you know about what happened, then?" I asked, thinking it was probably Tennessee's question too, and how I needed to talk to him about Mama.

"I know their daddy's on sick leave, and this girl's old enough to take care of herself and the little one at home. It's not like the two of you need any more to handle."

"Maybe if you were around more to help—" Mama said.

"Shhh." I stopped her. "There's something I'd like to talk with you about, Daddy. Maybe we can find some time tomorrow. Did you get my text?"

"Thought it was about the money. We'll see. Unlike the rest of you, I'm under a heap of work. Call me, same as everyone else has to, and we'll set something up. Can't say exactly when, right now."

"He's starting to think about the mines." Mama opened her mouth again and I wished she hadn't.

I started to tell her to stop before she said anything to make things worse for us, but then realized it might help Daddy meet with me sooner. "It's true," I said. "I'd like to come up there and have a look around."

"Well, I'm glad to finally hear that much," Daddy said, and set some cash next to Mama's ashtray. "Up to you how you spend it, but I'd be careful about feeding more mouths than need be," he told her.

She wouldn't look him in the eye but folded the money and tucked it into her palm.

"As for you," he said to me. "Folks are watching. Don't think I need to remind you of that."

"No, you don't," I said. "But if you'd like to explain what you mean to everyone else, that's fine by me." I was starting to see that he was not much more than a coward.

He pointed his finger at me and opened his mouth, but then looked at Tennessee and Omie and stopped himself and left without saying anything more.

"The way things have been going, we won't see him around here for a week or two now," I told Tennessee. "Don't let his talk bother you too much."

Mama counted the money in her hand and looked upset, which I took to mean that he'd given her even less.

"I want you to know that I haven't forgotten, and I'll call the hospital today," Tennessee said to Mama.

"I guess you've seen now why I'm on edge about it all," Mama said.

"Yes," Tennessee said. "And I don't want us to be any kind of a burden to you."

"You're not a burden," I jumped in, before Mama could say anything. "Hey, Omie," I said with a lot of expression because I didn't want his light to fade in all of the adult talk. "I was thinking yesterday that you were so good while we baked all day, maybe we should do something you'd like today. How's that sound?"

He nodded with enthusiasm and I raised an eyebrow to Tennessee to make sure she was okay with me saying more. She smiled and also looked relieved.

"What about fishing?" I asked.

"Yeah!" he said.

"I don't think you've ever been, have you?" Tennessee asked.

Mama set down her coffee and turned it in clockwise circles. "Reminds me of when Nate first took you."

"I know," I answered, but didn't look at her because it could set both of us crying. "I just need to get some things from the shed out back," I told Tennessee.

"We'll clean up and meet you outside," she said. "And thanks, Harlowe, right, Omie?"

Omie leaned toward me and, tilting his head to the side, simply smiled as big as his cheeks allowed.

CHAPTER 25

THE PADLOCK ON THE shed stuck a little when I first turned the dials, and I worried I'd gotten them wrong, but after I banged it with the base of my hand, it opened. I stepped over my saw and toolboxes, farther back into all the things Nate said he wanted to clean out but never got a chance to.

"Anything I can do to help?" I heard Tennessee say from behind me.

"Thanks," I yelled back, "but I wouldn't know where to point you. It's a mess in here," I said. "Might take a minute, but I'll find what we need. Just keep Omie busy."

"Yell if you change your mind."

The sight of Nathaniel's old things, his baseball bat and glove, Lego sets he'd put together when he was a kid, shoeboxes with his handwriting on them—hit me somewhere between my stomach and chest. I moved the bag with our old tent and then worked my way toward the back, restacking things and keeping my eye out for the tips of the fishing poles. Finally,

I spotted them behind a stack of boxes. I lifted one of the boxes and was surprised at how light it was. There was no label, but I heard papers inside, so I balanced it on my knee to look closer. Enough light came through the door for me to see the box was new, all the cardboard edges still crisp and clean. Sweat dripped from my hair into my eyes while I peeled back a corner of the clear tape. Inside was a pile of shipping labels and postage stamps. I set the box to the side and picked up the one just like it that had been underneath. The same things were inside, plus a few Sharpies. Nate liked to trade old car magazines, but there were at least a hundred shipping labels, and from what I'd already seen, hundreds of dollars' worth of stamps too. He'd never been that serious about it.

"You okay in there?" Tennessee yelled.

"Yeah, just one minute!" I answered, and moved the boxes out of the way so I could get to the poles and tackle box. It was hard to find my way back over the piles I'd made, and getting even harder to breathe.

"Grab these?" I yelled to Tennessee when I couldn't get the poles and myself out fast enough.

"I got 'em!" she said, and pulled them through. "Hang on, I just have to move this bag right here—"

When I finally got out of the shed, I wiped my forehead and gulped in air. "All right," I said. "Let's get Omie down to the water." I locked the door again and told myself that I'd deal with the boxes and all the questions they brought up for me later. There was no sense in letting it take over the rest of the day for everyone.

"I'm guessing Omie will use this small rod?" Tennessee held both of them in her hands.

"Yep. That one was mine when I was his age."

"It's hard looking at their things after they're gone, isn't it?"

"It feels strange. I'm sure I'll shake it off by the time we get to the pond."

"You don't have to, you know. It's not always so easy to do."

"Did you ever find anything of your mom's that made you wonder if you really knew her? Things that surprised or confused you?"

She thought for a few seconds. "I found some things from old boyfriends of hers—love letters and ticket stubs. That was a little weird, knowing she kept them and probably wondered what her life would have been like if she'd ended up with one of them instead of our dad. Why? You find something that's bothering you?"

"Just some things that make me think Nate had a lot more going on than I knew. I'd already guessed that some because of Tommy, but I still don't have the full picture yet. It's making me crazy."

Omie skipped ahead of us and wove a pattern of dust and flying rocks behind him.

"I think Mama Draughn's right about never being able to

completely know a person," Tennessee said, and then jogged ahead toward Omie before I could tell her that I didn't agree with either of them. They stopped to look at something on the side of the road, and I hurried to catch them.

"What is that stuff?" Tennessee pointed to the neon yellow sludge running down the mountain into the ditch.

"Yellow boy. You didn't have it in Chatham? After they blast the mines or dig, they rinse them, and this is the stuff that drains off. Don't let Omie get in it. It's like battery acid. Can burn the skin right off if it sits too long."

"God, that's terrifying. Where does it go?"

"You mean after it goes there?" I pointed to the ditch. "Into the ground."

"So it's in everything around here, then. All the plants. Water, even."

"Yeah, that's right." I realized I sounded pretty ignorant by not being more upset, but it was one of the things most of us learned to live with because it was all we had ever known. The yellow boy had always been there for as long as I could remember, and we always knew better than to play in it.

Tennessee fell quiet. She looked at the brown empty spaces between the sludge and the trees in a circle several yards away. The ones closest to the stuff were small and shriveled. The farther away they got, the bigger they grew, but when I looked close, I realized they all looked a little puny, and I wouldn't choose any of them to build something I wanted to last.

I steered our path to Mohosh, and saw that Tennessee and Omie shared my relief once we were in the cooler shade of the pines. The three of us stood on the same rock where Tennessee and I had sat together the day she found the geode.

There was a loud splash in the middle of the pond and Omie bounced up and down on his toes, screaming, "Fish! Fish!"

As fast as I could, I baited the lines, then handed him the small rod. Tennessee anchored behind him to keep him from flying straight off the rock and into the pond. I tucked away the rest of the tackle, then the three of us stood in a row, lines bobbing and poles pointed straight over the water. I tried avoiding it, but couldn't help noticing the poles took my eye to Amos's mountain on the other side.

After we'd been there close to an hour, casting and reeling and coming up with nothing more than pond scum, I looked over at Omie, and caught him in the middle of a yawn. He swayed back and forth, his excitement worn down to a calm curiosity.

"Think we should call it a day?" I whispered to Tennessee.

But before she could answer, my line pulled tight. I reeled just a little to make sure it was a fish, and not more scum or a turtle. There was too much fight for it to be anything else, so I reeled harder to sink the hook even deeper. "Got one!" I yelled.

Omie dropped his pole and Tennessee caught it right before

it fell into the water. He grabbed the leg of my jeans and tugged so hard that they nearly came straight off me.

"Walk around this way," I said, and Omie ran in front of me. I put his little fingers around the reel, and placed my hand over his. "Hold tight," I said, and we turned the reel together, his toothpick arms straining against the line. I was just as excited as he was, remembering my first catch ever with Nate, and how I felt like there was nothing I couldn't do once we got that fish out of the water.

"You ready to bring him in?" I asked.

"Yes, yes, yes," he said, with the last one sounding more like a question, probably because he just realized we'd have to get it unhooked somehow. I remembered worrying about that part, too, when I was his age.

"Come on, Omie, you can do it!" Tennessee cheered.

Omie went quiet with concentration. He stared hard at the line and gripped the reel so tight, his little knuckles poked into my palm. The fish fought both of us, with more strength than I expected. I worried that I would crush Omie's fingers while I turned the reel. He held tight and proved that even through the pain, he would never let go of that fish. Finally, we got the thing above water, all eight-something pounds I guessed, swishing and writhing, ugly whiskers sticking out in every direction. Omie was so excited when he saw it above the water that he finally let go and waved his hands back and forth over his head. The reel nearly slid from my grip, but I caught it and the fish just in time. Omie clamped his hands over the front of his pants, looking like he might pee himself, and it made me laugh so hard I thought I might do the same.

Once I had the thing in hand, I held it firm against the rock. It was an old fish, judging by its size and color, and I wondered how it'd survived so long in that water. Still, it fought and thumped its tail, nowhere close to giving up.

"You ever tasted catfish, Omie?"

Omie stopped bouncing and his smile went slack. He grabbed Tennessee and pulled her near, whispered something into her ear. I worked to get the hook out of the fish's cheek while it opened and closed its mouth around my fingers.

Tennessee crouched beside me and leaned in close. "He wants you to throw it back," she whispered.

"What?" It was the biggest fish I'd ever seen anyone catch at Mohosh, and I'd already imagined mounting it if we decided not to eat it.

"Shhh," she said. "Don't make a big thing about it."

"All right," I said, once I got ahold of my own excitement. "Omie, come over here."

He walked and stopped a couple of feet away from me, folding his hands together behind his back.

"Closer," I said.

Tennessee's knee touched mine when she crouched next

to me, and she motioned for Omie to come stand beside her.

"Put your hands right there, away from the fins. It's okay, I got him," I said.

Omie stuck out a finger and touched the fish once on the top of its head before he jumped back and laughed nervously, tucking his fingers under his chin.

"You sure? Last chance," I said, gripping the fish over the water.

The gills opened and closed, but the fish had stopped fighting. We didn't have long.

"Let him go!" Omie shouted.

"We caught him together, so you have to help me with this part, too, okay?"

Omie ran over, wrapped his hands around mine, and we lifted the fish together.

"One, two, three!" I counted, and we sent the fish flying into the air. I was a little worried that once it landed, we'd see it float to the top and flip over dead, but the thing swam away just fine, and Omie looked so happy.

"What do you say we take a quick dip? Might help us all cool off a little," I said.

"I don't have my suit," Tennessee said, "but I guess there's not much difference between a bikini and a bra and panties."

"I'm fine with it as long as you are," I said, probably a little too soon.

She gave me a courtesy laugh. "I bet you are."

We left the poles, tackle box, and most of our clothes in a pile, then found the deepest spot for jumping. Once we were all in, Tennessee glued her eyes onto Omie and kept them there, her eyelashes wet and dark against her freckles, and her hair floating out in soft yellow strands behind her. I thought of the mermaid in the fairy tale she'd told about her mom.

"Look, there's a crocodile." Omie pointed to the clouds above us while he floated on his back beside Tennessee.

"It sure looks like one," Tennessee said. "Glad there aren't any crocodiles down here, though."

There are plenty, just not the kind on four legs. "That one next to it looks like a tiger," I said.

"Yeah, it's got long teefs!"

"Oh. And that one." Tennessee pointed. "That's a baby elephant."

"We got the whole safari up there," I said, and they both laughed.

Omie closed his eyes and rested in the water. Tennessee swished him slow, back and forth, just two fingers underneath him. His hair whisked around his face and he looked so calm. He trusted her with every bone in his body. It was like the time me and Red and Jacob played "light as a feather, stiff as a board" at Josilyn's birthday party, except we were so drunk that we dropped her on the candle underneath. The water ran between Omie's fingers and toes, around his arms and legs. My eyelids grew heavy watching him and the rhythm of Tennessee's hands moving him back and forth. She must have sensed that sleep was coming to take us, because before I'd realized it, she was guiding us back to shore.

The sun's shadow on the rocks said it was around three in the afternoon. The heat wasn't so awful in the shade, and there was the slightest breeze—a new sign that summer was near over. I lay on my side and watched Tennessee comb her fingers through Omie's wet hair, his head resting against her shoulder. It didn't take long for all of us to give in to the afternoon sleepiness and close our eyes. By the time we woke, the sun had disappeared behind Amos's mountain, the animal clouds had all scattered off to another place, and the whole sky glowed orange. I didn't want to move from our drowsy spot, but I followed Tennessee's lead and helped her gather our things. Omie's stomach growled and he looked down at it like it surprised him.

"Wish we'd kept that fish for dinner?" I asked.

"Nah." He smiled.

"Me neither," Tennessee said. "You made the right choice."

CHAPTER 26

WHEN WE GOT HOME, Mama's bedroom door was shut and everything behind it was quiet.

"Is it okay if I pull some dinner together for us?" Tennessee asked.

"Of course. Ask me if there's anything you can't find, or I can help with."

"Just get Omie something to drink and I'll take care of the rest," she said.

I poured all three of us some Kool-Aid, then sat down with Omie at the table and gave him a piece of bread from the bag with the smiling bunny on it. Tennessee found the corn Mama Draughn had brought and cut the kernels into the skillet. She sliced up and added the last piece of ham, and a can of pinto beans. I started to imagine the three of us spending every night like this, but then told myself to stop, it was crazy thinking. I remembered how when Clarice first told Jacob she was pregnant, he said they'd marry someday.

That talk stopped after the baby. And now, according to her, he'd disappeared too.

"Take the plates to the table for me?" Tennessee asked after she filled each one with food.

Somehow she'd made the three things taste like they were always supposed to go together, even though it seemed a strange combination to begin with.

"It would probably be even better with a little hot sauce," she said.

"I think it's perfect, and look, Omie does too."

"Not exactly a tough crowd." She smiled. Both of their faces were pink from the sun and the water, and I felt the color coming up in mine, too.

As soon as Omie finished eating everything on his plate, his head drooped to the table, but he still held the spoon in his hand.

"Nope," Tennessee said. She jabbed his arm with her finger. "Bath first."

"But we went swimmin' today." He yawned.

"Yeah, in stinky catfish water. Go to the bathroom right now, and we'll make it a fast one. We need to at least rinse you off."

After they left the table, I listened to the running water, and their singing in the bathroom. Everything felt so much better with them there. I didn't worry about Mama as much, or any of the other things that pushed my thoughts deep underwater where I couldn't breathe.

Omie slid across the floor in his pj's, and I heard the shower running in the bathroom for Tennessee. "Can we go fishing again tomorrow?"

"Maybe," I said. "We'll have to ask your sister. If we can't then, I promise we'll go again real soon."

"I like Gary," he said.

It took me a second. "Is Gary the fish?"

"Yeah," he said. "He's a good fella." He sounded like an old man, shooting the shit on the porch with Mr. Draughn and his buddies. I had to cover my mouth to keep from laughing.

"I'd say you're right about Gary," I said.

"You're next," Tennessee said, standing behind me, wet strands of her hair falling across my arm.

"Oh really?" I argued, but only so I could hear her boss me around more.

"If you want me to get anywhere close to you, then yes, really."

I turned around to face her directly. "You know what I want."

She pursed her lips and squinted her eyes at me. "Go on, then."

I held the look for another couple of seconds then walked down the hall. What she'd said about the yellow boy in the ditch earlier had me thinking. There wasn't any way to really wash ourselves clean of that stuff. She was right, it was in everything, including all of the water that came out of our faucets. In the shower, I scrubbed my body with soap, rinsed my mouth and spit it out again. I guessed that sometime between when Mama Draughn still used to harvest crops with her family and now, the water ruined the soil and that's why seeds couldn't push up. I didn't like thinking about it, because it didn't seem there was anything we could do to change it now, like too many other things.

"That's much better," Tennessee said when I met them by the couch. She patted a spot beside her on the fold-out mattress. Omie's eyelids blinked slow while he watched Elmer Fudd chase Bugs on TV.

"Come see me again after he falls asleep?" I whispered, and stood up to go to my room, hoping that would get her there faster.

She looked at me from the corner of her eye, but it wasn't the same cute smirk she'd given me earlier—it was more of a "watch it" look.

"I took a shower and everything," I said, trying to get the grin back. It didn't work, and she looked at the cartoon instead of me. "Well, you know where to find me. I've canceled all my meetings," I said.

That made her smile just enough to give me some hope

that she wasn't completely disgusted with me. I waited for her in my room, bouncing a ball against the top of the bunk. My door opened, and I sat up, excited to kiss her again.

"Did you talk to them?" Mama asked, and I jumped.

"About what?"

"They need to go home."

I wanted to scream at her that she couldn't take away the one thing that made me feel good, especially with how much stress she was causing everyone. "I thought you'd find it in your heart to let them stay a little longer."

"This has nothing to do with my heart. More to do with the laundry I did today." She nodded at my closet.

I swallowed hard.

She shook her head and closed her eyes. "I told you—not in my house. No room for grandbabies you can't take care of."

My face burned more with frustration than embarrassment. "That wasn't what you think it was."

"Don't. I have to look out for my own, and you're making that mighty difficult these days."

"Why don't you ever take notice of the good things I do? I'd say I'm doing a pretty fine job of keeping shit together around here. And I care about them. They're almost like family to me now."

She glared into my eyes. "Listen to me good. They ain't your blood, they ain't your kin. You might think you already love this girl, but, Harlowe, there will be others. You're young and you don't know better. That's all." She reached for my shoulder.

I slapped her hand away. "You can't tell me what to feel!"

"If you want to break your own heart open, there's nothing I can do to stop you from doing it. Their daddy's out of the hospital now. Coming for them tomorrow."

"You called him?"

"Didn't have to. Suppose your own daddy took care of that."

"You have no idea what that man is like or what he might do to them."

"It's none of my business. Not yours, either."

"It's my business who I care about! Have you noticed I seem to be the only one you have left around here?"

"You expect me to treat you like a grown-up when you talk that way? Better get your head on straight real quick or you can find somewhere else to live." It was the hardest punch she could throw and she turned to leave before I could even answer. Tennessee stood behind her in the doorframe.

"Dad's coming for us tomorrow?"

Mama nodded. "He called today while y'all were gone."

"I guess that's best for everyone," Tennessee said, and looked back and forth between Mama and me, reading what had been said before she appeared.

"Things will settle," Mama said. "But right now, I'm worn out. You two leave the door open, if you're going to visit any. I'll see you both in the morning."

"Sorry about that," I said to Tennessee after Mama went to her bedroom.

"No, I'm sorry I put you in a tough spot with her. It won't help if you keep arguing with what she says, you know," Tennessee said. "We'll just both have to find time when we can meet together at Mama Draughn's."

"I'll meet you wherever you say, as much as you'll let me. You'd think Mama could see how much better you are for me than anything else around here."

"You know she's just scared and lonely, don't you?"

I looked into her eyes and took a deep breath. "Yeah. But everyone feels that way. Promise you'll come back here straightaway if you ever think he's going to hurt either of you."

She nodded. "We'll be okay. I watched Mama learn how to keep him calm. I can do the same, but not forever."

"I gotta tell you something," I said. "I wasn't sure when it would be the right time, and I still don't know if this is it, but it's starting to feel like a lie if I don't say something soon."

Her eyes widened and she set her jaw, waiting to hear what I was going to say.

"I didn't do anything bad." I rushed my words to ease her worry. "Thing is, I met your daddy before the other night. Well, kind of met him." And I told her about what happened at the station.

She squeezed her eyes shut. "Oh God," she said. "I'm so sorry."

"He didn't see me when they took him out of your house, but once he comes here to get you, I'd be surprised if he doesn't put it all together."

"I'll take care of it," she said.

"How?"

"I don't know, but what other choice do I have? I just need to keep things steady enough with him for me to graduate from school, and then I can take Omie and go somewhere else. That's the game I have to play right now. You've already seen what he's like. And that's not even the worst of it."

"Please don't talk about leaving."

"We have much bigger things to worry about," she said. "I hate it, but neither one of us can pretend our lives are simple."

"Take care of Omie and yourself. You're right, that's all you can do, and I know that already feels like more than you can handle."

She raked her fingers through her hair like she wanted to pull it all out. "What a freaking mess. Do you ever wish some of your family would disappear?"

"Yeah, seems like both of us lost the ones we needed most."

"Time for bed!" Mama yelled at us from her room.

"Do you think she heard what we said?" Tennessee whispered.

"No." I shook my head.

We heard Mama's door open, and she leaned across the

hall. "Now," she said.

"We're not done talking," I told her.

"Doesn't matter. Time for sleep."

I knew she hated that she couldn't control what the two of us said and thought, and that she felt I was the last thing she was trying to keep from slipping through her fingers. I also knew that if I didn't get away from her right then, I might say some things that none of us would recover from.

"We'll talk about everything tomorrow when we have more time at Mama Draughn's," I told Tennessee but didn't look at Mama. "Would you be okay here if I stepped out for a minute? I need to get some air."

"Where are you going?" Mama said.

"He's just got summer fever," Tennessee said. "We'll be fine. I need to get some good sleep before tomorrow."

"Thanks," I said, "I got my phone if either of you need me," and walked between them and out the door before Mama could argue.

CHAPTER 27

I WANTED TO PUNCH something, but instead of using my fists, I walked as fast as I could away from our trailer and everything that had just been said. Tennessee was the one thing I looked forward to. If she moved away, everything else would be unbearable. I couldn't move fast enough to get rid of the frustration that had built up inside of me. I was almost running down Kinley Road when I heard a voice yell, "Lowe!" and I looked down into the field where it came from.

"Over here!" Red called.

"What are you doing?" I asked once I reached him through the thick weeds.

"I don't know. Just needed to get out of the house. Mama has the quilting bee over. This seemed as good a place as any." He held up his mini cooler.

I swatted the mosquitoes and aphids hitting my face. "Come on," I said. "We can do better than this."

"I'm game." He made sure the cooler was closed. "Lead the way."

"You got liquor in there? Otherwise I might need to go find some right now."

"Yep. Shine. Bourbon too."

"Were you planning on meeting someone else?"

He kicked the road. "Josilyn said she would come. But that was hours ago."

"You don't need her," I said. "Glad I found you. I'm feeling restless myself."

"It's been too quiet with Jacob gone, and you always off with that new girl. Heard anything from him yet? I sent him some messages but got nothing back."

"Nope," I said. "But I'm not giving up. If you talk to him, you can tell him that."

"I thought he'd be back by now. I'm sure Tommy's long since moved on to something else, anyway."

"If neither of us hears soon, we need to find him. Or at least I do."

"I won't be going anywhere in the next week except to work," Red said.

"Shhh!" I heard voices behind us and clicked off the flashlight. We weren't too far up the trail, and could still see Kinley Road from where we were.

"You see that?" one of the voices below us said. A cell phone light glowed in our direction.

"Think you're imagining things," the other voice answered.

"You have to pull it together quick, you almost already fucked things up beyond repair."

There was no mistaking Amos's hoarse but high-pitched voice. I wished Red would stop breathing so loud, but then I realized it was my own breath I heard, and slowed it, hoping it would do the same for my racing pulse.

"Is that why you wanted me to meet you? There won't be any more problems. There wasn't one in the first place. Stupid kid called the ambulance. I was fine." Bob Moore's voice wasn't one I wanted to hear again, and now it was even more loaded than the first time he'd spoken.

"That's not what the report said. You don't get high on my goods or my time. I'm taking you off the mine and putting you on clinic runs. But if you get busted driving and using, I won't bail you out," Amos said.

"Shit," Red whispered. "Let's go."

I motioned for him to stay put and quiet. They were too close. Even if we ran and got away, Amos would see who we were and know what all we'd heard.

"I'm better off at the mine than driving with this leg," Moore said.

"Nah, there's less chance of you getting pulled over if you drive slow. I need someone now, and it's you."

"What about Tommy?"

Amos laughed. "You argue with me one more time, and

185

I'll send you right back to Chatham, but we know they won't have you anymore. Only thing my family runs is business, especially after that mess in Woodvale. You begged me for a foot in the door. So far, the only thing you've brought in for me is trouble."

"Mr. Prater, we made a deal before I came that I'd be above ground until you taught me the books, and then I'd take them over."

"That's the last word from you," Amos said, and must have gripped Moore's throat because the most pitiful sound came from it, muffled and strained. "Understand? One more and I'll do your other leg in, give it to my dogs, and leave the rest of you on Kinley for varmint."

A squeak escaped Moore's throat and we heard the sound of leaves slipping under his feet.

"I asked if you understand, damn it," Amos said.

"Yes." Moore barely got the word out.

Neither one of us breathed while their feet rustled and then padded away. It was hard to tell which direction they were going, and for a second I feared they were coming toward us. Red shook so hard, he lost his footing and gasped before he found balance again. I closed my eyes and prayed they hadn't heard the sound. Soon their steps faded, but neither Red nor I moved until the trail was silent again and there was no doubt they were gone. Then Red's breath came out in a whimper followed by a flood of tears.

"It's all right, they're gone," I said, and put my hand on his shoulder.

He opened the cooler and pulled the cork off the bourbon, took a long draw, and then handed me the bottle. The sting in my throat couldn't slow the questions firing fast in my mind. Amos had said something about Woodvale and Tommy. Nate must have found out about their pill run schedule, and for some reason told Jacob about it.

Red grabbed the bottle from my hand and drank again. "Clinics," he said. "They were talking about pills, I guess?"

"Yeah, that's what I took it to mean," I said. "Have you been in the office at the mines yet?"

"No, they don't let just anyone in there. You have to have a special badge, I think."

"Amos is like the yellow boy. Poisons everything."

"Huh?" Red said.

"Never mind. I guess we can head on now."

We didn't talk on our way out. There was a feeling that Amos or Moore could reappear any second, or someone else we weren't expecting. At the end of the trail, we each turned to go in opposite directions.

Except for the floodlights on the outside of our trailer, everything was dark when I got home. I was still a little buzzed from the bourbon, but sober enough to be mindful of my noise and footing. Tennessee and Omie were asleep on the couch, her arm draped over him, keeping him close. I envied that he never had to fear her leaving him the way I did. I knelt on the floor beside her so I could see her face better. Part of me wanted to wake her up and tell her everything I'd heard, but that would only be to unburden myself and wouldn't help her at all. Instead, I promised that I'd do everything I could to keep any harm from coming to her or Omie, no matter what it took. When I went to my room, I left the door open for her, just in case.

CHAPTER 28

MAMA WALKED THROUGH MY open door in the morning and said, "Thought you'd want to have breakfast with them before they leave."

My thoughts still couldn't catch up from all I'd heard the night before. Knowing that Tennessee was going home that day only made everything more frustrating. The smell of food came from the kitchen, and the sound of Tennessee's and Omie's voices singing together. I put on a shirt and jeans and went to the bathroom to brush my teeth.

"Everything okay last night?" Tennessee whispered when I sat down beside her.

My stomach turned. "I'll tell you about it later. Did you get some sleep?"

"Not as much as I should have, but some."

Mama took biscuits out of the oven and then set one of the jars of pie filling on the table beside them.

"We going fishing today?" Omie asked after he took a big

bite and left blueberry smears all over his face.

I saw that the look on Tennessee's face already said *No* and guessed she and Moore had decided on a pickup time. "Not today," I said, to give her a little break on being the bad guy. "But like I promised, I'll take you again real soon. Maybe Gary has an even bigger brother, you never know."

"Whoa," Omie said, and looked a little scared.

I reached for Tennessee's hand under the table, and she squeezed my fingers.

"Aren't we glad Harlowe showed up that day to welcome us with Mama Draughn's pie, Omie?"

"Yeah! And took us to Mr. Draughn's too!"

"You going to eat, Harlowe?" Mama asked, sounding a little annoyed with all the talk about the Draughns. "I made those from scratch."

"Of course," I said. "Can't remember the last time you cooked biscuits." I didn't have an appetite, but wanted to keep the mood as light as possible for everyone at the table.

There was a knock on the door and we all turned toward it, even Omie. Mama wiped her mouth and went to answer.

"Daddy!" Omie called when Moore walked into the room, leaning on a cane that seemed to beg more sympathy than use. There were three purple marks on his neck and I knew they were from Amos the night before. Those and the scar on his face must have been what made Mama take a step back right after she'd let him in.

Omie got up from the table and ran into his daddy's arms. Tennessee looked me in the eyes, inhaled deep, and walked over to join them. Still hugging Omie, Moore took Tennessee's hand and pulled her closer to him. My body tightened watching him touch them. I wished he'd leave us all alone. He hadn't seen me yet, but I figured it'd be better just to get it over with, so I walked over to them and stuck out my hand to introduce myself. The smile on his face slid right off and I knew he recognized me from that day at the gas pump. His jaw muscles tightened beneath his skin and the scar turned white against the red of his face.

Tennessee cleared her throat and said, "Dad, this is Harlowe." Only then did he take my hand, but he wouldn't shake it. He clasped it once and dropped it just as quick.

"Thanks for your hospitality to my children," Moore said to Mama, looking away from me.

"It was no bother. I'm glad to see you're back to health."

"Oh, it was more a misunderstanding than anything," Moore said.

I looked at Mama, thinking they shared more in common than she cared to admit.

Tennessee ran her hands along her arms like she was chilled, even though sweat shone on all our faces. Omie was the only one who didn't seem to feel the friction in the room. He stood on top of his daddy's good foot, holding his hand. I watched Moore's eyes narrow and his mouth tighten a little like he might push Omie off his shoe. He caught my look and forced a cold smile. I could tell that he could only hold the polite act a little longer, just enough to get them back out the door.

"Well," he said, "thanks again for your thoughts and care. I told the doctor it was just stomach troubles, but these days they want to milk you for every penny." He turned from Mama to stare daggers at me again.

"Good thing for the miners' insurance, right?" I couldn't stop myself from saying. The way he looked, acted, talked—it was so clear to me that there was nothing in him but spite. I wanted to scream right there that I knew what he was doing with Amos, and if he cared about Tennessee and Omie at all, he'd let them stay with us. Even though our home wasn't without its dangers, I felt I could take better care of them than Moore ever could.

"True, it's a mighty good thing," he finally answered me. "Don't know what any of us standing here would do without it."

Mama narrowed her eyes and crossed her arms. I could tell she'd also heard the poison in his voice. "The Lord sends plenty of lessons our way, doesn't he? Just a matter of listening. These two are a joy to have around. Special children you have," she said.

"And don't I know it. Their mother and me used to say

they might be the only things we ever did right. I'm real glad we got this whole mess behind us, now. Not that I blame you, son. I know you were only trying to do the right thing." His eyes never blinked whenever he fixed them on me. They said: *Watch out. I hurt you once, and I'll do it again,* as clear as if he'd said the words out loud. I held my breath and imagined pushing him out the door. Then I looked over at Tennessee. Her eyes were so tired but resolved. I didn't want to make it harder for her to manage him. She took Omie's hand and helped him off Moore's foot, a sign that they were about to leave. My heart sickened.

"We won't take up any more of your time," Moore said.

"Wait." I grabbed the one jar of pie filling left. "Don't forget this," I said to Tennessee, meaning: *Don't forget to meet me at Mama Draughn's as soon as you can get away.*

"Of course," she said, taking the jar. I hoped she understood.

Moore herded them to the door. Tennessee held her finger up and went to the side of the couch. She grabbed the trash bag of their clothes.

"Just let us know if there's anything else we can do to help," Mama said. It seemed that concern now replaced her stubbornness from the night before.

Tennessee and Omie followed Moore outside to the porch, then down the stairs to where the truck I'd first seen him in was parked. I felt the impact of each step that took her farther away from me. After Mama closed the front door, she stood and looked at it for a minute like she was trying to make sense of what she'd heard and seen. Then she rubbed her face as if her thoughts could be wiped away like sweat and went to clear the dishes from the table.

I pushed the curtain to the side and watched the Moores leave. Omie skipped to the truck, and Tennessee walked behind him carrying the jar, her head tilted down toward her feet. She stopped, looked back, and our eyes locked for a second. She nodded at me once before getting in the truck, and then they drove away.

CHAPTER 29

I LEFT WITHOUT SAYING a word to Mama. It was too early to go to Mama Draughn's, and I figured it would be a while yet before Tennessee and Omie were able to leave their daddy, if they even could. I didn't know where to go; my insides were wound tight around themselves. I kicked the rocks in the road and threw a stick off the side. Some fools in a jacked-up truck flew past and near ran me over. I screamed after them to watch where they were going. It felt good to yell at something, but the ball of nerves inside kept growing bigger, and bigger, like desert tumbleweeds on the old Westerns Daddy used to watch. At least the tumbleweeds had open spaces to roll around. Strickland closed in tight like a fist and squeezed all of the air out of me.

At first, Mrs. Devin smiled big when I walked into the Sip N Sak, but her face soon changed when she saw the look on mine. After Bobby Martin left with his cinnamon buns, and there was no one else in the shop but the two of us, I emptied all the change in my pockets onto the counter.

"I need beer," I said.

She peered at me over the top of her glasses. "Okay. But only the Pabst. Can't give you Bud for that amount. Don't tell the other boys—you know you're my favorite."

"Thank you," I said. "I'll pay back the rest, I swear."

She nodded, her forehead lined with worry. "You hanging in?"

"Best I know how."

"That's all any of us can do. That and wait."

"Yep," I said, because I knew it wouldn't make me feel better to spout off to her how tired I was of waiting, and how waiting never seemed to do one damn thing for me except bring the next problem along. "Have a good day," I said.

"Come back and gossip with me sometime. I miss seeing your face."

The door jangled behind me when it closed. I walked down the ravine to the creek and popped the top off a can. The yellow mud was thick below and I stared into it and drank, pushing my troubles deeper with each sip and numbing the places they bruised. By the time I emptied three cans, I felt something closer to better, or at least I didn't feel as much. My stomach rumbled, full of beer but empty of the two biscuit bites I'd managed at breakfast. I climbed up the ravine and headed to the Draughns', knowing that if I spent too much time alone with myself and the rest of the beer, things could only get worse.

I walked up the stairs and waved to Mr. Draughn, then stepped inside and was surprised to find Mama D, Tennessee, and Omie already sitting at the table together. My buzz fell away real fast when I realized they were all waiting for me. There were at least a dozen pies wrapped in plastic on the counter.

"Did y'all already do this today?" I asked, and then noticed the disappointed look on Tennessee's face.

"No, Mama Draughn baked them last night," Tennessee said. "Dad dropped us off at home, then went straight to the mines."

"I'm sorry, I thought it would take you longer." I set the bag of beer on Mama D's counter, then went to the sink to wash off my face and hands. I sat down next to Tennessee and tried to catch her eye again. "Hey," I said to her. "I'm here now, and I'm just as serious about doing this together and everything else I ever said to you. I had a moment, that's all. I snapped out of it now. Won't do me or anyone else any good to get stuck there. Just had to remind myself of it."

"Glad to hear it," Mama Draughn answered in a stern voice before Tennessee could. "Now start loading those pies. Market's already bustling by now, and it'll take us an hour to get there."

"We're going today?" I asked, and then noticed Omie's smile. "All right, then! I'll get us there in thirty minutes," I said, and walked over to the pies.

"I'll only let you drive if you promise to be careful," Mama Draughn said. "Be a shame to break them all before we had a chance to sell any."

"I promise," I said, carrying a stack and waiting for Tennessee to open the screen door.

"Want me to go with y'all?" Mr. Draughn asked once I was back inside the kitchen again.

"You'd only be crammed, hot, and bored," Mama D said. "But you're sweet to offer."

"You not going?" Omie said. "I want to stay here and play marbles with you."

"Tell you what." Mr. Draughn reached into his pocket and pulled out a dollar. "Take this with you and bring me back a treat."

After I had all the pies and jars of filling in the truck, Mr. Draughn followed us outside. Once we were all situated, he leaned through my open window. "It's been a good while since she's been gone from my sight," he said, looking at Mama D. "Promise me if you get lost, you'll stop and ask for help."

"Of course," I said, thinking of all the years they had between them and wondering how they'd managed better than most people I knew to still love each other so much.

After I pulled onto Kinley, Mama Draughn said, "Funny he'd tell you to stop for directions. I used to be the one always begging him to do the same."

"Guess he finally learned something from you then," Tennessee said.

"Sure enough," Mama Draughn said. "Patience has its payoff."

I felt her eyes on the speedometer while I drove, and it lightened my foot on the pedal a little.

Before we could even settle on a radio station, we were twenty miles from the Dickson County line. With any luck, we'd have several good hours of selling before things shut down. Diesel from the sixteen-wheeler in front of us blew through the windows, and Tennessee coughed and waved the fumes away from Omie in her lap. It was around two thirty when we exited the highway. At the market gate, colored lights flashed in front of tents and towers. Just beyond those, we saw the outlines of a roller coaster and Ferris wheel against the sky.

CHAPTER 30

"MY LORD, LOOK AT that," Mama Draughn said. "It's fair weekend, too."

"You knew about this all along, didn't you?" I said, driving through the gate.

She shrugged her shoulders and smiled. "Well. There was no reason to get everyone's hopes up for naught in case I was wrong."

Omie jumped up and down. "We go rides!" he shouted, almost directly in my ear.

Mama Draughn laughed. "I forgot how huge this all felt at his age. Daddy used to bring us here and set us loose for the day. It was better than Christmas, every time."

"Thank you for this," Tennessee said.

"There's nothing like these sights and sounds to bring a bit of wonder," Mama Draughn said, and patted Tennessee's knee. "Pull in over there, Harlowe." She pointed to a spot in front of a tent. I parked the truck and looked at all of the people rushing around and toward us—families and vendors, couples my age holding hands and sipping from flasks tucked into their pockets.

"Harlowe, grab a stack of pies and follow me. Tennessee, you sit on top of Omie and hold him tight for a few, as best you can, anyway."

I followed Mama Draughn through the crowded tent. Vendors offered everything from crops to tobacco, tube socks, guns, furniture both old and new, TVs—anything you could need plus a whole lot more that you didn't. People pushed against each other, fanning themselves when there was enough space and rushing to see what treasures were left and what kind of deal they might strike for them. A woman in a fancy dress ran toward me and dragged her kid behind, trying to get somewhere as fast as she could. She had the look of an animal on the hunt, and I wondered what it was she was so desperate to buy. The kid held tight to some blue cotton candy while he ran alongside her. His mouth was stained all the way around in a frown like a miniature sad clown and he cried that he wanted to go back on the Tilt-A-Whirl. All the people and noise moved in a fast, dizzy swirl. I was glad when Mama Draughn finally stopped at a table.

A skinny woman with long white hair stood up from a rocking chair. "Look, it's darlin' Darla!" she shouted, and wrapped her lean arms around Mama Draughn's soft neck.

Then she turned to me and said to Mama D, "Lord, you brought a handsome fella with you too?"

"That and a bunch of pies," Mama Draughn said. "You all right with sharing some of your booth today?"

"If the two of you stay and keep me company, you can sell anything you like, long as it's legal."

"Don't let Aida scare you," Mama Draughn whispered to me. "She's harmless. Mostly."

"Full of fire, but only fueled by good spirits," Aida said, her ears obviously still working just fine. "You really are a looker. Remind me of an old beau of mine. That's the last I'll say of it. Set those pies down right here."

"We got more in the truck," I said. "Filling, too."

"Bring it all. Only a few hours left, and my peaches are almost all gone, as you see. George left two hours ago and won't be back until closing time. Just the typical Sunday routine."

"Be right back," I said. "You rest, Mama D, you've done more than you should already."

"I'll take you up on that." She sat in a rocker next to Aida and fanned herself with a piece of cardboard from a broken-down box.

When I got back to the truck, Omie was hanging out of the open truck window and Tennessee held him by his belt loop to keep him from falling out.

"Found a spot," I said. "We got to hurry, though."

"Good, because I can't hold him any longer. Omes, get back in here and grab a pie. Careful. Carry it like it's a baby bird egg."

I grabbed one of the heavy boxes of filling jars and Tennessee stacked more pies, and handed one of them to Omie. While we walked, he concentrated and stared at the pie, his arms tense and steady in front of him. It was the first time he didn't try to run ahead of us.

"This must be the rest of your crew," Aida said when we all got to the table and set everything down. I exhaled and wiped my forehead. Mama Draughn must have told her about Tennessee and Omie, and I could only imagine what else while we were gone.

"Already sold the first two," Aida said.

"How much?" I asked.

"Eight dollars each. That suit you all right? Been told y'all starting a proper business," Aida said.

"That's right. Think you'd let us set up here again?"

"I don't see why not. Darla's already vouched for you; that's all it takes for me."

Omie pulled Tennessee's arm and pointed to the boiled peanuts two stands over.

"Here," Mama Draughn said, and handed Tennessee a five-dollar bill.

"I can't take that, you've already given us so much by bringing us, and that's on top of everything else you've already done."

"Please," Mama Draughn said. "Think of it as a favor to me. Watching y'all have fun brings me even more joy."

"Best listen to her," Aida said. "Her bloodline's Irish like mine."

"Part Irish," Mama Draughn said.

"Ain't a one of us under the sun that don't have roots first planted elsewhere, and I'll argue that with anyone 'til I'm in the grave."

"Amen," Mama Draughn said, and fanned herself.

Omie pulled harder on Tennessee's arm. "Can we go rides now?" He glued his eyes to the five dollars in her hand.

"Okay, but you have to stay close to me," Tennessee said, and waved goodbye to us over her shoulder while he pulled her along.

As soon as she left, a large man in a checkered button-down walked up and asked, "These pies fresh?" He looked closely at them.

"Yes, sir. Baked just last night," I said, and heard Mama Draughn and Aida whispering behind me.

"I'll take two. Ya got change for a twenty?"

Mama Draughn handed me some bills, which meant she was listening close enough. I counted out four dollars and handed them to the man.

"These worth eight dollars apiece?" he asked.

"Every crumb," I said. "They should cost more, really. If you're smart, you'll take a jar of filling too before it's all gone. It's delicious on just about anything. Tell you what, I'll throw in two jars with the pies for an even twenty."

He gave me back the four dollars and opened a pie right there, tearing off a piece of crust and digging his finger straight through, bringing out a sliver of apple. He tasted it, closed his eyes, and nodded his head in approval. "You here next week?"

I looked at Mama Draughn in the rocking chair, her eyes shut. Aida was bent over a notebook, scribbling something— both of them doing a fine job of ignoring me so I'd have to figure out every step.

"Absolutely," I said. "We'll have some new flavors. Tell your friends, too."

"I'll do that. Better bring several dozen with you next time," he said.

Aida closed her notebook and found an empty box for the man's pies and jars. When he walked away she said, "That there was the mayor of Dickson. I'd say you're off to a fine start. Natural salesman, aren't you?" Soon, there were so many customers in front of me that I couldn't hear Mama Draughn and Aida's voices over them.

Not much longer, and I'd sold everything we'd brought. As happy as I was about it, I hated missing out on the time with Tennessee and Omie. I turned to Mama D and Aida and said,

"If it's all right with the two of you, I'm going to try to catch up with them now." I held the cash out to Mama Draughn.

"What do we owe you for rent?" she asked Aida.

Aida laughed. "That's sweet of you, but you know better than that."

"Then put that money away, Harlowe, before someone else grabs it," Mama Draughn said. "That there's your startup. Be wise with it."

"I'll bring you back a treat, then," I said.

"That's not wisdom; you think this stomach needs any more cushion?" she laughed. "Go on, sun's starting to fade already."

Our neighbors were packing up their booths, and the owners and customers either walked to their cars or ventured out into the fair. I followed the crowd pouring out of the tent into the bright colors of flashing lights and spinning wheels. Balloons floated over costumes by the stand where people shot plastic ducks to win stuffed animals and candy. A man yelled that he could guess anyone's exact weight, and another sat on a plank over a tank of water below. People threw balls at him and laughed and yelled. He looked like he was exhausted from always waiting for the next dunk. As I walked past her, a woman with a silk scarf tied around her head and strands of jewelry hanging off every inch grabbed my hand. Her long fingernails were painted red and pressed into my palm.

"I can't stop right now. Have to go find someone," I said.

"I could help you with that and even more."

"Not today, thank you." I ran past her and, smelling something fried, remembered I hadn't eaten in a long time.

"How much?" I asked the man at the hot dog stand.

"Fifty cents," he said.

I handed him a dollar and took the change and dog from him. I ate it all in three bites, thinking Omie's eating habits must have rubbed off on me.

"Harlowe!" Tennessee's voice rose above the music of the rides.

I turned around in circles, looking for her, until I finally spotted her hand in the air waving at me from beside the carousel.

"Watch for Omie, he's coming around again soon!" she yelled.

I walked over, and she smiled as if it had been one of the best days she'd known, her eyes still glued to the horses going up and down. "Look!" She pointed to a flash of Omie moving along the metal pole on a mare posed in flight. He stood and whooped like he was a cowboy in his very first rodeo.

"We sold everything in four hours," I said. "We can make a lot more than I imagined next time."

"Are you serious? That's amazing! I was thinking I could design some labels, to make us look a little more professional. D-lish Pies, maybe? You know, for Darla Draughn?"

"Sounds perfect," I said. "And we should get boxes. Even up the price a dollar."

"Oh, that's a good idea. Look at that, I really can't remember the last time I saw him this happy," she said, pointing at Omie.

"And I love how happy that makes you," I said.

She turned and kissed me lightly, and then settled into my shoulder. I wrapped my arm around her waist while we watched the ride end.

"Again!" Omie shouted, and bounced up and down on the hard metal saddle, one of those things that hurts when you're older but you don't notice when you're a kid.

"I got a better idea," I said. "Let's try that one over there." I pointed at the Ferris wheel ten yards away, looming over us.

"Whoa. It's almost as tall as the roller coaster," Tennessee said while we walked, looking up into its outline against the sky. Omie scooted closer to her while he stared up at it so he wouldn't fall backward.

"Tell me if this is too much for him," I whispered to her. "Sorry if I jumped the gun."

"Unless he throws a fit, I say we do it," she whispered back.

A short man in a tall rainbow-striped top hat and suspenders measured Omie at the yardstick taped to the wall. Then he took our tickets and led us to the carriage. Once we had taken our seats, with Omie settled in the middle, the bar closed over our laps. When our carriage started to move, Omie clamped both of his hands over his eyes.

"Omie, watch, you'll want to see this!" Tennessee said, wrapping her arms around him.

Omie shook his head, his fingers pressing deep into his skin, but then Tennessee whispered something in his ear that made him laugh hard, and by the time he realized what had happened, he was watching the ground fall away beneath us.

When we got to the top of the ride, the wheel stopped and our carriage swung back and forth in the air. Tennessee reached across Omie for my hand. Both of our palms were a little sweaty, but Omie had lost all of his fear, straining to look out past me, then over at his sister.

"Those people look like marbles down there." Omie pointed to the ground below.

Tennessee followed his finger with her eyes. "You're right," she said. "Just tiny balls of color rolling around and bumping into one another."

We swung a few more minutes in the still air and watched the motion on the ground. From that height, I could almost imagine the things of Strickland in the same way that Omie saw all the people down below us—so much smaller that they almost disappeared. Or maybe it was me that I imagined differently, outside of what happened to Nate, and away from the Praters, mines, Mama and Daddy. I knew it would take some time and a lot of work, but if the three of us had more days like this one, we could have a start at something really new.

"That one's a puppy." Omie pointed to the clouds that were much closer to us than the ones we'd seen while fishing at Mohosh. They floated against a darkening lavender sky, the colors seeping through the white. It was the same sky I'd always seen from our valley, but right then, it looked like a whole different side of the coin.

I jumped when the carriage jerked and swayed, and the wheel began its way back down. The thoughts I'd had at the top scattered as if they were only passing through me like the clouds. I gripped the crossbar, each inch closer to the ground bringing back the thoughts of Mama, Nate, and the growing agitation of Jacob's silence.

Before the ride could stop at the bottom, Omie shouted, "Again!"

"What do you think?" Tennessee whispered to me.

"It's almost dark," I said. "I don't want to keep Mama Draughn waiting too long, especially not on our first trip here."

"You're right. Not today, Omes," Tennessee said. "We'll be back soon, and the next time we'll get on the Ferris wheel first, now that you aren't afraid anymore."

"Okay." He pulled a small plastic bunny from his pocket. "I take this to Mr. Draughn," he said.

"Where'd you get that?" I asked.

"I shot a duck!" he said.

"He really did, right on target," Tennessee added. "Still not sure how I feel about it, even for pretend, with a fake gun."

Our carriage clanged to a stop and I let go of the bar. I couldn't tell which was more real—the way I'd felt up there with the two of them, or the dread that was coming about going home, but I knew I needed something more often than a ride at a county fair to show me things could look a whole lot different from other places, depending from where you swung.

CHAPTER 31

AFTER I GOT US back to the Draughns' cabin, I turned off the engine and went to open the truck door, but a strange feeling came over me as soon as I looked out the window. "Hang tight, everyone," I said.

Something wasn't right. All the lights inside were still on, long past the time Mr. Draughn was usually asleep. My eyes followed the light across the porch and I saw the screen door had fallen off its hinge and was lying near the steps.

"We home already?" Mama Draughn yawned, but sat up quick when she saw the state of her door. She caught my eyes with her silent alarm.

Omie stretched his arms over his head, then fell against Tennessee again.

"Y'all stay put. I'll go check it out," I said, looking around the truck for some kind of protection. There was a rusty hammer in the back and I grabbed it. Tennessee and Mama Draughn watched me closely, but were both careful not to say anything that might frighten Omie.

After I shut the truck door quietly, I went up the stairs, and stepped over the fallen screen door. I didn't see anyone through the windows, so I walked into the kitchen. The scent of the pies we'd sold still hung in the air, or maybe it was baked deep into Mama Draughn's walls. There was the sound of someone walking out of the bedroom. I saw the shotgun first then Mr. Draughn behind it—one of his eyes bloody and swollen shut.

"Wait!" I said, shielding my face with my arm. "It's me, Harlowe."

He dropped the gun to the floor and stumbled toward me. "Is Darla here? Is she all right?"

"She's fine. What happened?"

He didn't answer, but shook his head and leaned against me, so I helped him to a chair and then ran to the door, motioning for everyone else to come inside.

Mama Draughn was the first one in, and ran to her husband's side. "Oh my Lord. Who did this to you?"

"I'm okay," he said. "Just glad you're safe. I worried after all the things he said." Mr. Draughn trembled and looked about the room, confused.

"Tennessee, take Omie to the bedroom, now," Mama D said.

Tennessee held Omie's head against her chest, trying to keep him from seeing or hearing too much. I couldn't tell if he had fallen back asleep, or was just pretending to. The bedroom door shut behind them.

"No Prater came near here, did they?" Mama Draughn asked as soon as the three of us were alone.

"No, of course not. You know better than that. It was the children's daddy. He came looking for them while y'all were gone."

"Bob Moore did this to you?" Mama Draughn asked. I wasn't surprised after feeling the strength of his grip around my throat.

"I'm sure it looks worse than it is. I'm fine. You know my eyes are already so bad, I don't know he could have made them much worse."

"No. I won't accept that for an instant," Mama Draughn said. "That man can't ever come back here, I'll make certain of that."

"He said the same about his kids—don't tell them that, though. They deserve something much better than him."

"Did you tell him where we'd gone?" Mama Draughn asked.

"You think I've lost my mind along with my sight? I told him you were at church, and I hadn't seen the children."

"Okay, good. But why'd he come looking for them here?"

"Said someone told him the kids had been hanging around your kitchen."

"Who would tell him that?"

"He didn't mention. Just gave me this to make sure they

don't come back here again." He pointed to his black eye.

"I hate to say it, but nothing good will come of this." Mama Draughn crossed her arms. "Harlowe, get me a wet rag, then tell them to come on out." She sat beside Mr. Draughn and gently cleaned his face, rinsing the rag in the bowl of water I handed to her. By the time I came back with Tennessee and Omie, she'd already emptied the bloody water in the sink, and Mr. Draughn held a fresh rag over his eye.

"Did you have some fun at the fair, Omie?" Mr. Draughn smiled the best he could from under the cloth.

"You knew!" Omie said. "I got ya something." He pulled out the Bugs Bunny that he'd won.

"Did I tell you I've been hoping for one of these?" Mr. Draughn asked.

"Nope, but I thought so," Omie answered.

I doubted Mr. Draughn could even see what the thing was with half his poor eyesight gone, but he wrapped his fingers around it like it was as valuable as the gold nugget he found years ago in the creek.

"Someone hurt you real bad?" Omie asked.

"Yep," Mr. Draughn said. "Mean old grizzly. I think I chased him off pretty good, though."

I wished it was true, but thought I saw something in Omie's smile change, like maybe he knew more than any one of us wanted him to.

"Come over here a minute, Tennessee and Harlowe," Mama Draughn said from the stove. The two of them huddled together and whispered beside me, outside of Omie's range. Tennessee covered her mouth with her hand while she listened to Mama Draughn. I took her other hand in mine and waited for anything she needed to say, but she only looked up at me and let the tears spill over her face.

Mama Draughn scooted in front of us to block Omie's view and Tennessee turned toward the sink to gather herself. "Your daddy don't know where we were today, and I beg you not to tell him," Mama Draughn said. "You know I want to help you two as much as I can, but this has all flown straight out of my hands. I can't put Herbert or anyone else at risk again."

"You're right, and I don't want to put either of you in danger either." Tennessee crossed her arms tight against her stomach and grimaced. "Oh my God, I'm so sorry," she said. I moved my hand to the back of her neck and rubbed it lightly, wishing there was anything I could say to make her feel better.

Omie peered around Mama Draughn and scooted close to Tennessee. "Why's everyone sad faces? Tomorrow we go on wheel again?"

Tennessee opened her mouth to answer but looked like she couldn't think of what to say. Mama Draughn jumped in for her. "I'm sure we'll all go back together sometime, sweetie, maybe not tomorrow. Right now, listen close to your sister and do whatever she says, because she knows how to take care of you better than anyone. And you take good care of her, too."

"Come over here a minute, Omes." Tennessee took him to the table and they sat while she talked with him quietly. I knew she wouldn't tell him everything that Moore had done, but just enough to explain why they wouldn't be coming back to the Draughns'.

"Listen," I said to Mama Draughn. "I understand why we can't use your kitchen anymore, but I don't want to give up what we started. You were right in thinking it'd be good for us. I can bake at home, and maybe Tennessee could too—I'll use Mama's car for the next trip."

"I'm sure Aida would still have you, but I can't—"

"I know," I told her. "You don't have to."

"Whatever you do from here on out, I'd think about it carefully. My guess is he came here for you as much as anyone," she said.

"Next time you show me the gold?" Omie asked Mr. Draughn.

"I'll keep it safe for you, all right," Mr. Draughn said.

We walked over to join them at the door and Tennessee said to Mama Draughn, "I want to find some way to fix what he did here."

"But this isn't yours to fix," Mama D said.

"You've made things better for us, and he ruined it," Tennessee said.

"We don't know what's around the bend," Mama Draughn said. "He can't take the things you hold in your heart, remember that." She brought Tennessee into a hug.

I waited until they let go of each other and then told Tennessee, "I won't show up at your place unless you ask me to come. Just please don't go silent on me."

"I won't," she said, and looked outside, through the broken door. "But it's going to take some time to bring him back down after this."

I pulled her into my chest and wanted to kiss her goodbye, but knew she wouldn't want that with Omie standing there, so I kissed her forehead instead.

She took a deep breath before opening her eyes and then let go of my hands. When they walked down the stairs and onto Kinley Road, I wanted to jump in Mama Draughn's truck again, pick them up, and go back to the Dickson fair, even though by now all the tents would be empty.

CHAPTER 32

"THIS SHOULD PAY FOR a new door." I took the cash from my pocket and set it on the counter beside Mama Draughn.

"No, no," she said. "Put that away right now. It's not yours to fix either, Harlowe, as hard as I know that is for you to hear."

"I'll find some way to make it up to you," I said.

"All you need to do is go home and keep good watch over yourself and your mama. I bet she's worried sick by now."

"There's nothing that will keep her from that," I said, "but I'll get back to her." I told them both goodbye, and began the walk home.

Before I went inside our trailer, I stopped at Nate's grave. *What did you know about Woodvale and why'd you have to stick your nose in all of it? You could have told me, you know. If you were still here, we could figure it all out together.*

Inside the trailer, Mama paced with a cigarette in her hand. "Near scared me to death. I had no idea where you'd gone or that you weren't coming back 'til now."

"I'm tired," I said.

"And you think I'm not? Tired of wondering where you run off to and if you'll get yourself hurt. I'm not the only one who doesn't like wondering all hours about my child. Mr. Moore came by here looking for his two."

"You told him about the Draughns, didn't you?" All of the blood rushed from my head to my chest.

"Only that you all were playing over there the other day. Woke up to you gone, and then him saying they were missing. I said it was my best guess, same as any other parent would have done had they been asked."

"But you know he's not the same as anyone else. You know that!"

"Alls I know is we were both worried over our children, and he said if you all were together, he'd bring you back to me."

"Well, he didn't, did he? Instead, he beat Mr. Draughn bloody. That's what he did with what you told him."

She dropped her eyes to the ground and then ashed her cigarette into the sink. "I'm sorry. I never thought . . . I just got scared, that's all." She inhaled again.

"We're all fucking scared. I'm scared all the time. Truth is, you're usually too high to even know what you're feeling. You're just numb now."

She pointed her finger at me and opened her mouth, but then fell against the sink. I jumped toward her out of reflex to make sure she was okay.

"I got it," she said. "I'm not a cripple." She pushed me away.

"Fine, then. What do you need, Mama? Shine? More pills? Something even stronger?"

She covered her face and her shoulders quavered with her sobs. I knew she wanted me to feel sorry for her, but this time I didn't feel anything except rage. "You took away the one thing that makes me happy because you're miserable. Does that make any sense to you? Do you want me to end up like you, Mama?"

She fell against the counter again like I'd punched her in the gut and taken her breath away. Her face hid in the crook of her arm. When she steadied her breathing, she looked up at me. "Go to your room," she said, her face blotchy and red and her hands quivering. "You might think I'm pathetic, but I'll never be as cruel as you."

I stared at her, my teeth clenched tight to keep from screaming that if I was cruel, it was only because she, and everyone else, had made me that way. I wondered how many pills she would take that night, scared to find that I was jealous she had something that could make her forget.

CHAPTER 33

IN THE MORNING, AFTER finally giving up the idea of ever falling back asleep, I pulled on my jeans, grabbed my phone, and went straight outside to the shed. I felt a little bad for not looking more into it before then, but with Moore coming for Tennessee and Omie, and then the fair and what he'd done to Mr. Draughn, I just hadn't had time to think of it.

It was only when I reached for the padlock on the shed that I noticed it was missing, and then found it lying a few feet away. It was still locked, but had been cut clean through one side with a bolt cutter, it looked like. I opened the door slowly, scared that whoever had been there might still be inside. It was empty of people, but the contents were ten times messier than they had been the day I drug the fishing tackle out. I cleared torn bags of old clothes from a heap and sighed with relief when I found my saw buried underneath. Whoever had been there found no interest in it, even though most anyone would know it could fetch some decent cash, especially being new. I moved it outside, along with piles of things that could be tossed and were cluttering my way. Little by little, I pulled everything out—scraps of wood, toolboxes, Nate's old card collections, and our tent. I made my way back to the corner where the boxes of shipping labels and stamps had been. I found one turned upside down with the labels spilled everywhere, and the other one with the Sharpies in the same shape. Underneath those I found a half-opened box that was much heavier than the others, and lifting one side, found stacks of smaller boxes tucked neatly inside. I couldn't read the writing in that light, so I took the box outside.

"What's going on?" Mama yelled from the porch with her coffee.

"Nothing you need worry about," I answered without turning around. I couldn't begin to explain any of it to her. It'd only make the time we had to spend together even more strained.

Tearing back both flaps of the box, I set it on the ground and hunched over to get a better look. Pulling one of the smaller boxes out then sifting through the others, I found that all twelve held the same Nikon digital camera. What made it even stranger was that the print on each of the boxes was in Japanese. I looked back at the porch, but Mama had already gone inside.

I didn't know how much cameras like that cost, but I knew

they couldn't be cheap, and there was no reason for Nate to have twelve of them, or even one. I couldn't remember him ever taking photos on anything but his phone. After searching the shed for any other surprises, I found one more box that had been overturned on its side, without any sign of what had been in it. Whoever had broken in must have found what they were looking for in that one.

I pushed everything back into the shed except my saw and the box of cameras. Those I carried with me into the trailer and set them in the corner of my room. I threw a bunch of my dirty clothes over them, just in case Mama decided to snoop around. I didn't have too much time to think about it, I just needed to get back out the door before I could change my mind about going to find Daddy.

Of course Mama tried to make a fuss when I grabbed her keys. "You could at least ask," she said, given up on any threats of taking them away. It actually felt worse than when she tried to pick a fight.

"Call me if you need me," I said before I left.

As soon as I got in the car, I dialed Daddy's number. It didn't matter that he didn't pick up after three rings. I expected as much, and put the gear in reverse anyway.

CHAPTER 34

IT HAD BEEN A few years since I'd been to the mining plant. The American Coal Council visited our school when I was in eighth grade, same as they'd done for years. They came to get us all pumped up about coal, to tell us how important we were to the rest of America—its bloodline and energy— and to ignore anyone who said it would ever go away. Daddy and Nate were underground when we went on the trip, but I saw plenty of bulldozers and ram cars from the loading dock where they gave us all hard hats and earplugs to muffle the noise of the drills.

The chain-link fences started about a mile away from the front gates. Pieces of fabric hung here and there from signs that protestors had tied up and then miners had torn down. I drove slower and spotted a couple still intact. "Stop Poisoning Our Children," one said, and the other, "We All Live Downstream." Next to it the yellow boy stained the ditch dark orange and ran toward the valley. When I was about ten,

Amos went to prison after thirteen people all died within a couple of months of the silicosis that ruined their lungs. But he paid the safety fines for hazardous breathing conditions and got out quick. No big surprise there. These battles had been going on as long as the mines had been running, I guessed, and probably would until they were gone.

"I'm here to see my dad," I said, leaning through my window toward Billy Curtis, the security guard.

"How ya doing, Harlowe?" he asked, taking his radio from his belt.

"I'm hanging in," I said, unsure how to answer.

"You gonna start up here with Red next week?" He tapped the radio against his leg and I wondered if it made a screeching sound for the person on the other side of it.

"Not sure about that," I said. "Hey, Billy, I know you were pretty tight with Nate, weren't you?"

"Yeah," he said, and looked past me. "It's been awful strange not having him here anymore. Sometimes I still go to call him for breaks here or beers after work."

"Trust me, I know what you mean," I said.

Billy scratched the back of his head, looking like he was trying to come up with something else to say.

"Hey, before you call for my dad, could you do me a favor?" I asked.

He looked up and waited.

"I just never got to see Nate's office. Always wondered what it was like in there."

Billy looked down at his watch. "It's almost lunch," he said. "Suppose I could take you by while it's quiet. Let me see if Howard can take over here for a little while." He pushed the orange button on the transceiver.

I picked up my phone and saw Daddy had tried to call me back. I decided to hold off on telling him where I was for the moment. I didn't want to see him before I had a chance to see the office first.

After a few minutes, Howard came and Billy said, "All right, mind if I ride up there with ya?"

The dust thickened while I drove, and I turned the wipers on just to try to clear the windshield a bit. Things looked a lot different than they had only a few years back. The front mine used to be almost hidden by the mountain above it, but now that, and almost everything else around, had been flat-topped. It was a wide expanse of rubble, the draglines towering higher than the neighboring mountains in the distance, all the driving equipment coated in gray dust. I felt much smaller near all the machines than I did in the valley.

A tinny-sounding bell rang so loud over the drilling that I stuck my fingers in my ears with the hand that wasn't on the steering wheel. "Where do I park?" I asked, knowing all the men would be heading to the cafeteria.

"How 'bout over there?" Billy pointed to an open spot by the side of the cinder-block building.

"Bet break is short and we don't have a ton of time," I said, crouching down in my seat. I wasn't worried about running into Moore, since Red and I heard Amos say he was putting him on pill runs, but I wasn't sure how often Amos came to check on things himself.

"We got 'bout twenty minutes or so," Billy said, and reached for the door.

"Just one more favor," I said, stopping him before he could get out. "Think I could have a little time alone in there? I'm just worried about someone coming in and I'll be crying or something. Embarrassing, you know? I mean, if it's too much trouble—"

"I understand," he said. "It don't mean you're not manly or anything, you know. Means you care. I'll watch the door. Only for a few minutes, though. Come on," he said. "Back door's this way."

CHAPTER 35

"THAT WAS HIS DESK right there." Billy pointed. "Henry Dalton has it now. All right, I'll leave ya to it," he said, his hand on the doorknob.

"Thanks," I said. "I'll be out soon." It felt strange being in that room for the first time, knowing Nate had spent so many hours there. It was dingier than I'd expected. From the way everyone talked about his job, I imagined something fancy, but the desks were chipped plywood and there were no windows in the concrete walls.

I didn't waste any more time and sat down in Nate's old chair and pulled open the front drawer. There were a few envelopes with Henry Dalton's name on them, some paper clips, and a stapler. Next I opened the two bottom drawers and rifled through the papers in file folders and the bags of snacks Henry had stuffed in the back. I picked up the picture of him and his wife from the desk. They wore matching sweaters and haircuts. I'd never met Henry, but right then I was mad at him for being happy. Even more, I was mad at him for being alive and taking Nate's desk.

I leaned my head in my hands and stared down at the peeling coating on the plywood, then turned the chair to face the rest of the room. The desk on the opposite side caught my eye and I walked over to it. It was much neater than the other two desks in the room, and it didn't look like anyone had used it in a long time. A *Sports Illustrated* swimsuit calendar that was two years old hung above it. I had a feeling about who it belonged to even before I saw Tommy Prater's face staring up at me from the identification badge in the top drawer. Before I could look in the drawer below it, the office door opened and I jumped.

Billy followed behind Daddy with a look that said he was sorry, but there was nothing he could do.

"What the hell are you up to in here?" Daddy asked.

I stood up from Tommy's desk. "I told you I needed to talk with you. You couldn't seem to find the time, so I came to find you."

"Doesn't look like it was me you came for," he said. "Let's go, right now. Do you know what could happen to you if they find you nosing around in here?" He walked toward me and grabbed my arm.

"Okay, fine," I said, and followed him out the door.

He spotted the car and walked over to it.

"I think Nate was trying to get the Praters busted for

running pills," I said, before he could tell me to leave again.

"Shhhh," he said tightly, and held his hand right in front of my face. "We'll talk about this later."

"I can't wait any longer," I said, my voice cracking from being quiet for too long. "Did you know Mama's taking them again?"

"There's nothing either one of us can do about that," he said.

"But you don't ever do anything! You're not even hardly there anymore. I'm the one who has to deal with her, just like Nate had to deal with her the last time."

He walked closer to me and lowered his voice. "Do you know what happens if I lose this job? We can't pay for anything—not her medical bills, or yours if anything happened to you, and certainly not mine." His face changed and he slumped against the car.

"What's wrong with you?"

"Nothing that doesn't happen to most after years of work here. Lungs. They're not giving out too soon, but I got three years before I can get pension, and the medicine alone is thousands a month."

I looked at him and opened my mouth to say something, but closed it again.

"You understand a little better now? Didn't think it'd do any good to burden either one of you with it."

"I'm sorry," I said. "I just can't let it go. I don't understand how you can be here, knowing what they did to Nate."

"Hang on," he said, and took his phone out of his pocket, the ring becoming louder while he lifted it to answer. "Yeah," he said. "Oh no. God damn it. All right, I'll keep an eye out." He hung up the phone and frowned at the dust covering his boots.

"What was that about?" I asked.

"Go home, Harlowe," he said. "Go straight home and stop asking so many goddamn questions."

The doors of the cafeteria opened, and all the workers filed out, putting on their hard hats, goggles, and masks they used to try to keep the dust from coating their insides as much as it did their outsides.

David Jenson spotted me and Daddy and came over to say hello, extending a gloved hand my way. "Did you hear about Tommy?" he said to Daddy.

Daddy only nodded, but I could tell he felt me watching and listening close.

"It's a shame. Hospital said it was a freak accident. Dogs in the house were dead too. Fentanyl powder. Guess he thought it was coke or something. Heard that stuff is everywhere, now," Mr. Jenson said.

I stared harder at Daddy, my jaw dropped open.

"Go home, Harlowe," he said again. "If you don't go right now, I'll drive you back myself."

There were so many thoughts and questions simmering to a boil in my mind. I needed to leave before I started spouting them without thought to whoever was within earshot. I turned to get in the car when a truck pulled up beside us. There was nowhere for me to hide when I saw Moore behind the wheel. "What's he doing here?" He pointed at me but looked at Daddy.

"I left my medicine at home, and he had to bring it for me," Daddy said. "He was just leaving."

"That's right," I said, swallowing hard and wanting to get away from Moore as fast as I could.

"Wait just a minute there." Moore stopped me before I could close the car door. "I reckon you've all heard about the tragedy. Amos feels certain it was no accident. Thinks someone was out to get Tommy. He's offering a reward if anyone knows anything. Spread the word. Don't think I have to tell any of you that now's not the time to screw anything up around here. Or anywhere else."

I nodded and chewed the inside of my mouth to stop from saying that Tommy got what he deserved.

"One more thing," he said, before I could get inside. "Be sure to ask your friends if they know anything. We'll be looking everywhere." He squinted at me.

I wanted to ask him if he meant like he'd looked for all of us at the Draughns, but bit my cheek even harder. "What about the sheriff?" I asked instead.

"Oh, he's looking too," Moore said. "You can be sure of that."

I drove away, my heart pounding. All of Strickland might be looking for the person who killed Tommy, but I wasn't about to forget that he was the one who killed Nate. Even if I was the only one who still remembered.

CHAPTER 36

THE PHONE SHOOK IN my hand, as I tried with the other to keep the wheel steady.

"Hello?" Powell said.

"It's Harlowe Compton," I said. "I just heard about Tommy Prater."

"I see," he said, and cleared his throat. "Is there something you'd like to report?"

"Yes," I said. "I overheard Amos and Bob Moore talking the other night."

"Go ahead," he said, and I repeated the conversation as exact as I could remember it.

"I'm sorry, and what do you think this has to do with Tommy's dying?"

"I heard them talk about clinics and pill runs, don't you understand? Amos said he took Tommy off of them after Woodvale, and Nate had written about that and other places in his notebook. Working in the same office, he must have gotten their schedule somehow. And there was a text." I stopped talking, realizing I was about to get Jacob involved too.

"A text to who?"

I took a breath and told myself to slow down. All of a sudden, I was unsure of everything I had set out to say. "Um, I just—I think Nate knew what the Praters were doing, and that's why Tommy killed him," I said.

"Bring the notebook to the station, and any other evidence you have," Powell said. "In the meantime, if you see or hear of anyone finding packets of powder, whatever you do, don't open it. All it takes is one spill, taste, or touch of that stuff. Don't know why anyone would even bother with it. There were about twenty of them stuffed inside a camera box, if you can believe it. Tommy definitely didn't know what he was dealing with."

My pulse pounded so loud in my ears that I could hear nothing else. "Okay, I have to go," I said. "I'll bring that notebook sometime soon," I muttered before I hung up and dropped the phone onto the passenger seat.

Sweat poured down my face and neck, and a wave of nausea almost forced me to pull over to the side of the road, but I didn't want to stop anywhere before I got home.

Mama was asleep in the recliner with the TV on loud, and I rustled her a little to make sure she was okay. When she shook her head and opened her eyes halfway, I said, "Never mind, everything is fine," and rushed back to my room.

I threw the dirty clothes aside and picked up the box underneath. I looked inside at the smaller camera boxes and considered taking the whole thing to the dump without looking any further, but I couldn't turn away from the pieces now that some of them were finally fitting together.

I took out one of the camera boxes and turned it over in my hands, looking for the best way to open it. Sheriff said the powder was in packets, but still, I worried. I lifted the back flap of the small box enough so I could see inside. As soon as I saw something white wrapped in clear plastic, I closed it shut.

My room wasn't close to big enough for the amount of pacing I needed to do, but still I walked back and forth across the floor, wondering what the hell I was supposed to do. I definitely couldn't tell Mama about it. And I don't think she'd be desperate enough to open a packet of powder without knowing what it was, though I couldn't be sure. Really, for anyone who found them, it wouldn't be strange to open one and smell it, maybe even taste it a little. Why the fuck did Nate have it in the shed?

Walking the same steps over and over wasn't getting me anywhere, so I put everything back in the box and taped it shut. I took my school backpack from the closet, dumped the papers still left in it from last year, put the box and notebook in, and then added a couple pairs of pants and shirts from my floor, some underwear and socks, a flashlight, and my toothbrush and toothpaste from the bathroom. I took the twenty-three dollars out of Nate's wallet and put it in mine alongside the pie money, then hid his wallet and phone behind a stack of old board games at the top of our closet.

My phone rang as soon as I got outside and when I picked it up, I saw it was Mama calling. "I know," I said, "I keep leaving," before she could say anything. "Just please trust me that I have to right now. If Daddy asks you, tell him you don't know where I went, because it's the truth. I'm not taking the car. And Mama, call Mama Draughn if you need any help at all. Promise me that."

"But what about—" she said.

"I'm sorry," I said. "I really have to go."

CHAPTER 37

"WHERE ARE YOU?" I asked as soon as Red answered my call.

"Swimming, come meet me," he said.

"Is it just you?"

"Yep, sad to say."

By the time I got to Mohosh, my shirt was soaked through with sweat and I wished I had thought to grab a drink before I left the house. I saw Red's cooler on the rock before I spotted him and hoped he had more in it than only the liquor he'd carried with him the other night. Two cans of lemonade along with a pack of cold cuts, saltines, and the bottle of bourbon were inside when I opened it. I popped the top off one of the lemonades and drank almost all of it in one go.

Red waved and started swimming toward me from the middle of the pond. I took a couple of saltines from the sleeve and ate them, hoping they'd soak up some of the nervous juice in my stomach. He pulled himself up on the rock and sat on his towel. "You getting in?" He shook water from his hair like a dog after a bath.

"No," I said, washing down the crackers with the last drops of lemonade. "Don't have time."

"Got an interview or something?" he laughed. "Oh, right, busy with the girl," he added.

"Neither," I said. "Well, I mean, I do need to see Tennessee, but that's not why I'm in a rush."

"Am I supposed to ask or something?" He reached inside the cooler.

"Nope. Red, I need you to answer something for me, and if our friendship means anything, you'll tell me the truth."

"Oh shit," he said, and dropped the silly grin. He looked out over the water and waited, listening.

"You know anything about Jacob or Nate you're not telling me?"

He shot a look back at me. "Nate? Don't you mean Jacob and Ryan?"

"Okay, start with that," I said. "Start with anything you haven't told me about."

"He'll kill me," Red said.

"Not if Amos gets him first," I said. "Tommy's dead, and they think someone planted the shit that killed him. Jacob will be a likely guess, considering what happened at the party. Go on."

"What happened to Tommy?" Red asked.

"I told you I don't have time," I said.

"All right. But none of this came from me. He never said exactly, but I guessed he was up to something after he started spending so much time with Ryan. And there was the cash and trucks and tons of booze all of a sudden. Everything you saw at the party. After Nate's funeral, when we dropped you at the Sip N Sak, he started acting really weird. Crying so hard he ran the wheeler off the road. He said something about how it was all his fault. I just thought he'd had too much to drink at the Crag, but then he took some pills out of his pocket and swallowed a couple. Right after that he stopped returning my calls, and then you saw what happened between Tommy and him," he said.

"Don't know how I didn't spot it then," I said. "I remember now his eyes were really bloodshot, and he was acting like a dick."

"You were upset about Nate," Red said. "And worried about the girl."

"He never said anything about Nate to you?"

"No," Red said. "You really think Nate knew anything about it?"

"He knew something, for sure," I said. "I just don't know how much or why. I have to find Jacob before anyone else does, though."

"I don't know where he is, if that's what you're asking next," Red said.

"I've got a hunch," I said.

"Don't tell me," Red said. "I don't want to know anything else about it. I go to the mines in two days. Last thing I need is Amos thinking I know anything about what happened to Tommy."

"You're right," I said, and was glad I hadn't said more. I stood up and put my backpack on again. "If you don't mind, keep an eye out for Tennessee while I'm gone."

"I'll do my best," he said, "but after hearing her daddy talk the other night, I don't think he leaves much room for anyone."

"That's why I need you to pay attention for me," I said. "Everybody's on high alert because of Tommy, her daddy included."

He nodded and rolled a small rock around in his hand. "Harlowe?" he said after I'd turned to leave. "You're the only friend I have left. Don't do anything stupid."

"Same goes for you," I said.

CHAPTER 38

I'LL MEET YOU IN the field by our holler, Tennessee texted when I asked if I could see her.

I found a bit of shade under the old poplar tree with the tire swing that one of the Murray brothers rigged for some of us kids when I was five or six. The tire was coming off in pieces and could use replacing soon, but the rope was still strong. I sat on it halfway, walking my feet along the grass, and remembered when I was scared as a kid because it felt so high off the ground.

"Hey," I said, and stood up straight, dropping the rope when she surprised me from behind.

"Don't stop because I'm here," she said, and tied her hair into a kind of tucked-up ponytail on the top of her head with a rubber band from her wrist. "Omie's with Mrs. Hemlock for a minute."

"I was hoping," I said. "There's some stuff we need to talk about."

She sat down at the base of the tree, between two gnarled roots, and leaned against the trunk, pulling her knees up. "I'm listening," she said when I sat down beside her.

"I heard your dad and Amos talking the other night," I said. "Has he said anything about leaving town?"

She looked at me from the corners of her eyes, took a deep breath, and nodded slow. "He said there's a miners conference. He's leaving tomorrow."

"I don't think that's where he's headed," I said. "Amos said something about putting your dad on clinic runs. I guess that's where the Praters get the pills they're selling, except now with Tommy dead—"

Tennessee crossed her legs and leaned over them, her head in her hands.

"I know," I said. "It's all fucked up. I think Nate knew about it all. Jacob too. I've got to find Jacob and get it all straight."

"That seems dangerous," she said. "Shouldn't you wait until things die down a little after Tommy?"

"I can't. I'm sure they're looking for him too. Nobody's heard from him and no one can get ahold of him. Something might have already happened to him, I don't know. But I have to try. I already know too much to not know everything there is. Listen, the only reason I'm telling you this is because when I get back, I think the three of us should leave."

Tennessee sat up straight and looked me square in the face.

I tried to read her expression, but she kept it hidden. She was thinking, I saw that much in her eyes as they moved back and forth across my face.

"We already know that we could make money with the pies," I said. "And I can fix things for people while I'm still working on my furniture. We could find a school for you and Omie so you can finish."

"Where would we go?" she asked.

"I don't know, I haven't gotten that far yet, but almost anywhere seems better than here. Things are only gonna get worse with your dad and Amos, I can feel it. No matter how I try, I can't pull Mama out of her funk, and most of the time I think she might pull me under with her."

"Harlowe, wait," she said, and put her hand on my knee so I would slow my words down. "I called my aunt yesterday, and told her about what Dad did to Mr. Draughn and that I'm worried he might hurt Omie or me. You know I'd never forgive myself if anything ever happened to Omie. I can't pretend anymore that it's not a possibility."

"I thought they weren't speaking to you?"

"They weren't. Because of how he always treated my mom. But as soon as I admitted to Aunt Celeste that I'm afraid of him, she wanted to help. She runs a motel and I can make some money working there while I finish school. I have cousins who can help with Omie, too." She pulled at the strings around a hole in my jeans that was wearing through. "They're coming to pick us up in three days."

I swallowed and looked away before I said anything I might regret. "Were you going to tell me?" I asked, still trying to get my head around what she was saying.

"Of course, I was already planning on it today. Then you texted first."

"Have you told Omie yet?"

"No, because I don't want him to accidentally slip and say something to Dad. It has to happen while he's at the conference—or wherever."

"What if you hate it there?"

"Then I'll figure something else out, but I have to do what's best for Omie, and I have to finish school."

"I understand that," I said. "But you could do those things with me. Look, I won't be gone long. I'll be back Wednesday at the latest. Just don't go anywhere until I'm back, okay? Can you promise me?"

"As long as nothing else happens, I promise I won't go until Celeste gets here on Thursday."

"And you'll call me if anything happens. So I can get back to you."

"Yes, I promise you that." She took my hand. "You really feel you're sure enough about us to start over somewhere together?"

"I know I am," I said.

"I won't go unless you have a plan."

"That's fair enough."

"I'm only thinking about it for now. I'm not giving you a decision yet."

I leaned toward her on my knees and kissed her. "That's okay," I said, and then kissed her again. "I'll take your 'maybe' over a 'no.' You better get back to Omie. I saw your dad up at the mines a few hours ago, and he sounded like he was delivering messages around here for Amos. No need to get him suspicious before he leaves tomorrow."

"Yep, you're right," she said. "Thanks for thinking about that."

"I'm looking out for you," I said. "Both of you. Not because you wouldn't do fine without me—I know you would. It's just that I want to. And I really hope you'll let me." I stood up first and held my hand out to her. She took it, and while she pulled herself up, I dug my heels into the ground and held fast.

It was always hard to end a kiss with Tennessee or say goodbye, but that time was especially awful. The thought of having to maybe say goodbye to her forever was so terrible that for a second I thought about not going. But I had her promise, and if I didn't find out what happened with Nate before I left Strickland, I'd never be able to really leave it behind.

CHAPTER 39

AT THE SIP N Sak, I walked straight to the cooler, grabbed three bottles of water, then a handful of jerky sticks and several bags of peanuts.

"Did you forget something?" Mrs. Devin asked when I dropped all of it onto the counter.

"Nah, this is it. No beer for me today."

"Camping trip with no beer?" she asked, looking at my backpack.

I was in no mood to answer her questions, and wished she'd just ring me up and let me go. "Something like that," I answered.

"You're looking a little thin," she said. "You sure you're all right, Harlowe?"

"It's just too hot to eat most of the time, and I guess I haven't had much appetite."

"You've still got to keep up your strength. This heat can't last forever."

"I hope not, for all of our sakes," I said.

She reached for a paper bag.

"You don't need to do that," I said. "I can put everything in my backpack." I set it next to the register and opened it, making sure the box at the bottom was covered with my clothes.

"Looks like you're going away for a while," she said, glancing inside and handing me the bottles.

"Just a night. This thing doesn't hold as much as it looks like," I said, thinking again of what was in the bottom.

"I'm throwing these in for free. Make sure you eat them before they melt." She set two big Snickers bars on top of everything else in my bag.

"Thank you," I said, and felt bad that I'd gotten annoyed with her earlier.

The pack hugged my shoulders and settled between the blades. The weight wasn't too bad. It was the water that weighed the most, and that wasn't something I could go without. I jumped over a ditch where the yellow boy ran thick as glue on my way to Mama Draughn's.

The screen door was back in its rightful place, but there was a tear in the mesh, a reminder of Moore's visit that, even patched, would remain. Mr. Draughn was in his usual spot too and rocked a gentle rhythm, his bruised eye black around the edges, but at least open by now.

"I'll only keep her a few minutes this time," I said, climbing the porch stairs.

"You take however long you like, you know that." He spat

some tobacco juice off the side of the porch and wiped his chin. "How those children doing?"

"Okay, but I wouldn't mind if you listened a little more closely for them the next few days."

He nodded and shut his eyes, the tune starting in his throat by the time I reached for the door. I stopped and faced him once more. "Is Mama Draughn mad at me about what happened here?"

"Oh, she's plenty mad," he said. "But it ain't at you."

"Thanks."

Mama Draughn opened the door to let me know she'd been listening to us the whole time. "At least something good came out of all this trouble." She nodded at the steady screen door. "It'll take a little more mending, though."

"No squeak now, that's good."

"How 'bout you? You back in working order?" She held the door until we were both through to the other side.

"Depends on what you mean," I said.

"Set." She pointed to the table. She must have said that word to me a thousand times since I was Omie's age. And anyone else who ever said it would always remind me of her.

She brought over a cherry pie and two glasses of tea, then settled into the chair across from me.

"You still having trouble sleeping?" I looked at the other pies on the counter.

"It's the arthritis meds." She rubbed her hands and looked at me. "Didn't notice until this minute, but you've gone skinny and dark-eyed on me. I don't like it one bit. Can barely see the sparks in those green eyes. We need those back straightaway."

"That might have to wait a spell." I dipped my fork into the pie. It was the first thing I'd eaten all day other than the saltines.

"So," she said, settling into her chair and watching me eat. "I heard about Tommy, and I gather you did too."

"I'd say he had it coming, wouldn't you?"

"Harlowe Compton, I don't like that kind of talk, especially not from you. That's a human life that's gone. If every sinner deserves to die, where do you think it stops?"

I set my fork down. "I think a lot less people will die now that Tommy's gone."

"I don't think that's the way the world works," she said. "There will always be hurt people who hurt other people. It's only when the pain becomes too great, or the grace is even greater, that people change. Maybe there's still a chance for Amos. Losing his son might be the only thing that could break him open."

Her words felt like a betrayal. "How can you say that, knowing what the Praters did to Nate? Knowing how they've always gotten rid of anything that stood in their way?"

"The longer I live, the more I understand that there's very

little that separates any of us from each other. Right now, your fire for the truth worries me. It will burn you alive if you don't learn how to temper it."

I took a sip from my glass and thought about her words before I spoke. "If people were better about telling the truth, I wouldn't have to go hunting for it." I took a deep breath. "That's why I came here. I need to borrow a gun. It's only for protection, and I'm sure I won't need it, but I'm going up the mountain to find Jacob, and I don't know who else I might meet along the way. I've been thinking, and my best guess is that he's at Ryan's family's cabin. Heard anything about that?"

She pursed her lips down at her hands and then lifted her eyes to mine. "I'd say that's a good guess. Wait right there," she said, and walked to the bedroom. Her feet dragged a little over the creaking boards. She returned with something wrapped in a piece of burlap cloth. "You can take this," she said. "I hope you don't need it, but you're right, I'd rather you have it in case. These too." She passed me a box of bullets. "It's loaded already, so take care. You know how to shoot, don't you?"

"Yeah, Nate taught me when I was eight. Is this Mr. Draughn's? I don't want to take his gun from him."

"No, love, it's mine. You know that man can barely load a shotgun with those eyes. You think he could manage a revolver?"

I unwrapped the gun, put it in the back of my jeans, and tightened my belt. The piece of burlap went in my backpack, over the food. "I'll bring it back," I said.

"The only thing I care about you returning is yourself."

"I care about that too. Oh, one other thing if it's not too much trouble. Well, two really. I need a plastic bag and something to dig a hole."

"You already done something that needs burying?"

"No, it's not mine. Just—" I tried to think of a way to explain. "I don't know who it belonged to, but I need to get rid of it. Safely."

She pushed herself out from the table and bent down to look under the sink. "Will this do?" She held up a trowel. "Or you need something bigger?"

"I think that'll work," I said, and took it and then the black plastic bag she held out for me. I put them both in my pack, and then zipped it again. "I better get going. Thank you," I said, and reached to give her a hug.

"Just tell me one thing," she said, her arms still around my middle. "Why do you need to know exactly what happened to Nate? What will it change?"

I wasn't sure how to answer her at first, and looked around the room while I thought about it, my eyes finally landing on the photos of June. Mama Draughn let go of the hug and I looked into her face. "Because I can't know where I'm going without knowing who I've come from. Nate was showing me the way. I have to know the turns he took before I can find my own."

Mama Draughn snapped her eyes shut for a second and then nodded like she was listening to my words again in her head. "Well, I have to say, that makes a lot of sense to me. I trust you, Harlowe. I hope you do too."

After I said goodbye to Mama D and Mr. Draughn, I headed toward the ditch at the start of the trail where the yellow boy ran. It seemed like the best place to bury the box. I didn't want to carry it any longer, and if I tossed it in the trash somewhere, it could end up spilling or getting into the wrong hands, or both. I wrapped it in the plastic bag and then dug a hole with the trowel Mama D gave me. Anyone from Strickland knew to stay away from the mine sludge and they wouldn't go digging near it. I almost felt like I should put a caution sign by the fresh mound of dirt above the ditch, but I knew that could be as much an invitation to some as a deterrent to others. I got a bit of satisfaction from burying the shit that had buried Nate, but it wasn't enough. There would always be more of it, and that wasn't a battle I could take on by myself. But what I could do was find out how much Nate knew about it all and why it was important enough for him to risk everything.

CHAPTER 40

HOGAN'S CROSS, WHERE RYAN'S cabin sat, was at least twenty miles from Kinley Road, and those miles went much slower on foot than they did in a four-wheeler. Walking was my best bet—it wouldn't have been right for me to take Mama's car from her for that long, even though I didn't especially like the idea of her driving on pills, either. After an hour of hiking, my pack grew heavier than I expected and pushed against the gun in the back of my pants. I stopped and took one of the bottles of water from my bag, careful not to drink too much. If there was any clean water left hidden somewhere deep inside the mountain, I didn't know how to find it, or have a thingamajig to make it drinkable. Then I moved the gun to the front of my pants, under my belt, adjusted the straps on my pack, and hoped things would get easier.

When I found my pace, my body settled into the rhythm of the walk, and so did my mind. Thoughts speak loud when you have nothing but quiet and time and the tap of your feet against the earth with each step. I'd spent hardly any time on the mountain alone, and whenever I'd gone, it was usually with the boys, wheeling. It probably would have done me some good.

Hawks swirled over the trees and squirrels ran from my step. Some of the leaves had already turned color from the summer drought and fallen to the ground. They cushioned my feet and gathered around the stumps where trees had been cut down for lumber. Before Amos bought the company, he promised to double replanting efforts, but of course he never followed through. He said the same thing about surface mining, but I don't know why he thought anyone was dumb enough to believe that you could rebuild a mountain after you'd cut it down. That afternoon, even the dried and ruined parts of the mountain sparkled with the sun's descent and hummed like one day, the mountain might rise up and take its revenge. Soon, the navy shadows grew longer and faded into the deepening sky. I wished Tennessee was there beside me, and thinking of her waiting at home for me made me walk a little faster.

I figured if I kept traveling through the night, I'd reach Ryan's cabin by noon the next day. When I couldn't ignore the rumble of my stomach any longer, I stopped only long enough to eat a supper of jerky and a Snickers, the chocolate just slightly melted. I was so hungry I would have licked it all off the paper if I had to. I was a lot more grateful then that Mrs.

Devin had thought to give them to me. I took the flashlight from the bottom of my pack, zipped everything back in place, and moved with a little more haste now that it was starting to get cooler in the dark. Owls woke from their sleep and hooted to one another. Two eyes blinked at me and then bounced away, a white tail flipped up at its rear, and two more deer bounded after it. I'd never seen or heard the mountain come alive that way when I'd been up there drinking with Jacob and Red. Then again, I guess we'd done so much hooting ourselves, we wouldn't have heard anything else.

The quiet was nice for a while, but it turned lonely fast. The purple shadows went black and I could only see whatever was within the flashlight's reach. Every once in a while, I noticed the speckled glow of foxfire, or what the old-timers called fairy fire, growing wild on rotted stumps and branches. Tennessee and Omie would have loved to see the blue-green glow on the carpet of the woods, luminescent like a million fireflies. I imagined both of their faces lighting up alongside it. I gripped the flashlight tight, and kept its beam close to my feet and the ground ahead. Stumps and trees jumped out only in time for me to quickly dodge them, and I near tripped and smacked my head several times over. I'd pass one, then be faced with another straightaway, like I was trapped in one of Ryan's pinball machines in his basement. My feet slipped on the leaves already damp with dew. When I came to a tree three times my size, I stopped and leaned against it to catch my breath.

I looked for the road, but couldn't find it, and wondered if I should keep going in the same direction I was headed, stop and look harder for it, or wait it out until the light of day. A coyote howled and, by the sound, was close enough to smell me. I panted and quickened my steps, scared that the coyote or something worse might pounce before I could manage the gun.

The flashlight flickered and I banged on the bottom of it, thinking that maybe it just needed a little slap to stay awake, but no such luck. The darkness rattled my nerves. I reached into my pocket for my phone, but the battery was dead and I cussed myself for not thinking to bring either batteries or my charger, not that I'd be able to plug it in. I stood for a second and blinked into the night, and after a few minutes, noticed my eyes adjusted a little better. Enough light traveled from the moon and stars through the branches for me to see the outline of my fingers when I held them up in front of my face. Slowly, I put one foot in front of the other. After a little while I was more confident and quickened the pace again. Soon I was dodging trees and the sound of small animals as I ran. If I could keep it up, I might get to Jacob even sooner than I thought.

Then the ground opened and there was only air under

my feet and a swift pang of terror through the rest of me. I bounced off a root and landed on my back. My head felt like an ax pierced it. My ears filled with the sound of blood rushing. I lay there, not wanting and not able to move, and confused about where I'd missed a step. Finally, I sat up slow and carefully touched the back of my head, finding a wet knot as big around as one of the roots beneath me. My hand was damp with blood, and soon the side of my face was too. *That's what you get for rushing*, I thought through the throbbing in my skull. I'd been so hell-bent that I thought I could beat the darkness and this gaping hole it'd covered from view. Now I'd be behind, and I had no idea how much farther I had to go to the cabin. I hadn't left much room for the unexpected, obviously not the smartest bet.

I slid the pack off my shoulders and searched inside for something to soak up my blood, finding only the burlap that had been wrapped around Mama D's gun. A new pain shot up through my ankle and all the way into my shin, and I realized the revolver was no longer tucked under my belt. I felt around until finally my fingers touched metal.

I tightened my belt around the gun again and balanced on the ankle that didn't hurt. It grew even darker then, the moonlight falling short of the hole. If there was one thing I should have been looking for on the mountain, it was sudden drops where earth and trees were missing, but this was something different, I was sure. Holding my hands out in front of me, I found the edge of the ditch. It felt like someone had hacked the earth clean through, the drop was so sharp. Feeling my way around, I realized the thing had four definite sides. Judging the depth and width, it wasn't just a hole I'd fallen into, but a grave waiting to be filled. Panic filled every space of me and I stumbled backward.

My throat closed, and the throbbing in my head grew stronger. The only thing I needed was to get out as fast as I could. I gripped an edge to pull myself out, but the grass above came free in my hands and the dirt crumbled beneath it. My arms shook, all the strength in them leaving. I couldn't breathe, and worried that soon the earth would swallow me whole. The same panic I'd felt at the lake about Nate poured over me, and my heart sped, sickness spreading from my stomach to my fingertips until they went numb. *Just breathe, Harlowe. Breathe,* I remembered Tennessee saying.

I managed to slow my mind a little and sat down, my back against one side of the grave. I waited with the gun in my lap. Each minute stretched too long, and it seemed that dawn resisted coming to me on purpose. I tried to take my mind off things by figuring out how far I'd already come, guessing I must be at least halfway to Ryan's cabin, though I might have lost some distance by losing my way. Part of my mind wanted to give up, and the other fought against it. I listened to the two sides argue with each other until my eyes grew heavy, but I couldn't let them shut for the animals that might be lurking. I was wounded prey, trapped where I couldn't escape.

A few minutes later, still unable to move, I decided to wait patiently, the thing I should have done as soon as my flashlight went out. The moon came into sight again and shone through the branches above, casting crossed shadows on my skin and the dirt around me. Here and there, stars speckled the bit of sky that the branches couldn't block from my view. The pieces of light and the sound of small feet scurrying through leaves kept me awake. I strained to see the creatures beyond the edge of the hole, still sure they were waiting to pounce, their eyes flickering invitations to one another.

I let myself imagine getting out and going home without finding Jacob. Maybe this was as far as I would make it. But then I thought about Nate, who worked so hard to get into the office at the mines but hated working for Amos, Daddy sick without telling any of us, and Mama glued to her recliner living every day half-asleep. I thought about Jacob with a baby that never saw him and secrets that kept him hiding in the woods, and Red, who would likely spend most his life paying off his mama's debt. Tennessee and Omie deserved more than what Strickland made of people, and by the same right, I figured I did too.

I held my hand steady on the gun and settled myself into

the dirt. It was just dirt. The animals above me couldn't fight a gun, and the sun couldn't stop itself from rising again. There was nothing else I could do until there was light enough for me to see. Once I really accepted it, there was a strange comfort in having to be still, like someone had given me a blanket when I hadn't yet realized I was cold. And soon enough, the night began to lift as if it had only been waiting for me to stop expecting it.

Before it was fully light, I heard footsteps walking toward me. When it peered over the edge at me, I was so glad it was human and not a wolf or grizzly that I almost yelled, but reminded myself that mountain people could be jumpy and even more mistrusting of people. As far as I could tell by the frame and hair, it was a woman, with a shotgun slung over her shoulder. I gripped the gun under my fingers, just to be sure of it.

"I bet you weren't looking for a soft place to lay your head down there," she said, standing directly over me.

"No. It was a hard landing," I said. "You have no idea how happy I am to hear a human's voice." I pulled myself to a squat and squinted up at her, still unable to see anything but her outline against the brightening sky.

She leaned over the edge and extended her hand. I gathered my things, and when I reached for her I was surprised by her strength while she pulled me up and over without strain. Once I was out and could see her face, I noticed her features were sharp and strong, with something a little familiar in them. A shock of white fell from her forehead, stark against the rest of her long dark hair. She swung her shotgun around to her back.

"My name's Nuna," she said.

CHAPTER 41

"YOU'RE DARLA DRAUGHN'S SISTER?" I asked.

"I am. Hand me your things."

I looked at her another minute, wondering if she could be trusted after the falling-out she'd had with Mama Draughn. My ankle ached worse now that I was standing on it, and I needed to at least clean up a little before getting to Jacob. I handed her my pack and she threw it over the shoulder that held her shotgun. Now that I was on somewhat even ground, I noticed a large mound beside the grave, the grass already grown over it, plus a covering of fallen leaves. I wondered who the grave was meant for, and why it had never been filled.

"This way," Nuna said, and took off walking.

I followed her, but the pain shot from my ankle all the way into my thigh, and stopped me. I limped behind her as fast as I could and tried not to whimper.

"That won't do at all," she said, and came up alongside of me. She wrapped her arm around my waist, and threw mine over her shoulder.

"Did she tell you I was coming up here?"

"Do you always ask so many questions?"

"Your sister would probably say as much," I said, sensing already that Nuna wouldn't be as forthcoming as Mama Draughn was with me.

She remained silent until we came upon a small cabin, one I hadn't seen the last time we were all up at Ryan's, or any of the other times we'd ventured that far on our four-wheelers.

There was an old truck and an outhouse behind the cabin. Nuna brought me limping through the door, my arm still around her shoulder. Then she pulled a chair out from the table in the middle of the one-room cabin and set me in it. She stood at the sink with her back to me and I took a quick look around. There was a bed in the corner, a small table covered with books, crates of supplies against the back wall, and in the kitchen, next to the wood-burning stove, a shelved cabinet holding pots and pans, metal tins, and some gardening tools.

"Darla called me yesterday and told me to be on the look-out," she said, deciding to finally answer my question. "Been a long time since we've spoken to each other, so I figured you must be pretty important to her." She handed me a mug of water. I swallowed it all in one gulp and she filled a pitcher at the sink before placing it beside me. Then she lit a fire under the stove and set a kettle over the burner.

"You should put that foot up," she said, her back to me. "Only way to get the swelling down." She came over with a bowl full of water and a rag. "Let me take a look at your head. No squirming, now." She cleaned my face first. I felt the dried blood and dirt come off in pieces, and then she went around to the back of my head. "It's not all that bad," she said, but when she put the wet rag on it I jumped. "Small cut. Probably bruised more than anything."

"I'm familiar with that feeling," I said, and pulled one of the chairs closer, resting my foot on it. My eyes grew when I saw the size my ankle had become, and the dark color it had already turned. Nuna moved quickly around the kitchen, and I watched close, wondering what she was planning to do next. She looked like one of my teachers, Mr. Elliot Ward, when he concentrated so hard on a science experiment that he forgot we were in the room and set off the fire alarm. Nuna wasn't the kind of person anyone would call graceful, but there was something spectacular in her movements, and the way her arms moved about like slender forklifts. Her laced boots clunked against the wooden planks, each step an exclamation mark. More than anything, she made me very nervous.

The kettle screamed on the stove and the sound pounded against my head. Nuna walked to the shelf and took down a metal box, opened the tin, and dropped whatever she'd taken from it into a clay teapot. The screaming stopped when she lifted the kettle from the stove and poured the steaming water. She stirred it once, set the lid on the pot, and brought it over to the table.

The tea rested between us, and Nuna stared at me in silence, her hands folded in her lap. I looked away from her steady gaze and shifted my ankle on the chair. She filled the mug with strong tea and the room with an even stronger smell.

"You need to drink all of that down," she said.

"What is it?"

"Arnica, calendula, horsetail, a little valerian to help you relax."

I stared into the green liquid and then raised my eyes to her, skeptical of the smell. "You trying to knock me out or something?" I asked.

"Look, I don't know if Darla tried to scare you about me or not, but I've no reason to wish you ill. Think you might have guessed that by now, seeing how I took the time to find you and bring you into my home. It's true that I prefer to keep to myself, and don't mix much with strangers, so I'd say you should count yourself lucky more than anything," Nuna said.

"Mama Draughn didn't say much about you, just that you don't visit anymore." I lifted the mug and blew on the steam, wincing at the stench. "I don't mean to seem ungrateful. I've just become careful lately," I said, and took a sip. I must have made another face because Nuna passed me a small jar of honey.

"That's from this year's hive," she said.

I drizzled some into the mug and then licked what had

dripped onto my finger. "Are there any sourwood trees left up here?" I asked, thinking of Mr. Draughn's story of the bees.

"Only a few, but I'll shoot anyone who tries to take what's left. I'm glad you know about them—they bring the best honey."

"That's what your sister always says." I took another sip of tea. "Looks like I'll have to wait a little longer for the swelling to go down," I said, nodding at my foot. "Mind telling me what happened between the two of you?"

CHAPTER 42

NUNA SANK FARTHER INTO her chair and then swept away the white streak that had fallen across her face, before crossing her arms. "You don't mind pushing people, do ya?"

"What's the worst that could happen? Like you said, you went to all the trouble to save me once. I don't think you'd shoot me now, considering what we've already gone through."

She let out a single deep-throated laugh and, leaning forward again, rested an elbow on the table. "Remember, I don't keep much company. I'm not used to talking."

"Well, I'm in a hurry, so you don't have to worry about me overstaying my welcome or anything."

"That's a comfort at least," she said, and then her face became serious again. "How much did she tell you about June?"

"I know she's sad about her leaving and never calling. Kind of the same as she is with you, come to think of it. I only knew June a little before she left Strickland, but I was so young. She didn't turn out the way Mama D hoped she would. Is that it?

Is Mama Draughn ashamed of her?"

"No, Darla's more ashamed of herself than anyone."

"Why?"

"That isn't my story to tell," Nuna said. "You'll have to ask her yourself." She reached for my mug and when I handed it to her, she filled it again. "Your turn. What are you looking for up here?"

"I think a friend of mine is at Hogan's Cross. And yes, I need him to answer some questions for me. About my brother."

"You sure he wants to be found? Most people who come this far up don't."

I had managed to down half of the second mug by then. "No, I don't think he wants anyone bothering him, me included, but it's come to a point that I have to." I realized that probably didn't sit all that well with Nuna.

"I hope it's worth your while," she said. "Whenever you're able to move around freely again, anyway. Your ankle needs wrapping, if not a splint," she said, leaning over the chair where it rested.

She pushed up my pant leg to my knee, and we both saw that there was more damage than either of us knew, with a gash along my shin. "That's on its way to infection if we don't take care of it," Nuna said. She stood up, went to the rack of shelves, and came back with a pair of scissors. "Sorry about the jeans, but there's really no other way," she said, and cut from the bottom up. She went back to the shelf and dug around in another tin box. Mama Draughn was a master with flour and butter, and it seemed Nuna was the same with herbs. After she boiled some more water and steeped something in it, she returned carrying a bowl, rag, and another small bottle.

"Where'd you learn all this stuff?" I asked.

"I've never trusted doctors much, so I found some things I could do instead. Our grandmother taught us remedies, and then I read a bunch about it later on." She cleaned my knee with the stuff from the bowl. I grabbed my leg when the liquid hit my skin, but the sting eased up pretty quick. Next she cut off the part of my jeans that was split open, so it looked like I had shorts on one side, and pants on the other. I looked ridiculous, and was glad Tennessee wasn't there to see it. Nuna cut the extra material into strips, and then wrapped and tied a few of them around my ankle. I marveled again at how strong she was; the wrap was so tight I don't think I could have bent it had I tried. "That will speed your recovery time," she said. "You finish the tea yet?"

I looked into my cup and drank the rest of it down in one gulp.

"Look at that. You're not such a bad patient after all."

"Now that I'm not scared you're trying to poison me or turn me into a toad."

"It's not the first time someone's wondered if I'm a witch. I've been called plenty worse than that."

"Do you ever leave here? You must sometimes, to get all

of those supplies." I looked at the corner of the room where all the crates were stacked.

"Couple times a year I'll go to Lexington to stock up. I have friends—not many, mind you—but a couple that come visit regular and will bring anything I can't grow or catch."

I yawned and stopped myself midway, covering my mouth.

"That's the valerian kicking in," Nuna said. "And I reckon you didn't sleep much last night in the hole either. Best thing for healing is always sleep. I'll fix the bed for you right quick." She straightened the sheet and blanket on the mattress, and then helped me hobble to it by taking a strong grip around my ribs.

As soon as my butt hit the bed, I gave in to the drowsiness washing over me. "Just for a little while," I said, laying my head on the pillow.

Nuna laughed. "You valley people are always ruled by the clock."

"I have to get to Jacob and back home to Tennessee."

"I thought you were from Strickland?"

"Not Tennessee the place; the girl. She's waiting for me." I was already too far on my way to sleep to remember anything else I might have mumbled after that.

When I woke from a deep, dreamless sleep, I sat up too fast and pain seared through my foot and leg.

"Sore, huh?" Nuna said. "That's to be expected. I'll help you to the table." She came to the bed, where I was now sitting up. "It sounded like you were fighting a battle in your sleep."

"Really? I don't remember anything, but it doesn't surprise me," I said. "And now I have to pee." I scooted to the edge of the bed and winced. "If I can manage to get outside, that is."

"Take this with you." She crossed to the other side of the room and came back with a walking stick. "If you want, there's a shower beside the outhouse too."

If anyone had been watching me take off all of my clothes and then shower, holding my wrapped ankle out of the water and using a walking stick to balance, they would have laughed themselves drunk. The water felt good once I managed to stand under it, though. It didn't have the same smell as the stuff that came out of our faucets at home. In fact, I found it a little strange that it didn't smell like anything at all. I was dirtier than I realized, and watched the water wash the grime from my skin. Drying off and dressing was tough, but more than anything, I was glad I'd thought to pick the pants up off my bedroom floor and throw them into my pack.

As soon as I opened the cabin door again, Nuna's cooking filled my nostrils and I realized my stomach had been empty for a while.

"Looks like you're feeling better now," she said.

"Much. Might have gotten my ankle wrap a little wet, though."

"That's all right. After tonight, you should be able to take it off. Wouldn't advise that you walk too far on it, though."

"How long do you think it will take to heal?"

"Hard to say, because no one heals at the same pace. It'd be best if you could stay off of it for a week, though." She stirred something in a cast-iron pot and the growling in my stomach turned to pangs.

"I can't stay off of it for a week!" I said.

"It's your call, Mr. Hurry. I'm not going to force you to do anything. You asked for my opinion, and I gave it."

"I'm sorry, I didn't mean to sound upset. I'm just on a bit of a schedule."

"I heard that," she said. "A schedule named Tennessee."

It sounded to me like she thought I was fussing over a stupid crush, but I let it go. "Is there anything I can do to help?" I couldn't stop staring at the pot. Whatever she was cooking smelled as good as Mama Draughn's kitchen.

"You and the questions," Nuna said. "Sit down. Standing certainly won't get you to heal any faster."

It was much harder for me to stop than it was to keep going. Whenever I got still, I felt restless again because that was when my thoughts got loud. It felt like Nate, Tennessee, Mama, and Daddy were all crammed into my brain together, talking all at once. Sometimes it was hard to hear my own voice over all of them.

Nuna brought two bowls to the table and then a loaf of

homemade bread. The stew she'd made had some kind of dark meat, with carrots and potatoes. I watched the steam rise and inhaled the scent. It didn't quiet all the voices, but like the times I'd slowed down at Mama Draughn's table, it made me feel much better. I settled a little deeper into my chair and picked up the spoon. Nuna tore off a chunk of bread and handed it to me, then took one for herself. "Go ahead," she said, and dipped into the bowl.

"This is incredible," I told her after the first bite. "I don't know how you and Mama Draughn turn just a few things into something so different."

"I'm glad you like it. It's venison. I don't hunt too many deer, but this year, they were overpopulated. They're running out of space up here."

"Seems everyone is," I said. "Or Amos is pushing them out."

"There's a name no one likes to hear at dinner," Nuna said.

"Even up here, huh?" I reached the bottom of my bowl fast.

"In this house, anyway. I'll get you some more stew." She took my bowl and carried it over to the stove.

"What has he done to you?"

"You're still hungry, aren't you?"

"Yes." She was avoiding my question again, and it got me thinking. "Was it Amos that caused trouble between you and Mama Draughn?"

"What? The spoon clanked louder against the sides of the

pot. I had hit something inside of her.

She came back to the table, set my bowl in front of me, and leaned over hers like it took all of her concentration to eat a bowl of stew.

"I don't think anything about Amos would surprise me now," I said, sticking the spoon in my mouth.

"Mmm," she said, chewing on a piece of bread.

"Look, Mama Draughn has been more of a mama to me than my own, many times. She's family. I guess that makes you like my aunt or something. You can trust me."

She laughed, and it was enough encouragement to keep me talking. "You're relentless," she said.

"I know." I remembered Nuna's hand on little June's arm in the photograph, and her asking me how much I knew about her earlier. "Does it have something to do with Amos and June?" I asked.

She shot a quick look at me and narrowed her eyes just enough that I saw the answer in them.

"Did Mama D ever—" But I jumped at loud banging on Nuna's door and my spoon fell to the ground before I could finish the question.

"Shhh!" Nuna whispered, and grabbed her shotgun before walking soundlessly to the door.

CHAPTER 43

"WHO'S THERE?" NUNA YELLED, and the knocking
stopped.

"I can't find my key," a voice said from the other side.

Nuna unlocked the door. "Damn it, Peter, why didn't
you say it was you in the first place?" She leaned her shotgun
against the wall and let a tall man walk through the door.
"Shit, what's happened to you?" she asked.

The man was covered from head to foot in black grime.
The whites of his eyes stood out, but nothing else. "My house
caught fire," he said, then leaned back against the door to
steady himself and catch his breath. "Trees behind it are still
burning to the ground."

Nuna covered her mouth, then wrapped her arms around
him, and pressed her head into his chest. "Here." She pulled
a chair from the table for him. Then she brought three mugs
and a bottle of whiskey to the table. She gave him a generous
pour and splashed a little in the other two mugs. "Let me bring

you some food," she said. "What happened?"

The man walked to the sink first and washed his hands and face, then sat down at the table. "Don't exactly know. Could be this was Amos's way of showing he won't take no for an answer. He's been after me for so long to sell him the land."

"What makes you think he's done something now?" Nuna asked.

"You going to introduce us?" the man asked Nuna, and looked at me uneasily.

"This is Harlowe," Nuna said. "And that's Peter."

I swallowed another sip of whiskey. "Wait, is your last name Macnab?"

He glanced up at me from his bowl. "Inquisitive, ain't he?" he said to Nuna.

"You've no idea." She smiled.

"That's right," he said. "You live in the valley?"

"Yep."

"Can only guess the stories you've heard about me," Macnab laughed.

"I've heard a few," I said.

"Fine with me. For the most part, it's made people leave me alone. Until now, of course."

"I'm sorry about your house," I said.

"So go ahead." Nuna leaned across the table toward Macnab. "Harlowe's a friend of Darla's. He's safe, for the most part."

"I was only gone for an hour. Went to town for the things you asked I bring here tomorrow. Before I got back on Kinley, I saw the smoke. I ran in, but the flames were already too high, and I had to leave quick before the roof fell in. Noticed a can of gasoline that wasn't mine on my porch."

"Makes me sick," Nuna said. "Though I wondered if it'd come to something like this."

"I thought you were going to speak with Darla about it. He's always left her alone."

Nuna's eyes cut back toward me. "I don't want to get into all of that tonight," she said to Macnab.

She pushed her hair back from her face, the white streak of hair like a skunk tail warning. Then she stood, went to the shelves, and came back with a wooden box and a set jaw. She handed Macnab a joint, and when he took it, his fingers wrapped around her hand and held it for a moment. Then he leaned over the candle, inhaled, and fell back into his chair on the exhale. After another hit, he passed the joint to Nuna. She brought it to her mouth and blew streams of smoke through her nostrils. I wondered if Nuna was mad at me for asking too many questions, until she passed me the joint and said, "No more talk of Amos from anyone here. He's burned enough bridges, and we don't need to add fuel by giving him more thought."

"You're right," Macnab said. "I need to get cleaned up,

then I'll bring in your things."

"I'll get them," I said, feeling I should do more than eat and drink at such a time.

"Not with that ankle, you won't," Nuna said.

It was strong weed, and I'd forgotten about the pain.

"Go on, love," Nuna said to Macnab. "I'll get the things from your truck."

I stared at the candle and wondered what could have ever made Mama Draughn fall for Amos. I remembered her saying he hadn't always been such a bad person and what she'd said about Tommy's dying maybe straightening him out. But if it really was Amos that set fire to Macnab's place, it seemed the only thing Tommy's death had done was make him even more cruel.

Nuna came back with two bags and started putting things away in the small icebox, and on the shelves next to it.

"Seems like you've both known each other a long time," I said, speaking my thoughts even more freely.

"We're an odd pair; I won't argue with anyone about that," Nuna said.

"Will he move up here now?"

"Oh no," she said, her back still turned to me. "At least not for good. He loves his land, and knows I want to stay here. Sometimes I think that's what draws us together, a bit of distance—keeps our longing for each other alive."

"But you never wanted a family?"

Nuna laughed. "You're sentimental, like Darla. No, love doesn't look the same for everyone. The house, kids, always together and never apart—someone wrote that novel and then made a movie out of it. Peter and me wrote our own. It wouldn't have worked any other way for either of us."

Macnab walked through the door with water dripping from his hair and beard, but not a stitch of clothes on his body. I laughed out loud at the sight of him, but was glad I caught myself before either of them seemed to notice. Nuna looked at him and rolled her eyes, then threw him a towel.

"You never complained before," Macnab said to her.

"And I'm not complaining now. It's good to see you without all the soot."

He tucked the towel around his waist and pulled her close to him. "It's good to see you too," he said, and kissed her long enough for me to feel uncomfortable, and look away. "You might be stuck with me for a little," he said.

"Fine by me," Nuna said. "We've made it through worse."

I saw they needed some time alone, as much as they could have with the three of us in such a tight space. "I'll make a pallet and lie down for the night, if that's okay," I said.

Nuna broke free from Macnab and I followed her to the corner of the room, where she spread out a bear skin and a quilt, and threw me a pillow. After I lay down, I listened to them talking and laughing until I fell asleep. The next morning, Wednesday, Macnab was still snoring on the bed, and Nuna was making breakfast in the kitchen.

She handed me a mug of black coffee and said, "How's the ankle?"

"Much better," I said, and realized I had walked from the bed to the kitchen without the stick or too much pain. I cleared my eyes and lifted the mug to my lips, feeling a little groggy from the weed and whiskey the night before. "I think I can take the bandage off now," I said, and leaned over my foot. "I'd like to get going soon."

"Up to you," she said, and set a plate of corncakes in front of me. "But you already know my thoughts on the matter."

Macnab walked up behind Nuna and grabbed her around the hips. She leaned back into him, and even from where I sat, I could tell there was a smile on her face. He carried his coffee to the table and sat next to me. I thought of how I'd told Tennessee that he was so weird when we passed his cabin on the way to Ryan's party, and wished she'd been there to meet him and Nuna right then. I knew she'd love them.

"So what's your plan, unless you'd like to tell me that it's none of my business," Macnab asked.

"I was hoping to hike the rest of the way to my friend's place at Hogan's Cross today," I said.

"But he has a sprained ankle," Nuna added.

"Well, I can drive you there, if you like." He took one of the corncakes from the plate and ate half of it in one bite.

"If you're sure you don't mind, that'd be great," I said.

"No problem." He grabbed another corncake and smiled at Nuna. I figured he would be glad to have the cabin back for just the two of them. I couldn't blame him. I couldn't wait to have that kind of time with Tennessee.

CHAPTER 44

"THANK YOU FOR EVERYTHING. There's no telling what shape I'd be in right now if you hadn't found me," I told Nuna as I packed up my things.

"You would have found your way out. In fact, now that I know you a little, I'm sure you would have."

Macnab waited for me by the door while I hugged Nuna goodbye, and then pointed the way to his truck, parked about a hundred yards from the cabin. By the time we reached it, my ankle was throbbing again, and I was even more grateful that I wasn't hiking the rest of the way to Ryan's place.

While Macnab drove, things were quieter between the two of us than they'd been in the cabin with Nuna. I guess a man who lives alone most of the time gets used to silence and doesn't always feel the need to fill it. He turned on the radio, and through the static, we listened to a news channel, until he turned it to classic rock.

"Don't know about you, but it doesn't bring me much

comfort knowing things are hard for everyone all over," he said.

"I'll take the Eagles over that," I agreed.

"Impressed you know who they are."

"My brother was into all the old stuff," I said. "Good stuff," I added.

"Heard you lost him. Sorry about that."

"Thanks."

That was the whole of our conversation until I spotted the tin roof of Ryan's cabin ahead and said, "That's it."

Macnab put the truck in park and waited while I slung my pack over my shoulder and reached for the door handle.

"Once I rebuild my house, you're welcome to come visit," he said. "I'm sure you've already guessed I'm not the best company. I'm lucky Nuna disagrees. But we're neighbors, after all."

"I'll remember that," I said, thinking of how Tennessee and Omie and I would be on the road to somewhere else by tomorrow night.

We said goodbye and waved, and it wasn't until I was close to the door of Ryan's cabin that I heard his truck drive away.

The cabin looked like no one had given it much thought since the last time I was there two years ago. The weeds around it had grown three feet high, and the roof was covered in brown leaves. After seeing Ryan's decked-out basement the night of the party, I expected that things here would have been upgraded, too, but it almost looked like no one had been there at all. It made me even more nervous when I knocked on the door. I didn't hear anything from inside, so I glanced around the side of the cabin, but there was no sign of Ryan's Dodge. I hadn't thought what I would do if I didn't find Jacob, and suddenly that struck me as pretty stupid.

Then I heard the sound of something falling to the floor inside, and a voice say "shit." I knocked again, and heard footsteps coming toward me.

"What is it?" the voice asked through the door, sounding hoarse and sleepy.

"It's Harlowe," I answered, and wondered if I shouldn't have. "I'm looking for Jacob and Ryan."

There was silence—then the sound of a lock and chain rattling. I wasn't sure why at that moment, but I remembered the gun was in my backpack if I needed it.

When Jacob opened the door, I wanted to unsee him. He'd dropped at least fifteen pounds and his eyes were red and bulging. He swayed back and forth on his feet and his eyelids drooped like he might fall asleep standing up. He looked nothing like the Jacob I'd last seen, only a fading shadow of the kid I grew up with. He squinted at the sun shining behind me, but said nothing at all.

I stared at him, trying to figure what to say first, and finally landed on the only thing that I felt mattered. "Let's go," I said.

Jacob opened his mouth and what came out sounded like

laughter underwater. "Nah," he said, and leaned against the doorframe.

"Let me in," I said.

"Can't. Promised Ryan I wouldn't let anyone in." He yawned.

I tried to see around him into the cabin, but he blocked my view. "Just for a minute," I said.

He blinked at me, arms crossed against his sunken chest. "Only if you promise to go as soon as I say."

The place smelled like rotten milk and mold. I took in as much as I could in one glance, and then wished that I hadn't when I saw stacks of bottles in clear boxes, and next to them, a pill press that took up almost the whole table.

CHAPTER 45

JACOB WALKED AWAY FROM the open door to a couch in front of the TV and fell into it. I wanted to scream at him, shake him, drag him away from it all. I shut the door behind me.

"How long?" I asked.

He wouldn't look at me, but stared at the TV screen instead. "Like this?" He glanced down at himself. "Got bad after Nate, I guess."

Red had been right about that.

"Did Nate know? That you were using?"

Jacob chuckled once.

I couldn't take it anymore and walked over to the couch and stood between him and the TV. "Tommy's dead," I said. "Fentanyl powder." I looked over at the pill press. "There's more, but I need you to tell me what Nate had to do with all of this."

He didn't lift his head from the back of the couch, but scooted up a little higher. Finally, when he saw I wasn't going anywhere, he looked into my eyes.

"We found we could beat the Praters at their game," Jacob said. "Well, Ryan did, and we knew Nate could find out where Tommy was picking up and when."

"That was what he wrote in the notebook, and texted you about Woodvale?"

Jacob nodded.

"Then what?" I asked.

"Ryan started intercepting the pickup. He'd call the clinics first and tell them he was working with Tommy. It was crazy, but we got away with it, for a while. Once we saw how much money we could really make, we couldn't stop."

"Did Nate know about that part?"

Jacob nodded again.

"And then Tommy found out."

"Ryan screwed up the Woodvale pickup and the guy called Tommy to double-check when he suspected. Tommy put it together that Nate got info from his work computer."

"What did Tommy want from you at the party?"

Jacob squirmed on the couch and looked at the door.

I walked even closer to the couch and blocked his view of anything except me.

"What he found in the shed?" I wasn't going to accept silence this time.

"Our recipe," he said.

"That was why he opened the powder," I realized. "And I guess the other boxes—it was easier for you to ship the stuff."

"Other than pickups, we don't have to leave. What were you saying about Tommy?" His eyes darted back and forth like he was fighting falling asleep.

"He found that shit in the shed," I said again. "What if it had been me? Did you ever think of that? Or someone else? What are you still doing up here? What about your kid, Jacob? I saw Clarice. She told me they haven't seen you in months."

"Shut up, Harlowe. You always thought you were better than everyone else."

"Did you talk Nate into doing it? Or did Ryan?"

"We didn't talk him into anything. He saw a chance to make money, and took it, just like us. Just like plenty others would have done."

"But it got him killed. And it's gonna do the same to you, sooner or later."

"Well, it's either that, the mines, or cancer, far as I can see."

"This is a fucking waste," I said, looking around the room, feeling nauseous at the stink coming from the piles of trash in the kitchen and the sight of Jacob wasting away.

"The thing is," he said, rolling his head back and forth along the couch, "I don't even care anymore. It feels so—" He stopped when we both heard the sound of an engine outside the cabin.

The back door flung open and bounced against the wall, but Jacob didn't even lift his head. Ryan crossed the room in wide steps until he stood in front of us, his eyes big and round and his fists clenched. "Told you not to let anyone in," he said. "What's he doing here?"

"Ask him," Jacob mumbled, and blinked, trying to focus his eyes.

Ryan looked at me like I was someone he'd only ever met in passing. "Guess you're coming with us, then," he said, "because we have to go right now."

"I'm not going anywhere with you."

"We're running late, and we're supposed to be in Knoxville by tonight. Come on, let's go. Grab some of those." He pointed to the boxes on the counter. "Pull it together, Jacob, we're leaving."

Jacob looked at him like he hadn't heard anything he'd said, or even remembered him walking into the room.

Ryan took a bottle from his pocket and opened it, then walked over to Jacob and pushed something into his hand. "That'll set you straight," he said. "Go on." From the sound of his voice, he'd already taken whatever kind of upper it was he'd just given Jacob.

Without even looking at it, Jacob put the pill in his mouth and swallowed. I wondered at what point he'd stopped thinking for himself entirely.

"Won't take long," Ryan said, and started stacking the boxes. "Just a fast pickup. We'll be back by morning."

Jacob stood from the couch and walked toward Ryan, but bumped into the counter before he could reach him.

"All right," Ryan said, holding the boxes under his arm. "Let's hit it." There were still two trays of pills left on the counter, and some on the kitchen table, surrounded by empty beer cans and half-eaten rotted food.

Jacob followed him to the door.

"I'm not going," I said.

Ryan pushed the boxes onto Jacob and crossed the room to where I stood. He grabbed the collar of my shirt and pulled me into his face. "Listen," he said. "If I hear anything from anyone, I'm coming straight after you."

"That's not fair," I said. "You know Amos is already looking and will find out about this soon enough. It will have nothing to do with me."

"You better make sure he doesn't."

I looked at Jacob and hoped to find traces of my best friend left in his face, but saw only a stranger as he looked away again.

Ryan let go of my shirt and scooped up the last of the trays from the table. "Now that I think on it, you're no threat to us," he said. "You'll always go along with the flow because you're too scared to do different. That's probably why Nate said you could never be a part of this." He grabbed Jacob's elbow on the way to the door.

I was left standing in the cabin alone, holding my backpack in one hand by a strap. I tried to understand what had just happened, how I felt hearing what Nate had done and how much he'd kept hidden from me. I'd never understand how he could have gone through everything he did with helping Mama get clean and then choose this.

The door opened again and Jacob walked inside. "Hang on," he said, walking back to the bedroom. He came out again and handed me a brown paper bag, the top folded over. It weighed a couple of pounds at least. "That's Nate's cut," he said. "Forget what Ryan said. Nate didn't want you involved because he wanted to get out. If you want to blame someone, it's me. I asked him to snoop on Tommy's computer."

I opened my mouth to say something, but there were no words that would do. Jacob was standing at the back door again. "I'm sorry, Harlowe," he said, and then he was gone.

There were twelve tidy stacks of hundred-dollar bills inside the bag, each stack a thousand dollars. I should have felt like the people jumping up and down on *Wheel of Fortune* to be handed so much money, but the bag couldn't hold the weight of what that money cost. I looked around the filthy cabin once more, put the money in my backpack, and left before the smell of the cabin could make me vomit.

I started the trail back home and my ankle screamed that

it was far from healed. If there was any place that should be burnt to the ground, it was the cabin I'd just left, I thought, not Macnab's home. Part of me wondered if I had ever really known my brother at all. He'd shown things about himself to Jacob that he'd never share with me. I thought I'd leave the mountain with all of the stories straight, along with my ideas about who Nate would always be to me. Because I wanted to keep him alive. But he'd tossed both me and Mama aside for the hope of buying a ticket—even if he thought he could get one for all of us, I couldn't believe that he hadn't learned better by then.

Limping down the mountain and catching myself from falling again when I slipped on a pile of leaves, I remembered how slick the rocks had been under our feet when me and Nate looked for crawdaddies in the creek during summers that weren't so dry. One time he'd fallen, and his toes got stuck under a rock. At first I laughed at him, thinking he was making too big a deal of things, but then he looked up at me and I saw the truth of the pain in his eyes. "I'm stuck," he said. I waded over to where he sat and lifted the rock from his foot and then helped him walk home. Through my tears and my own pain there on the mountain, I realized that more than being angry at Nate—I just missed him.

By the time I made it close to Nuna's cabin the pain of my ankle was unbearable and I decided to stop and ask her for help. Again.

CHAPTER 46

"HAPPY TO GIVE YOU a ride home," Macnab said after I told them what happened.

"How 'bout I wrap your ankle again?" Nuna asked when she saw me limping and the tears on my face.

"Thanks, but I should really get back as soon as I can," I said.

"You know how I feel about rushing, but have it your way," she said. "Here, take these at least." She poured something into her hand from a small bottle and then handed me two brown pills and a mug of water.

"What are they?" I asked.

"Advil," she said, like I was silly for not knowing.

"Thought you only used natural stuff," I said after swallowing them.

"Sometimes you have to reach for a little more," she said. I thought of everything I'd just seen at Ryan's place, and figured that one way or another, that's what everyone was doing—reaching.

After we got in his truck I asked Macnab if he knew anything about the grave I'd fallen into on my way up the mountain.

"Nuna's seen a lot of strange things on the mountain over the years," he said. "It hasn't been there long, I know that. Maybe a couple of weeks at most. If I had my way, I'd bury Amos in it."

I wondered if Tommy had dug it for Nate and then changed his mind and brought him home to us instead. I'd never forget the relief I felt when I realized it wouldn't be mine, and wished Nate could have known the same feeling.

Macnab drove me down the mountain, and turned into our driveway, where I told him to stop. "You know where to find us now," he said.

"I'm not sure how much longer I'll be around here," I said. "Could I get your number?" I felt kind of strange asking for it, but never talking to him or Nuna again didn't feel right, either.

He found a scrap of paper tucked in the seat and a pencil on the dashboard and wrote it down for me, then waited until I was on the porch to pull out of the drive.

Walking through our front door, I felt a familiar heaviness return that I hadn't even noticed had lifted while I was gone. The door was locked when I tried to open it. I knocked and a wave of panic rolled through me when I realized I hadn't taken any keys with me. I couldn't help but wonder if anything had happened to Mama while I was gone, and banged against the door even louder. When she finally came and opened it, her eyes held the same glassy expression that had been in Jacob's. She stepped away from the door to let me walk through it, and this time, didn't even bother asking where I had been or why it had taken so long. She just leaned against the counter, her head bobbing a little and her robe falling halfway down one of her arms. She wouldn't like what I was about to do, but there was no way around it, so I walked past her to my room and began packing.

I didn't take much. Only what would fit in a duffel, plus my saw and blades and what was already in my backpack, including the money. I took Nate's phone and wallet from the closet, and before I left our room, grabbed the photo from under the bunk of the two of us with the fish and cousin Beau.

"I want to buy your car," I told Mama, setting my saw and bags on the floor in front of her recliner.

She gripped the arms of the chair and rustled, pulled herself up a little straighter. "How are you gonna do that?"

I reached into my backpack and pulled out two stacks. She fumbled with the arm of the recliner, and I helped her get it down. She stared at the money in my hand and leaned forward. "Why do you need to buy it? You use it whenever you need it."

"I won't answer any questions. Not right now. You could take this and get some new clothes, get some help, if you want to. I promise I'll call very soon. I'm not disappearing, but I have to leave. Now, before I'm stuck here forever. Or I end up like Nate."

She pushed herself out of the chair and tied her robe around her. She lifted her hands as if they'd help her find the words, and then dropped them. Then she looked into my eyes, and for a moment, the glassiness cleared and a softness I recognized from too long ago took its place. Her feet shuffled a little closer to mine, and I reached my arms to wrap them around her. Her face pressed into my chest. Tears pushed from my eyes into her dirty hair. I felt her trembling, crying, and remembered the times when I'd woken from a nightmare, before I could even talk, and she'd rocked me back to sleep. With my arms around her and the money still gripped in my hand, I wished that I could take both of us back to before we became so hard. But I knew I'd only get harder for staying.

"Okay," I said, and loosened my arms from her. It hurt me to see the glaze return to her face when we stood in front of each other again, both of us wiping tears from our faces.

"I don't know how—" she said.

"I know, I don't either. But I think you can find out if you really want to. And if you ask for some help along the way. That's what I'm believing for myself, anyhow. I'll call you. Promise." Before she could say anything in return, I walked over to the counter, picked up her keys, and then all of my things from the floor. Mama stood on the porch in the same spot where we'd found Nate and watched me leave the house where she'd raised both of her babies, and now was left to take care of only herself.

CHAPTER 47

I TOOK A CHARGER from the glove compartment and plugged it into the cigarette lighter. Once my phone got a little juice, it said it was 2:19. I had one last stop before picking up Tennessee and Omie.

Mama Draughn opened the screen door for me as soon as I got out of the car. "Get in here," she said once I was on the porch, and scooted me through the door.

I dropped my pack under the table and sat down in my usual spot.

"Hungry?" she asked.

"I'm in a bit of a hurry," I said.

"You're here to say goodbye, aren't you?"

I nodded and found it wasn't any easier telling her than it was Mama. "I promised I wouldn't leave without it."

"I knew this day was coming," she said. "I just hoped that maybe it would take a little longer. But that was for my sake, not yours."

"Did you talk to Nuna?"

"I did. You must have rubbed off a little on her. She said she'd like to visit soon. She also said you might have some questions for me after your time there."

"No. I'll listen to anything you want to say, but if there's one thing I learned up there, it's that answers just lead to bigger questions. That's fine and all, but right now, I've got plenty of questions I need to answer for myself, and no one else can do it for me."

Mama Draughn tilted her head a little and smiled, then rested her chin in her hand. "What?" I asked, wanting to hear her thoughts behind the expression on her face.

"Was just thinking about when you stayed with us here for a little. I'd watch you playing outside. You'd run in these circles, over and over, and I knew it was because you were doing the same thing in your head. I'd wonder when you'd finally take off running in another direction and start exploring. Here you are. You're doing it."

"I might ask you to remind me of that again sometime," I said, and looked around the room, taking a last mental snapshot to remember. The pictures of June that were curling around the edges, the yellow curtains Mama Draughn washed and ironed every month, with the holes she mended, and the ghost smells of everything she'd ever cooked in her kitchen.

"I have one favor to ask you," she said.

"I owe you more than that."

Mama Draughn glanced at the closed bedroom door where Mr. Draughn was napping, the sound of the fan turning around coming through softly. "He doesn't know. About June. And—"

"Amos," I said, so she was clear on the fact that I knew what she meant.

"Right. That's what drove Nuna away. That I never told him, and I never will, because I feel it would be cruel to break his heart over a foolish night that I've spent more than half my life paying for in guilt. And if that makes me a liar, so be it."

"I understand," I said. "A lot more now than I could have before." I reached down for my backpack and pulled it into my lap. In the bottom, I found the revolver she'd lent to me. "Here," I said, putting it on the table.

"You don't want to take it with you? I'd hate to think it, but you might need it."

"I might. But I'd rather leave it behind, along with some other things that aren't as easy to get rid of. Might as well start there." I stood from the table and hung the pack over my shoulder.

She walked around the table and pulled me toward her, her knotted fingers that had worked love into countless crusts and dinners pressing into my back.

"I'll be talking to you," I said.

"I believe you. That says a lot."

When I got in the car, the sadness of two goodbyes mixed with my excitement about finally getting to Tennessee. She was the beginning at the end of everything else we'd soon put behind us.

CHAPTER 48

I WALKED AROUND THE side of her trailer and made sure that Moore's truck was gone before I knocked. I'd parked the car near Widow Hemlock's, beside the row of holly bushes that partly kept it from view of the road.

As soon as my knuckles lifted from the door, I heard soft footsteps from inside and the sound of the TV volume dropped. Then there was Omie's little voice, and Tennessee saying "Shhh," while she came closer.

"Hello?" she said, through the still-closed door.

"Hey, it's me." I listened to her unlock the chain first, and then the lock.

"Come in," she said, standing behind the door and opening it just enough for me to get through, then pulled me inside and stretched her arms around my neck. "You're safe," she said, and I noticed the dark circles under her eyes like she hadn't slept for a few nights.

Omie got up off the couch and ran to me, squeezing my

legs in his little arms.

"Come on, Omes," Tennessee said to him, and took one of his hands. "I'll put the Mickey Mouse video on for you in our room so me and Harlowe can talk a minute, okay?"

I waited in the kitchen while she set up the DVD player and headphones in their room. I wondered how many times she'd relied on those headphones to try to keep Omie from knowing about their dad, and how'd she'd handle it when he started asking questions himself. There was a casserole dish half-covered with foil on the table, an opened bottle of orange juice, and a box of cereal.

When she came back, I pulled her toward me, and the tightness in her shoulders released a little beneath my hands. She lifted her face to mine and I kissed her, thinking how when I was in the grave on the mountain, I wasn't sure that I'd ever get to do it again and how much I was looking forward to countless others. "Are you packed?" I asked. "Everything's ready for us to go."

She settled back onto her heels from her tiptoes that had lifted her further into my lips a moment ago. "Some things happened while you were gone," she said.

My stomach flipped. "I'm listening," I said, and rested my backpack on the floor.

She pulled one of the chairs out from the table, and I reached for the one next to her, scooting a little closer once we were both sitting.

"Almost as soon as Dad left, he started calling constantly. He sounded paranoid, saying that someone was following him and that he thought Amos was out to get him. A couple of times he cried and said God was punishing him for not taking better care of Mom, but then in the same breath he'd say random awful things I can't even repeat about the black guy sitting beside him at a traffic light or the Hispanic woman in line at the restaurant."

"Or the kid who pulled up in front of him at the gas station," I added.

"Yeah," she said, and frowned down at the fingernails she couldn't stop picking at. "It all sounds really familiar, doesn't it?"

"It's why we need to get both of you out of here," I said. "Because he's right on the edge, and you don't know how much longer he can stay there."

"Where do you think we should go?" she asked.

I hadn't had any time to think about it, or look at a map. "We can pick somewhere together, and if we don't like it, we'll go somewhere else," I said.

"I can't jerk Omie around like that all over the place."

"And I don't want you to. Listen, I'll tell you while we're driving, but I can take care of us now."

"What do you mean?"

"I have money. Plenty of it to get us settled until I can find work. You won't even have to worry about it, you can just go to school and take care of Omie."

"Wait a minute," she said, and shifted in her chair, leaning a little farther away from me. "Having money doesn't mean you can be there in the ways I need you if we're really going to do this."

"No, I know that. It won't fix everything, but it will make it easier, you have to admit that."

"Not if everything else is a struggle and we don't have a place we can call home."

My stomach sank and my heart rose up in my throat.

"After the calls from Dad, I phoned my aunt Celeste. They're coming for us tonight instead of tomorrow."

"Tennessee," I said, but she cut me off before I could say any more and put her hand on my knee to get me to calm down.

"They just sold their house and decided to move outside of Williamsburg," she said. "So Dad won't be able to find us there. There's an even better school with an honors program so hopefully I can get a college scholarship, and a bigger house where we'll have our own rooms. They're changing everything for us. So we can have a better chance. I can't say no to that, no matter how much I care about you. I told you from the beginning, my life isn't my own right now. As soon as Mom died, it became about Omie, and it will be for the next fifteen years, until he's ready to go out on his own." Her voice grew louder and she pressed one of her palms against her forehead like she was getting a headache. "I don't want to do it all by myself anymore, Harlowe." She took a deep breath and looked into my eyes. "Not if I don't have to. I'm so tired," she said, and ran her fingers along her wet cheeks.

"But I want to be there with you," I said.

"I know you do, but you can't right now as much as they can."

"What if I wanted to move there too?"

"Harlowe, please don't make this any harder. I already feel awful because I know you had this idea that we could start everything new together—and for a little while, I thought maybe it could work, too, but it just doesn't feel right. The timing's all wrong."

My tired heart dropped into my shoes. "If it's about timing, then I'll wait," I said.

The front door opened and Moore walked into the room.

CHAPTER 49

"WHAT IS HE DOING here?" Moore crossed the room and walked straight toward us, his false leg dragging a little behind the other.

I gripped my backpack but didn't answer him.

"You let him in here?" Moore turned to Tennessee when I was silent.

"Shhh!" She held her hand up like she wanted to silence everything. "I need to check on Omie," she said.

"Stay back in your bedroom," he said while she walked away, and fixed his sight on me.

I stood from the table. "I'll go now. Tennessee told me it wasn't a great time. This is all my fault."

"Damn straight it's your fault. I knew as soon as I laid eyes on you that you were one to stir up shit whenever you got a chance, and then you went and proved it. Several times over, too."

I thought of how many times I'd kept my mouth shut about

all the things that had made me mad for so long. "You didn't know anything about me then and you still don't. You were just looking for someone to blame and I got in your way."

Moore flung his hand toward me like his reach for my throat was automatic. I dropped my backpack on the floor and backed away from him. From the corner of my eye, I saw Tennessee standing at the back of the room. He came toward me again, and this time got ahold of my face, his fingers stretched toward my eyes. I couldn't see him or anything anymore when his hand covered my vision and pressed against my nose.

"Leave him alone!" Tennessee screamed.

"You can fuck up your own life if you want, but not hers," he said, when I managed to push his hand off my face, but the one around my throat tightened even more.

I swung at him, but he held me out so I couldn't reach him. I sensed something behind him, but knew better than to take my eyes away from his face. There was a loud thud against the back of his head. Then came the sound of glass and clay crashing against the floor. Tennessee cried from behind him, and pieces of a light bulb and lamp scattered in the scuffle of their feet.

Moore let go of my throat, and then turned around to look for Tennessee. As soon as he found her, he grabbed a handful of her hair and pulled it so tight that her neck stretched back and she fell to her knees on the floor. She tried to catch her breath through her sobs. I rushed toward them along the ground, but Moore kicked me away. He took hold of the locket Tennessee's mom had given her, the chain shining bright against her skin.

"You don't deserve this," he said, and tore the locket from her neck. It flew into the air and then spun on the laminate floor. Tennessee scrambled after it. I tried to reach her, but before I could I saw Moore open the kitchen drawer and bring out a knife.

"No!" Tennessee screamed at him from the floor.

We turned toward Omie's shrill cries in the hallway. He stood there, watching all three of us, wetness spreading across the front of his shorts and running down his leg. Tennessee ran over to him, swept him into her arms, then down the hallway to their room.

The knife turned in Moore's hand, and butane sparked in his eyes. The scar pulled his face back into the smile that held nothing but hate. Through the adrenaline pounding in my veins, I realized I'd turned my ankle again at some point during the fight and it throbbed along with the heartbeat in my ears.

I backed slowly away from Moore and then froze, hoping to throw him for just one instant. In his confusion I bolted for the door and managed to get out onto the porch. He followed me into the yard and swiped the air with his knife. His eyes filled with the kind of crazy that left no room for anything else. Just like at the gas station, I knew I could have been anyone, as long as it was someone he could hurt.

Two kinds of screams flooded from the front door of their trailer. Omie ran onto the porch, Tennessee yelling after him, unable to hold him back any longer.

"Stop!" Tennessee yelled at Moore, and at everything else that spun beyond our control.

Moore kept his gaze on me while he inched forward. We were almost to the end of the drive by then. I stumbled on a rock behind me and he swiped the knife in my direction. I ducked just in time for it to miss my throat and nick the front of my shoulder instead.

Through the pain, I heard Omie's and Tennessee's cries from the porch matching mine. Moore found his footing fast this time and sprang toward me once more.

There was the sound of tires in the drive behind me, and Moore looked away from me for one instant to see the car. Then I heard it. The shot rang through our valley and echoed against our shredded mountains before sinking into the earth along with the bones of our people.

A look of surprise came over Moore's face when the breath left him, and he fell toward me. This time he missed entirely, and once he had fallen to the ground, he never moved again.

In a shaken blur, I turned to find Mr. Draughn holding his shotgun, and, standing close behind his elbow, Mama Draughn.

CHAPTER 50

I LIMPED AROUND MOORE'S body, toward them.

"Widow Hemlock called," Mama Draughn said before I could ask. "Are you hurt at all?"

I pressed my hand against my shoulder and then looked down at the smear of blood on my fingers. "It's not too bad," I said, then left them to walk toward the porch, where Tennessee and Omie stood.

She held Omie in her arms, his head against her chest. I wrapped my arms around them both, hoping that maybe I could blanket her trembling and sobs at least a little. We watched Mr. Draughn leave the shotgun in the bed of his truck, and then both of them walk toward us.

"Tennessee, I'll go inside and make some calls," Mama Draughn said. "You don't need to worry about the details." I knew she would most likely call Amos first, because it was the fastest and easiest way to get these things taken care of.

"I can't stand out here any longer," Tennessee said. Mr.

Draughn and I followed her and Omie inside. Once she saw that Omie would let her, she set him down beside Mr. Draughn on the couch, where he curled up against him. Mr. Draughn pulled his old watch and chain from his pocket, the same one that I coveted as a kid. I knew Omie would have plenty of questions for Tennessee in the months and years to come, but I was glad to see that right then he was still as trusting of Mr. Draughn as he had been the first day he met him. Watching him, though, he seemed much older than he had been less than two weeks ago. That summer had done the same to all of us, I was sure of it.

Tennessee took my hand and pulled me into a corner where we could talk without anyone hearing us. She leaned into my chest and I rubbed her back. "I don't know what I feel right now," she said. "Or what I'm supposed to feel. I think I'm sad, but I'm also a little relieved, and oh God, that feels so terrible to say." Her tears soaked into my shirt.

I didn't know what I could possibly tell her, so I asked, "What do you need from me?"

"The same you needed from me. Just to know you're there. Even if we aren't in the same place. Celeste should be here soon."

We heard the sirens, same as the night when we'd found Moore in the bathroom, but Mama Draughn walked out onto the porch to answer the questions this time. I was glad that I wouldn't have to see the look on Moore's face again, and hoped the memory of it would lift for all of us at some point, too.

"I'm sorry if I made things harder for you earlier when we were talking. I've never felt better in my life than when the three of us are together, and I really wanted to have that all the time. I still want it."

"I know," she said. "Thing is, neither of us can fix this stuff for each other."

I sighed and then said, "Yes, but that doesn't mean I'm not mad about it."

She looked over at Omie and Mr. Draughn and drew a deep breath. "I'm mostly packed, but need to grab a few more things. Come with me?"

We walked down the hallway, past the open bathroom to her room.

"I don't want to take too much," she said, looking at her still-full bookshelves and then around the room at Omie's stuffed animals on the bed.

"I feel the same way. I don't need too many reminders. Except I'd like to have one of you."

She walked over to the table by her bed and picked up the geode she'd found the first time we went to Mohosh Pond together. "There's this," she said. "Would you like to take it?"

"We should break it open," I said. "So we can both take it with us." I looked around for anything that might help me crack the rock.

"Outside the window," she said. "There are some tools by the stack of wood. We used them for the fort." She pushed the bottom of the frame and then lifted the screen.

I found a rusted sledgehammer and ax, but was worried they'd splinter the thing into shards. A little farther back, half-hidden by a stack of broken crates, there was a pipe splitter, tossed as if no one ever had any use for it. It took some work, and my hands ached from the pressure, but I managed to break the rock into halves, with only a few slivers falling from each part.

Tennessee sat on the edge of the bed and leaned over her knees, staring into space, when I came back through the window. She jostled when she saw me stand in front of her, like I'd pulled her back into the room with me from someplace else.

Without looking at them closely yet, I handed both pieces to her.

"Amethyst," she said, running her fingers along the crystals. "Look at that."

"Do you think we changed it that day at Mohosh?" I sat down on the bed beside her.

"I'm sure we did. So much has," she said, and handed one of the halves to me.

We sat together in the quiet until we heard footsteps nearing from the kitchen, and a woman's voice I didn't recognize, asking if she could come into the room.

CHAPTER 51

I HELPED THEM PACK the car and couldn't help thinking that I still wished they were coming with me instead of leaving. I wanted Tennessee to know I was still there with her, until the minute that I couldn't be any longer. Moore's body had been gone for at least twenty minutes. Celeste started the car and the air-conditioning, and Tennessee and Omie said goodbye to Mama D and Mr. Draughn. Then Tennessee put Omie in the car seat and, leaving the door open, turned to me.

I took Tennessee's face in my hands and she lifted it toward mine to kiss me.

"I won't ask for any promises from you this time," I said, pulling away only enough to speak. "But I'll make one that I know I can keep. If you ever need me—whenever you need me, no matter how old we are or what happens in between—I'll be there. I mean that."

She closed her eyes, took a deep breath, and then kissed me for the last time before she got in the car.

I leaned through the open door and took Omie's hand in mine, but when the tears sprang to my eyes, I let go and mussed his hair once before standing straight, knowing he'd already seen more than enough tears that day. When Celeste started driving, I began walking and followed them onto Baxter Creek until they were gone from my sight. Back at my car, I set my pack in the passenger seat, the geode half-tucked safe inside, along with everything else. I didn't feel good about leaving Strickland without Tennessee or with a bag full of Nate's drug money, but I knew the most important thing was that I was leaving, period.

I unhooked my phone from the cigarette lighter and went to my contacts. Beau answered on the second ring.

"I know it's been a long time," I said.

"I've been trying to reach you, man, did you get my messages?"

"No," I said, "but things have been crazy here."

"Broke my heart to hear about Nate. I know he was working hard to get both of you down here."

"He never said anything to me about it," I said, adding it to the long list of things I wished I'd known. "But what if I headed that way now?"

I drove until I was well past the Strickland County line before I stopped at a gas station. I didn't want to risk anything getting in the way of my leaving. When I parked at the pump,

I stopped and looked at the cars and people around me. There was no sign of anyone like Moore, looking to pick a fight.

I stepped inside to pay for my gas before I pumped, and found a map near the register. The guy behind the counter held up the hundred-dollar bill to check the watermark before putting it in the drawer and finding my change.

"Wait," I said, and handed him two Snickers bars to add to the bill.

He gave me my change and then turned his attention to the woman in line behind me without bothering to ask where I was going, or how I was doing. Already I missed Mrs. Devin at the Sip N Sak and all of her questions.

After the tank clicked full, I unfolded the map across the steering wheel. It would take me thirteen hours to get to Florida. Thirteen hours and almost nine hundred miles from the place where I was born for the chance that I might really live.

ACKNOWLEDGMENTS

Thank you to my fierce and dear agent and friend, Cindy Uh, for believing so strongly in this book and in me. Your faith inspires me daily, and I can't wait for the journey ahead of us. Thank you, Meg Thompson, for picking up my manuscript at Ade and Cory's apartment in Nashville and getting it into Cindy's hands. Cory Chisel and Adriel Denae, thank you for writing the song "Tennessee" that inspired this book. Roseanne Cash, thank you for introducing me to Cory and Ade, and for all your wisdom and encouragement over the years. I am incredibly blessed to know such talented artists and to be intrinsically inspired by all of you.

Thank you to my editors, Alex Arnold and Rebecca Aronson, and everyone at Katherine Tegen/HarperCollins. I am so proud that you brought this story to life and taught me so much in the process.

Thank you to my early readers, who offered critical advice and encouragement: Stephen Parolini, Nora Pelizzari, Kelly Morrison Zumwalt, Kristy Robinson, Ben Pearson, Scott Laudati, Johnny Duke, Allie Levick, and Jonathan Lewis. To my book club women who read drafts and have always championed me in both writing and life: Jessica Kimbrough,

Tammy Rutherford, Liz Scowden, Jaime Bryan, and Marna Taylor, I love you all dearly.

A special thank-you to Jonathan Lewis, JR Davis, and Kyle Hittner for taking me deep into the mountains and sharing your passion for its beautiful people.

Thank you to the Foxfire organization for preserving Appalachian culture for so many years, and for being an incredible resource. Thank you to *Bitter Southerner* for caring about the South, the rights of all people everywhere, and fighting for a better, more inclusive South.

Thank you, Lisa Donovan, for Mama Draughn's pie recipe. I hope I got it right—no one can match your wit and baking skills.

To my North Carolinian parents, Scotty and Darlene Smith, thank you for taking us to Boone, North Carolina, every year and for not having a television for many years and for raising us on good stories and music. My brother, Scott Smith, thank you for loving me so well and for sharing your ardor for nature and fishing with me. You are imbedded in these pages.

Thank you, Rann Russell, for being a great father to our son, Finn, and to Elise Russell for being a great stepmom, and Sam a great stepbrother. It always takes a village, but especially for a writer-mum.

Bill and Gail Vinett, thank you for books, brunches, and unwavering belief in your hairstylist, now bonus(?) daughter.

Finn and I love you both so much. Here's to never falling down stairs again.

Jana Smith, thank you for putting up with my neuroses at the salon, and for reminding me to not take everything so damn seriously all the time.

Ruby Amanfu, thank you for loving me and being a force. We're doing it. Natalie Paige, thank you for our feminist taco talks, and being a touchstone of growth over the years.

Jeff Zentner, thank you for befriending me, and answering all of my novice-author questions without ever being condescending.

Thanks to my Barre 3 community in Nashville for keeping me somewhat sane in mind, body, and spirit and balancing the time I spend in my head.

Parnassus Books of Nashville, thank you for being my home away from home for so many years and supporting my book addiction. I'll never feel lonely within your walls.

Dearest Finn, it's an honor to be your mom. Thank you for lighting my path. Keep asking all the questions.